FOR LOVE AND GLORY

BY POUL ANDERSON

FROM TOM DOHERTY ASSOCIATES

Alight in the Void
All One Universe
The Armies of Elfland
The Boat of a Million Years
Conan the Rebel
The Dancer from Atlantis
The Day of Their Return
Explorations
The Fleet of Stars
For Love and Glory
Genesis
Going for Infinity
Harvest of Fire
Harvest the Stars
Hoka! (*with Gordon R. Dickson*)
Kinship with the Stars
A Knight of Ghosts and Shadows
The Long Night
The Longest Voyage
Maurai and Kith
A Midsummer Tempest
Mother of Kings
No Truce with Kings
Operation Chaos
Operation Luna
Past Times
The Saturn Game
The Shield of Time
Starfarers
The Stars Are Also Fire
Tales of the Flying Mountains
There Will Be Time
The Time Patrol
War of the Gods

POUL ANDERSON

FOR LOVE AND GLORY

A TOM DOHERTY ASSOCIATES BOOK

NEW YORK

This is a work of fiction. All the characters and events portrayed in this novel are either fictitious or are used fictitiously.

FOR LOVE AND GLORY

Book design by Jane Adele Regina

A Tor Book
Published by Tom Doherty Associates, LLC
175 Fifth Avenue
New York, NY 10010

ISBN: 0-312-87449-9

Printed in the United States of America

TO GEOFF KIDD

for help above and beyond
the call of friendship

ACKNOWLEDGMENTS

A dozen years ago, the late Isaac Asimov created a science fictional cosmos to serve as a narrative background for other writers. It was interesting to see how differently they handled it while trying to stay consistent with the premises. I contributed to two of the ISAAC'S UNIVERSE volumes, *The Diplomacy Guild* (1990) and *Phases in Chaos* (1991). Now Janet Asimov and editor Martin Greenberg have graciously given me leave to incorporate these stories in an independent novel.

It has turned out independent indeed. The concept of several intelligent spacefaring species, who come upon relics of unknown predecessors, is still there, but that is scarcely unique in our literature. Otherwise little remains except that pair of episodes, much altered. To avoid conflict with anything in the original series or constraining any future volumes, the history, the races involved, the individual characters, most place names, and the general course of events have all been changed. This tale stands entirely on its own.

Still, I wish to acknowledge my debt to Isaac, Janet, and Marty.

POUL ANDERSON

FOR LOVE AND GLORY

1

At first sight Lissa thought it was an island—a strange one, yes, but this whole world was strange to her. Then as she and Karl came out of the woodland and went on toward the river, she knew it could not be. It lay in midstream, dully iridescent, about twenty meters long, perhaps a fourth as wide, curving up to a gently rounded top one meter or so above the water. Someone or something had made it.

But there were no native sophonts anywhere around this star. Scant though exploration had been in the seven Terran years since the system was first visited, that much was certain.

So who, and when, and why?

She halted. "What the chaos? Have you any idea what that might be?"

Karl stopped too. "None," he said. "I do not recall any such artifact from my experience or other sources of information. A slight resemblance to some dwellings of the Orcelin civilization." The tip of his tail gestured at the camp near the shore. "Obviously it is not the work of yonder persons. I presume they are studying it. They may have learned something."

The translator clinging to Lissa's backpack rendered his answer into flat-voiced Anglay. He could follow her words readily enough. If he had tried to utter them the result would have been grotesque. For her part, she could not hear most of his language, let alone pronounce those trills, whistles, and supersonic melodies. Once it had struck her funny that such a huge creature should have so thin a voice. But that was in her silly girlhood. She had since met beings much more paradoxical and less comprehensible, and learned that to them humans were likewise.

She did still sometimes wonder whether Karl—her name for him, honoring a friend at home—really spoke as academically as the device rendered it. He was a scientist, but also a top-class waymate. Yet she would never understand the nuances of his personality, nor he hers. They could never be more than comrades.

"Let's have a better look." She unsheathed her optic, raised it to her eyes, and activated it. His keener vision had already made out what she now did. The surface was not actually smooth, it was subtly, bewilderingly complex. Increasing the magnification gave small help. Noontide shadows were too short to bring out enough relief.

The idea struck her like a fist. Her hands dropped. "Forerunner work?" she cried.

Amidst the tumult in her head she felt that the translator's level tone was, for once, conveying an emotion. Calm. "I immediately suspected so." Somebody with Karl's size and strength might not be very excitable. Interested, yes; delighted, maybe; but free of the chills that ran up her spine, out to the ends of her fingers.

Steadiness returned. She lifted the optic again.

Two beings poised on the thing, with a variety of instruments set forth. One was a male human, the other an anthropard from Rikha or a Rikhan colony. She watched them come to full alertness, peer her way, and hasten down the whaleback curve. Their boat lay alongside, tethered by a geckofoot grapnel. They got in, cast off, and motored toward the land.

Lissa swung her gaze about and found their camp, which from here was half screened by brush. She put her optic back.

"Do you recognize either of them?" asked Karl.

"No," she said, "nor why they haven't been in touch." She scowled as she started off again. "We'll find out. We'd better."

The camp amounted to three dome shelters. But the vehicle standing by was no ordinary flyer adapted for this planet. Twice the size, it was clearly capable not simply of flitting through atmosphere, hovering, vertical landings and takeoffs, but of making orbit. Indeed, when last she and Karl heard from headquarters, personnel had detected a small spaceship circling farther out than theirs in a sharply canted plane. Apparently those who had been aboard would rather not be noticed.

Otherwise the landscape lay primeval, hills rolling low in the east and on either side of the valley, thickly wooded. The vegetation was unlike any she knew of anywhere else, curiously shaped boles and boughs, foliage in shades of dark yellow and brown, eerie blossoms—another world, after all. Animal life was as alien and as abundant; the sky was full of wings and clamor. The fundamental biochemistry resembled hers in a number of ways, and the basis of life itself was microbial here too. But that was due to the working of the same natural laws on more or less Earthlike planets. How many centuries until the biology of even this single continent would be even sketchily charted?

Depends partly on how much of an effort scientifically oriented sophonts feel is worth making, passed banally through her mind. The galaxy's so huge, so various, and always so mysterious.

Odd, how high and steep the riverbanks were. In fact, it flowed at the bottom of a rocky canyon. Farther inland, its sides were low, begrown to the very edge of the water. Only as she neared did she see that here the stream had broadened to almost a kilometer.

She reviewed the local geography as scanned by a satellite. Flowing westward, the river became wider still. Fifty kilometers hence its estuary was salt marshland. There it emptied into a channel that in turn led to an ocean.

Evidently local topography had made it cut this gorge. Hadn't that taken time on a geological scale? But the rock wasn't wind-sculpted, merely littered with boulders where ledges and cracks offered resting places.

Nor was the ground above richly forested, like upstream. A strip of thin, poor, rocky soil reached back some fifty meters from either verge. Tough-looking, deep-rooted little bushes stood sparsely, interspersed with lesser plants that she guessed were evanescent opportunists. She saw just a few tiny animals scuttering between, though winged creatures continued plentiful. The camp was at the edge of the semi-desert, half surrounded by fairly large shrubs, trees behind it.

One of countless puzzles. . . . At the moment, she had too much else to think about. Surely in due course somebody would reason this out.

She eased her pace. In spite of a noticeably denser atmosphere and higher partial pressure of oxygen, in spite of her being in athletic condition and having trained beforehand, a surface gravity fifteen percent above Earth normal added nine kilos to her weight.

Karl slowed to match her. By his standards, he was taking baby steps. Carrying nearly all their field equipment on his back, as well as his own mass, he seemed to move effortlessly.

With him at her side she'd scarcely need the pistol at her hip. Not that she supposed the pair ahead of her had violent intentions. Still, however mild-mannered, Karl was bound to be a trifle overawing. Looming a meter above her, he was not wholly unlike a, well, a tyrannosaur. Longer arms, yes, and four-fingered hands; short muzzle, big green eyes, tall ears, gray skin; the taloned feet bare rather than booted. His many-pocketed coverall resembled hers, though open in back for a formidable tail.

The air had cooled, while keeping a medley of odors, sweet, pungent, acid, sulfury. Wind boomed from the west, where clouds lifted massive. Their hollows were dark blue, their heights amber, against a sky almost purple. The sun brooded overhead, two and a fourth times the size of Sol seen from Earth. To the human eye, an M0 dwarf is pale yellow, and you can look straight at it for a moment without being blinded. To Lissa, the summer light recalled autumn at home.

And the noontide would last and last. This planet orbited close in, with a two-thirds rotational lock. A hundred and twenty-three of Earth's days would pass before noon came back.

She thrust her stray thoughts aside. The man and his partner had reached a wooden dock that a robot—they must have one or two along—had doubtless constructed, and were debarking. In a few minutes she'd meet them.

II

The spot was about halfway between. All four halted. For an instant only the wind spoke.

After an appraising look, the man apparently decided that Anglay was their likeliest common language. "Greeting, my lady, sir." She didn't recognize his accent. The voice was resonant, though she guessed from it that he couldn't carry a tune if it had handles. "Welcome. Maybe." He added the last word with a grin. She suspected it was not entirely in jest.

"Thank you," she replied. Her glance searched him. He stood tall in his rough garb, thick-shouldered, slender-hipped. The head was round, the face blunt, blue-eyed, weatherbeaten; a stubble of beard showed he hadn't bothered lately with depilatory. The light-brown hair grew a bit thin on top but peeked abundantly from under collar and sleeves. By no means unattractive, she thought. "I'm Lissa Davysdaughter Windholm of Asborg—Sunniva III. My companion's name for human purposes is Karl."

"What language does he prefer? I know a few."

"His own. The dominant one on Gargantua," as humans called the mother planet of that race, a back formation from their name for the race itself. "He understands us quite well."

"We'd like to understand him, though, wouldn't we?"

"Shouldn't my translator be set for that?"

He laughed. "A touch, my lady! Well, I'm Torben Hebo. My partner is Dzesi, from her native world."

The other made a gesture involving her knife. *"S-s-su alach."* She switched to Anglay. Her species could render human sounds fairly well, with hissing overtones and an underlying growl. "Peace between us, Lissa Windholm and Karl Gargantuan."

"Peace in truth, Dzesi," Karl answered through the device. "I request knowledge of your origins, that we may address you in seemly wise."

Lissa realized, startled, that he had some familiarity with Rikhans—must have had dealings, probably scientific. Fortunate! Her acquaintance was minimal, almost entirely from what she had learned in school and from occasional anecdotes. They were said to be innately proud and touchy.

The anthropard's eerily humanlike mouth made a smile, baring pointed reddish teeth. Otherwise the visage, with its slit-pupilled amber eyes, flat single-nostrilled nose, upstanding tufted ears, and long cilia, suggested a cat more than anything else. The body, nude except for orange-hued, black-spotted fur and a belt holding two pouches and the knife, was also not unlike Lissa's, in a huge-chested, breastless, wasp-waisted fashion. The long legs brought the height to about the same as the man's.

"Yes-s," she said. "I am of the Ulas Trek in Ghazu."

"In honor," Karl responded.

"Accepted and offered."

Lissa turned to Hebo. "But where are you from, sir, and what's your allegiance?"

He shrugged. "Everywhere, and to my friends." With another laugh: "Hey, this is an unexpected pleasure. Welcome for sure, Lissa—and, uh, Karl, of course. Come on, we're being rotten hosts, let's get you settled down and have a drink for openers."

He was scanning her with imperfectly concealed lust. That was natural under the circumstances, even a compliment if he kept it under control. She was not tall but full-bodied, supple, tawny of skin and high of cheekbones, short-nosed, heavy-lipped, stubborn-chinned, mahogany hair banged and bobbed. Her last rejuvenation having been eighteen years ago, time had thus far only laid a few laughter lines at the hazel eyes. And she always carried her biological age well, whatever it was at any given time.

"We thank you, but we must take your hospitality provisionally," Karl said toward Dzesi.

"Your warning satisfies," the Rikhan told him.

"For now, anyway," said Hebo. Quickly: "We've got a lot to talk about. Plus that drink."

He led the way. Dzesi came well behind.

Karl signed to Lissa that she should lower the volume of the translator before he explained: "Her ancestors seldom went about without a rearguard. To provide one was an amicable act. The feuds are now ended—or sublimated—but traditions endure. And, I believe, instincts. Ghazu is largely steppe. Its inhabitants are the only known beings who, nomadic, independently developed high technology."

Lissa nodded. What a diverse and wonderful universe she lived in!

The habitation dome was clean, and neat where neatness counted. Hebo's things showed a certain bachelor disarray. Dzesi's things were few. The humans sat on folding chairs, the Rikhan on her haunches, the Gargantuan balanced on his tail. Hebo broke out a bottle of excellent whiskey for Lissa and himself, not diluting it much. Dzesi poured water from a gilt bottle into a decorated drinking horn and sipped ceremoniously, almost religiously. Karl had tea from his own canteen. Everybody knew how poisonous alcohol was to his kind.

Hebo lifted his tumbler. "Here's to friendship."

"Indeed." No matter how much she enjoyed the dram she took, Lissa tautened. "I must say, though, you haven't seemed eager for it."

"Business is business," Hebo replied, unabashed. "Now that you've found us, let's make the best of it."

"What's your business, then, if you please?"

"I might ask why you care. A whole planet should be plenty big enough for all, no?"

"If nothing else, we're concerned about possible damage. You can't be unaware of what ecological havoc can start if strict precautions aren't taken, especially when biochemistries are strongly similar." She was sounding like an elementary school teacher, she heard. Amusement flickered across his face. She didn't want that. "And now, this object in the river—what's it mean, what's its scientific value—and you haven't reported it. I imagine you counted on sheer area to hide you."

His grin flashed afresh. "Hey, I like your frankness. It's a long story on both sides, I'll bet. You're with a scientific expedition, right?" She nodded. "Yeah, Dzesi and I guessed that, when we detected your ship and base as we approached. Whose are they?"

"You could have learned that when you arrived." His gaze on her stayed shameless. "Our expedition originated on Asborg. Several Houses there sponsor what planetary exploration and research their means allow. This time it's mine and one other. Jonna has been neglected since it was first found and skimpily surveyed."

"Jonna? Your people's name?"

A second sip glowed along her tongue. She relaxed somewhat and smiled. "Better than a catalogue number."

"Seems like your party's awfully small. To judge by the glimpse we had. No offense, but how much can you do, working out of one camp in—how long a stay?"

She sighed. "Two years. Asborgan, that is; twenty-one months Earth standard. The most the consortium can afford at this stage." Too many worlds, she thought, too full of unknownness, and we sophonts too few. "But a beginning. There's no such thing as useless information, insight, is there?" Enthusiasm surged. "Who knows? We could make a discovery important enough that major institutions on several planets will mount a real effort." She curbed it. "You may have made one, Captain Hebo."

"Torben, Lissa. Formality doesn't belong hereabouts."

The Rikhan surprised her by taking her side. "Tradition is not a shield to lower lightly."

"Speak for your own folk, partner. Uh, not to get forward, Lissa, or m'lady Windholm if you'd rather. How did you find us?"

"A monitor satellite of ours captured a view." Happenstance, as enormous as the region was, but not too improbable, given the capabilities.

"I reckoned so. We'd figured it was lucky for us your base is on the next continent. Well, our luck didn't hold out. Not that any harm's necessarily been done. For sure, none was intended."

"You didn't respond to our calls," she accused.

"Is that compulsory? They weren't distress signals."

Her amity dimmed. "You hoped we didn't receive more than an inadequate image that could be misleading, and we'd be too busy to investigate just on the strength of it. Didn't you?"

He laughed again. "That was sort of what we hoped. At least, we were buying a little time. But, say, if you wanted to check, why not send a flyer directly?"

"We are busy," she admitted. "Undermanned, underequipped, under a deadline because of supplies—" She stiffened her backbone. "It chanced that Karl and I were in this vicinity. Base asked us to go have a look."

He raised beaker and brows together. "On foot?"

"Our flyer is parked about fifty hours' journey away by the most direct route," Karl put in. "Our mission is to conduct a random-sampling investigation of nature in these parts, on the ground, for comparison with data from elsewhere. Brief, superficial, inadequate in itself, granted; but trained observers may conceivably come upon a clue that causes research to redirect itself. Since, in our ignorance, one direction was as good as another, we readily agreed to make for this point."

Hebo kept his attention on the woman. "So you're a xenobiologist, Lissa?"

"No, Captain Hebo," she said. "I'm a—generalist. I've simply done a fair amount of wilderness exploration on more than one planet, and the forest here is not too unlike others for scouts afoot to cope with." The joy of it! "Karl's the scientist."

"And the muscle, I see. Not that you don't have mighty good-looking muscles yourself," Hebo purred.

She felt herself flush, and snapped, "Very well, here we are. Now it's the turn of you two to explain what you're at."

III

A shelter window let in the deceptively mellow sunlight. From where she sat, Lissa could see over the scarred ground to the edge of the canyon and, beyond, wanly sheening amidst the gleam of water, the thing.

"Fair enough," Hebo was saying. "Yep, fair enough. We're absolutely legitimate."

She swung her gaze back to meet his. "Then why the stealth?"

Dzesi stirred. She touched her knife. "S-s-s," she hissed. "That is not a pleasant word about this."

Karl took a short step forward and loomed at her.

Lissa had experienced a multitude of situations in the course of—going on a hundred years, was it? she thought in sudden astonishment. That long? Already? She lifted her free hand and made a smile. "No offense, as you put it, Captain Hebo, nor to your honorable companion. Shall we say you've been remarkably discreet?"

The atmosphere eased. The man laughed once more. "We could spend the rest of this large economy-size day beating around the bush. I don't want to, do you? Sure, Dzesi and I have been sneaky."

Again he was likeable. In fact, Lissa admitted to herself, he had a good deal of raffish charm. "Would you care to explain? No, I don't imagine I have any authority, but others do."

"I'd argue about that. But put it aside for now." Hebo leaned back in his chair, crossed his legs, and took a long swallow. "All right. To start with, I'm a free-lance entrepreneur, to give it a fancy name. I keep my senses and sensors open, and when I get wind of a possible profit to be made, I go there."

Lissa half gasped. "On your own?"

"Yep, my little spaceship is mine free and clear, along with the assorted gear and such, including enough capital to keep me solvent till the next success. More ventures don't work out than do."

"But, but what government *licenses* you?"

"Oh, this one or that one, depending. I've been at it a long while. When some fly-by-night nation goes under, I find me another." He saw her frown. "Yes, I know a spacecraft mishandled can do as much damage as a crashing asteroid. Mine hasn't done any yet; and I've been flitting a long while, I said. With several tribes, countries, sovereignties, globalities, what-have-you, I'm kind of grandfathered." He leaned forward and patted her knee. "Don't worry, brighteyes."

She drew back, also in her spirit, but was nevertheless gripped. "Why are you on Jonna?"

He nodded toward the river. "What else but yonder?"

"Which is—"

"That's what Dzesi and I would like to find out. So far, between our tests and my database—I keep a whopping database, if I do say so myself; and I do—we've established that it wasn't made by any beings we know of, and includes technology none of them have ever heard of."

A fresh shiver passed through Lissa. "Forerunners?"

"I suppose so, whoever they were. Or are."

"Yes-s-s," breathed the anthropard.

"Let us make certain we understand each other," said Karl. He was right, Lissa admitted to herself. If you didn't trudge through the obvious at the outset, you might learn the hard way that an alien—even a member of your own species, come from another world, another society—meant something quite different from what you did. Language was often too subtle, too mutable for the capabilities of a translator program.

"I assume we refer to those mysterious beings whose ancient

relics have infrequently been come upon," the Gargantuan continued. "It is not known whether the creators are still extant, but certainly they are no longer present in such parts of the galaxy as any of today's spacefaring societies have visited."

Hebo nodded. "You've got it. Myself, I favor the notion that they weren't interested in colonizing, for whatever reason, and just had a few scientific missions in these parts. But why they never came back for a later look—" He shrugged. "That's another good question. They must know that geological time has gone by. If they're alive yet."

"One may well doubt that," said Karl. "Surely, however few and fleeting have been the expeditions to remote parts of the galaxy, so mighty and long-established a civilization would indicate its existence somewhere in it—by radiation from power sources, for example, detectable across many parsecs."

"But the galaxy's so bloody goddamn big. Oh, yes, our ships can jump to anywhere in it, but what microfraction of the total volume have we even touched? Especially at much greater distances than our usual rounds go. Wouldn't you at least expect that the Forerunners' home region would show lingering signs of their influence? Instead, everyplace seems to be the same on average, a few planets where the sophonts have gotten into space themselves, and that's *it*."

Unless the Forerunners are something utterly other, thought Lissa, so strange that we can't ever find them—or couldn't recognize them for what they are if we did—maybe beings or machines that can survive at the core of the galaxy, maybe off in a whole different universe, maybe— It was not the first time she had wondered, nor was she the first one.

Hebo slapped his knee. "All right," he said impatiently, "have we told each other enough of what everybody knows?"

"No, rather, of what no one knows," answered Karl.

"What is this thing here?" Lissa whispered.

Hebo laughed. "I thought you'd never ask. Well, that's what we're trying to figure out. There could be one blue giant of a lot to learn from it. Including, maybe, a clue or three to the makers."

The little she knew whirled in her head.

Found, almost always by purest chance—

A great field of rock on each of three airless worlds, fused by something not natural, optically flat save where meteorites had gouged craters.

Two nickel-iron asteroids that had been shaped into perfect spheres and set in the Trojan positions of the orbit of the planet humans called Xanadu.

On another living world, a single crystal the size of a high hill, which may have been the core of a huge machine or—or what?

Small metallic objects of peculiar shapes, brought to sight by erosion of the rock around them, conceivably tools or components that had been dropped and forgotten, as modern explorers might leave a hammer or some bolts behind, but the uses of these were unguessable, though when their perdurable alloys were finally analyzed it opened up a whole new field of materials science.

Six-meter bubbles of similar stuff afloat in the atmosphere of a Jupiter-sized planet, hollow, emptied of whatever they once contained, though maybe that had not been matter at all but a resonance of forces.

Fossilized traces of foundations removed and activities ended, like dinosaur tracks, and one maddening impression that might have been made by some kind of circuitry—

Where datable, perhaps ten million years old, but the probable error of those measurements might be up to fifty percent.

And few, few—

How much more waited undiscovered, at the half-million or so stars that spacefarers or their robots had come to, however briefly, and the three hundred billion or more in this one galaxy that none had yet reached?

Lissa stared back toward the river. "This may be . . . the best preserved Forerunner object . . . ever found."

Hebo nodded. "As far as Dzesi and I can tell. We even suspect it's in working order. Though we can't tell what that would signify. It can't be hyperbeaming, this far down in the gravity well. Maybe there was a relay satellite, or maybe a ship called now and then to collect the data."

"But this is incredible. You can't keep it hidden." Anger flared. "You've no *right* to!"

She jumped to her feet, spilling her drink. The Rikhan glided up, hand on knife, lips drawn off teeth. Karl whistled and stirred his bulk.

"Whoa, there!" Hebo rose too. A cloud passed over the sun, blown from the west. A wild creature screamed.

Hebo picked up Lissa's beaker and busied himself with a fresh one. "Here, let me make you a refill," he urged. "Come on, we're friends. Just listen, will you?"

"Go ahead," she agreed after a minute. She accepted the drink. He'd mixed it stiffer than before. She'd better be careful.

Hebo returned to his chair, outrageously relaxed. "Well, now, to start with, I told you I make my living where and how I can, as long as it's more or less decently. Decency's got a lot of different definitions, human and nonhuman." His tone smoothed. "But I assure you, milady, I'm not a worse man than most.

"So a couple of years ago I caught word about the discovery of, uh, Jonna. Obscure, only another sort-of-Earthlike planet—'only!' " he exclaimed. Calm again: "Sooner or later, somebody would try to learn more, but no telling who or why. Nobody can keep up with everything that everybody's up to. Well, why not me? Nothing to forbid. No one's laid any claim. No jurisdiction except the Covenant of Space, and you know how much that means."

"A statement of pious intentions." Did the Rikhan sound contemptuous?

"A basic common-sense agreement," Karl reproved.

"Anyhow," Hebo said, "we weren't about to commit banditry, conquest, environmental destruction, or cruelty to politicians. We just intended a look-see. Dzesi's partnered with me before, now and then."

"For the fame and honor of the Ulas Trek," said the anthropard.

And Dzesi's own, Lissa thought. She isn't altogether unlike us.

"How did you find the artifact when we didn't?" the woman asked.

"Partly luck, no doubt," Hebo conceded. "However, we did have our particular motives. You people are after basic scientific knowledge, planetology, biology, et cetera. The planet's loaded with that, anywhere you go. We were looking for something that might pay off."

"How?"

"Oh, maybe a region someone would like to try colonizing. These long days and nights, swings in the weather, and all—in some areas, at least, maybe they'd not be too much for, oh, possibly the Sklerons. Of course, they'd want very specific information before deciding it was worth their while to investigate further. So we were random-sampling, with a close eye out for anything unusual. When our optics spotted this from orbit, naturally we came down to see what it was."

Indignation resumed. "And you haven't considered reporting it!"

"We will, we will, and meanwhile we won't have harmed it. We figured somebody—a news agency, a scientific institution, whatever—would pay well to be told about it. Contract drawn up beforehand, payment on proof of truthfulness. Same as selling any other information. Information's really the one universal currency."

Anger gave way to a certain sympathy. She wished it were not she who must dash his hopes to the ground. "I'm afraid we—can't keep the secret for you. Not ethically."

Dzesi snarled.

Hebo shushed her. Astonishingly good-humored, he responded: "Luck of the draw. Can't win 'em all. Though I do already have a couple of notions about deals that could maybe be made—" He finished his drink. "Hey, let's knock this off. Stay a while, why don't you? We'll help you set up your camp. We'll show you around. And then you can decide what to tell them at your base, other than that you're safe and sound and having a good time."

IV

Dinner became jolly, at any rate for the humans. Hebo kept an excellent larder. He poured the wine with a liberal hand and did most of the talking. Lissa soon had nothing against that, even after it became rather boastful. If half what he told was true, he'd had some fabulous adventures. And he had also absorbed considerable culture. Much of what he quoted or mentioned in passing was unfamiliar to her—who were Machiavelli, Hiroshige, Buxtehude?—but she didn't think he was making it up. The worlds and histories were simply too manifold.

"Yep," he ended, "we'd've been rescued plenty sooner if it hadn't been for the squabbles back on the satellite."

"That *was* a tense situation," she said. "The rivalry between the Susaians and the Grib—I didn't know it can get so bitter."

"Actually, that didn't cause most of the trouble," Hebo explained. "Sure, those two breeds don't get along, and it was a big mistake including several of both in the expedition. But they're too different for any real, deadly feuding, let alone war. Nope," he said, turning a bit philosophical, "I don't expect there'll ever be an interstellar war. Between species, that is. Inside a species, though—races, religions, tribes, factions—in this case, two Susaian creeds. Not that we humans are saints. We may be the worst of the lot."

You might almost call him handsome, in a rough-hewn fashion, Lissa thought. "You must have a wide basis for comparison," she murmured, "with all the roving you've done for—how long?"

"I was born about nine hundred years ago, Earth count."

"What? But that's amazing!" Minor scars and the like suggested his latest rejuvenation had been about twenty years back, which would put him biologically in his forties. He didn't look it. "Why have I never heard of you before, at home on Asborg or anywhere else?"

"Oh, I've been on Asborg now and then. You've got some beautiful country. But it's a while since last, and anyway, a planet's so big and patchworky and changeable. Not to speak of a galaxy. I'm not interested in doing anything worldshaking."

"Though the, the revelation here—"

They had finished coffee; she had declined to share brandy with him. "Tell you what," he said, "if you want, we can go out. I'll give you the guided tour."

She accepted eagerly. Aglow, his tongue still clattering, he nonetheless walked as steadily as her. Karel accompanied them to the gorge, but not on the scramble down its steep, rocky side. The boat could scarcely hold him together with the humans. He turned back. He and Dzesi, eating their separate rations, had apparently become interested in fathoming one another's personalities.

The boat slipped forth onto the water. Clouds westward loomed ever higher and darker. The wind had strengthened. "A storm seems to be brewing at sea," Lissa remarked. "Do you think it'll come this far inland?"

"I'd guess not," Hebo replied. "Though by now, don't your people, with all their instruments and observations, know the weather patterns pretty well? Dzesi and I haven't been here but a short while, and have hardly gotten around at all."

"Coming straight down, with scarcely any study from orbit first—wasn't that a little—reckless?"

He shrugged. "Life's a crapshoot, however you play it."

Some of his words and phrases were strange to her; she had to take their meaning from context. Archaic, she supposed. Well, in many ways he was archaic himself.

The boat arrived. He made fast and offered a hand to help her up the metal flank. She didn't need it, but enjoyed the contact.

Mainly, her attention was underfoot, on intricate low-relief patterns that possibly bore—circuits, receptors, transmitters, receivers—?

They halted on top and stood mute. The wind tossed her hair and ruffled the stream. The sun glowed dull and huge. Creatures leaped briefly out of the water or winged in noisy hordes.

She looked to and fro, the length and breadth of the mystery. Awe nearly overwhelmed her. "What is it?"

He chuckled. "Wouldn't Dzesi and I like to know?"

"You must have learned something."

"Of course. I think."

Eagerness throbbed. "What?"

He shook his head. "Uh-uh. The idea is to sell information, not give it away. We haven't got any institution supporting us, nor professional prestige to gain by publishing."

She had been turning that question over at the back of her mind. "I can't promise anything," she said slowly, "but I can do my best—and I know some influential people who'd probably agree—I can try to arrange that you be rewarded for what you've done."

He beamed. "Hey, that's really sweet of you." He moved in on her.

She retreated a step, pretending she did it casually. "Only fair. The discovery is a tremendous contribution. And whatever you've learned is that much work already done." Keep this practical, impersonal. "However, I'll have to know what to tell those people."

"Quite the little bargainer, aren't you?" he said, more amicably than she liked. "Well, reasonable. But I've got to dicker too. I'll give you a quick and dirty outline if you want, and keep our exact facts and figures under the table till later."

She smiled. "Besides, this is hardly the place for a scientific lecture." Nor are you in shape to give one, she judged.

"No," he agreed. "We can talk comfortably over a drink, the two of us."

"Our partners deserve to be there," she answered warily. Divert him. "Could you give me some slight notion of, of what to expect?"

"A sketch of that outline? Why not?" He gestured grandiosely. "This is doubtless a self-growing, self-renewing device. Same principle as we often use, but way superior. Nothing we can make could maintain homeostasis anywhere near as long as this has. Well, of course the plan, the chemistry, everything's entirely unlike our stuff." His words gathered momentum. "We've traced its configuration electronically, sonically— Hm, am I a poet? Anyhow, it sits on the river bottom, but extends deep roots to anchor itself and extract the minerals it needs to repair the, uh, ravages of water and weather and radiation and what-all else. Deep. Clear through bedrock, way into lower strata. Dzesi and I think it is, or was, an observatory, taking data on everything that comes in range, geology, atmosphere, life, everything, maybe down to the molecular level."

"Yes, it's usually supposed that's what the Forerunners wanted in these regions, information. Why they then abandoned their network and never returned—"

"Who knows? This thing isn't dead. We register traces of power, probably drawing on solar energy. As you'd expect, since it still resists erosion. Self-repair. But we can't find out exactly what's going on."

Lissa shivered in the wind.

Hebo gave her a broad smile. "There, will that do for a synopsis? How about now we relax and enjoy ourselves?"

"For a while, perhaps. With our friends. Frankly," and honestly, "I'm almost ready for bed."

"Me too. Though not sleep, huh?" He leaned close. "Not right away."

She took another backward step. "What do you mean?" She knew full well.

"You're a mighty attractive woman, Lissa. Even if it hadn't

been quite a dry spell for me, you'd stand out." He laughed. "In every way, but especially two."

"Hold on, there," she snapped.

"Been a while for you also, I hope. Our partners are of opposite sex to us, but that doesn't help, does it? They aren't built right. Come on," he coaxed. "I'm good. I'll bet you are too."

"No."

He reached and caught hold of a buttock. She sprang from him. He lumbered ahead, grinning and beckoning. She drew her pistol.

"No," she said. "I mean it, Hebo."

He slammed to a stop. "You do," he said, as if astounded. "You really do."

"Take me back ashore."

"All right, if you're cold."

Fleetingly, she confessed to herself that, earlier, she'd been tempted. "No," she blurted. "You're crude."

He lifted his palms. "All right, all right, I'm sorry. You shouldn't have acted like—"

"Stop. We're going straight back to camp. Behave yourself after you've slept this off, and I'll let the matter rest. Otherwise Karl and I will send word to the base and make for our flyer. Meanwhile, I suggest you keep Karl in mind."

"All right, all *right,*" he mumbled sullenly. "I said I'm sorry."

They returned in a thick silence.

Puzzlement, more than anger, tumbled through her. How could he have been so stupid? He was intrinsically intelligent, he'd had centuries of experience, surely space itself had schooled him in patience, he hadn't lost coordination, which showed he could hold his liquor when he chose—what ailed him?

Torben Hebo woke with a foul taste in his mouth and a worse temper. Damnation, but he'd bungled! Misgauged, at least. He'd have sworn the girl was hinting, her eyes, her hips, her tone of voice. He should have remembered what manners and mores were like on Asborg. Every society, including every human society, had its own. In fact, people might think and behave one way in one part of a planet, otherwise in another. How was he supposed to keep such things straight? He'd forgotten whatever he once learned about her homeland. If he'd actually been there. His visits might have been to areas hundreds, maybe thousands of kilometers from it. He'd forgotten to ask about her background. And about herself.

He'd been forgetting too much, too often, these past years.

Nevertheless, she didn't have to take such offense, did she? He'd backed off, apologized, hadn't he?

He and Dzesi needed her goodwill. What did she want for restoring it?

Maybe she'd be in a forgiving mood. Maybe she wouldn't. If not, what could he say to soothe her?

While he brooded, he rose, cleansed, and dressed. Dzesi had already left. When Hebo returned from the river, the anthropard had said wryly, "I wondered whether you would prefer I rest elsewhere," which hadn't helped.

Outside, the sun had shifted less than a degree across the sky. Cloud cover hazed it. The wind blew stronger and cooler, with a salty tang. It sent russet waves over the crowns of the forest on the hills.

Lissa's puffball tent lay shut, near the storage dome. Was she sleeping late? Because anger had kept her awake late? Hebo entered the dome for cooking and dining, almost afraid to find her there. Karl and Dzesi sat conversing. "Greeting," said the Gargantuan politely. Had she told him?

"Coffee is ready," the Rikhan said.

In spite of everything, Hebo chuckled. "God bless you." He strode to the pot and drew a large mugful.

"What are your plans for the immediate future, if I may inquire?" asked Karl. "Or would you prefer to postpone talk until after breakfast? I have observed that many humans do."

"Don't want breakfast." Hebo gulped the hot brew. "A trail bar will be plenty. We've got to get started, Dzesi."

"To the relic?" Karl's question was not entirely ridiculous, for he added, "The tide is flowing up the river. Do you know how far it will come or how high it will crest? A sun close to a planet raises large tides."

Dzesi's whiskers bristled. "That is obvious," she said, miffed.

"In this case, the force is eleven or twelve times Terran maximum," Hebo added. "Anybody can calculate that."

"But topography causes great variations," Karl said.

"We know that too," the Rikhan snapped.

"I beg your pardon. No condescension was intended. I have learned that humans like to make—small talk, do you call it in Anglay?—but have found it virtually impossible to formulate what the appropriate occasions and subjects are."

Dzesi relaxed. "Honor is mutually satisfied," she said.

Hard enough for humans to please each other, Hebo thought.

His spirits lifted the least bit. Maybe he could cultivate this being, who could then put in a kindly word with Lissa. Or, for that matter, with those influential people she'd spoken of.

"We haven't been here for a tidal cycle," he said. "But, plainly, the object will be submerged. We'll take what further measurements we can, then retrieve the instruments out there.

While we wait for ebb, we can try reducing some more of the data.

"We'd be glad of your help and milady Windfell's in that," he added, "and I guess you'll be interested."

"Indeed. I will tell her when she rises." Did Karl sound anxious? "I do recommend alertness."

Impatience took over. "We're still alive, aren't we?" Hebo emptied the mug and pocketed his ration. "Ready to go, Dzesi?"

The anthropard came lithely erect. Now her whiskers quivered. "For these past three hours." Her species slept too, but ordinarily in brief naps around the clock. Which made it a lot easier for them to adapt to other planets than it was for humans with their long circadian rhythms, Hebo thought for perhaps the thousandth time.

In spite of which, he also thought, humans had done pretty damn well, and they weren't the very first local race who set forth to the stars.

Therefore let's get on with the job at hand.

Which was to collect as much further information as possible before the tide covered the relic, and prepare an arrangement that would keep on probing while it was underwater—increase what he and Dzesi would have to bargain with—and afterward make up with the woman. He'd think of some way to do that. Right now he was too busy.

Karl stayed by the tent. He himself didn't bother with shelters. His gaze followed them till they had gone from sight down the canyonside. Maybe it still did when their boat came into his purview.

Already the river roiled within thirty centimeters of the top of the artifact. The wind from the darkling west raised choppy, chaotic waves. Spray blew off them, sea-bitter where it struck lips.

Having debarked, Dzesi leaped to the crystallometer. Like the other instruments in place, it had been sending its input to the computer ashore, but this hadn't lately been analyzed and she wanted to adjust it. The array of atoms here was evidently different from any other that was known. What kind of potential did that imply?

When races sundered by space and time finally got together, what marvels they discovered!

Hebo sought the far side to inspect a vibration analyzer. Water gurgled around the attachment of its cable and lapped at its geckofoot stand. Damn, but the river was rising fast.

Unease struck. "Dzesi," he called into the wind, "I think we'd better load our stuff on the boat right away."

"There is not that much haste," answered his partner, absorbed.

"Well, soon," Hebo yielded. Currents set even this material slightly ashiver, which provided clues—

And then waves lifted, to wash over metal and ankles. Noise rolled, crashed, and deafened. Eastward up the river, glinting green and foam-white, raced a wall of water.

VI

The thunder shocked Lissa out of sleep. She squirmed from her bag, crawled from the tent, and jumped to her feet. In horror and instant understanding, she knew.

Karl was headed for the gorge. His legs scissored. She ran after him, unable to match that stride. He stopped on the rim, wheeled around, gestured and shrilled at her. The translator lay amidst other gear, but there was no mistaking what he cried. *"Go back! This can kill you!"*

She recoiled. He turned again to the river. Over the brink he went.

"No, Karl!" she yelled. "You can't either! Don't do it! Please!"

He didn't heed. Nor could he have heard through the roar. She looked, helpless.

Hebo and Dzesi were in their boat. The flood engulfed it. Water swept onto the ground above. Lissa stood fast. It swirled about her feet and drained away. The surge sped on. Behind it, the river level fell, with a hollow sucking sound. She saw the wave damp down too, as it climbed to higher levels. But that mass must pour back here from a narrower channel upstream. The bottom of the canyon went aboil.

The boat bobbed into sight, down again, up again, tossed to and fro. It had capsized. Through the foam she glimpsed Dzesi. The Rikhan must have clung to a thwart, then gotten hold of the rudder. She clasped herself to it, catching breath at every moment her face was in the air.

Where was Torben?

Karl hove into view. His legs kicked, his tail threshed. Crosscurrents raged around him. He battled through them. His head stayed well aloft. Thus he spied Hebo when Lissa did. Torn loose, the man was, somehow, desperately swimming. She could barely make out the distance-dwarfed form amidst the violence. He vanished, drawn down. He emerged, he went back under. No human, however strong, could live.

No human.

Karl reached him, caught him, started for shore. The man kept his wits, didn't struggle, let his rescuer carry him along. Well, he was a natural survivor, Lissa thought crazily.

They vanished under the canyonside. Karl doubtless left him on the boulders, for in a minute or two the Gargantuan reappeared, bound for Dzesi.

The water and the turmoil were slowly, raggedly dropping. Lissa ran back to the tent and slipped on shoes. Otherwise still in pajamas, she returned and picked her way down the steepness.

She found that Hebo had begun to crawl up. "Thanks," he gasped when she came to help. By the time they reached the top, Karl was bringing Dzesi ashore.

Hebo collapsed. Lissa slumped beside him and panted. It had been a tough climb.

Hebo struggled to his knees. "Holy Mother of God," he stammered, "I, I thank you for your mercy. Hail Mary, full of grace, the Lord is with you—"

Lissa watched, astonished. She dimly recalled the prayer from one or two historical documentaries. Who would have expected anything like this from anybody like him?

VII

Rain drummed on the dome and made the outside view a shadowiness in sluicing silver.

Recovered from shock and, in part, exhaustion, the four sat trying to assess that which had come over them. "I should have guessed," said Lissa contritely. "The canyon, the scoured soil along it."

Hebo shook his head. "No," he growled. "The blame's mine. You and Karl weren't prepared, you were doing entirely different studies, you wouldn't have come here if you hadn't been diverted to us, and then we kept your minds too full of other things." He grimaced. "Including my gross behavior. Can you believe I haven't been in the habit of acting that way?"

"It's all right, Torben," she murmured.

"Nor was Dzesi at fault," he plodded on. "She's a drylander. Her people had no experience. But me, I'm from Earth. That was long ago, but still, I've stood on Severn side, I knew about the Bay of Fundy—and I forgot."

He sighed. "It should've been plain to see from space. An estuary opening on a channel that leads to the ocean. A funnel; the exact conditions for a tidal bore. And the tide on Jonna is huge. And now it also had a storm at sea to push it higher.

"I could at least have stayed longer in orbit, observing. But no, I was in too much of a hurry to get us down and started, before your outfit noticed us and our nice little monopoly on the information evaporated.

"I was *stupid*."

She found she hated seeing such a big, adventurous man humbled. Seemingly Dzesi did too, for the Rikhan said low, "I could have held us back. I have fared enough in space to realize that every new world is a snarefield of surprises. But I was likewise impatient."

"Everyone makes mistakes," Karl added. "You would soon have perished if you were incompetent. Instead, you have coped for century after century."

"I will see to it that you get proper payment for the work you've done," Lissa told the man and his partner. "Without you, the artifact might never have been found."

Hebo smiled lopsidedly. "Thank you," he said. "Thank you both, for everything.

"But this has driven the truth home to me. I've grown too old."

"No!" Lissa exclaimed. "You aren't due for a rejuvenation. Are you?"

"It isn't that." She saw and heard how determination gathered itself. "Maybe you've never met a case before. You must have read or heard something about it, but it's not the sort of thing anybody likes to dwell on. My foolishness was to keep shoving it aside. Later, I always told myself, later, someday, there's no need yet. As the condition crept up on me, ignoring it got easier and easier.

"The problem is memories."

"Oh, yes." A chill passed within her. "Yes, I see."

"I do not," said Dzesi in quick irritation.

You probably wouldn't know, thought Lissa. I daresay every member of your species expects to die a violent death. Or hopes to.

Hebo looked grim. To spare him, Lissa explained: "Rejuvenation makes the brain youthful again, of course, like every other part of the body. But it doesn't erase memories. It refreshes them. Well, the brain's data-storage capacity is finite. Worse, the correlations increase geometrically. In the end, it's overwhelmed."

"Surely, in humans, as in my kind, selective erasure is feasible," Karl said, as if offering comfort.

"Oh, yes." Lissa turned back toward Hebo. "I'm not familiar with the details, Torben, but I do know we have excellent clinics of every sort on Asborg. At least one of them must be equipped for the service."

He eased a bit, smiled wryly. "Editing. Thanks, but I think I'd rather get the job done on Earth, if I can."

Surprise jarred her. "Earth?"

"I'll have to choose and decide, you understand. Earth is where my oldest memories come from. And some of my dearest."

He looked away from her, outward into the rain and the distance.

VIII

Her team did not come to a real understanding of Jonna and the life thereon. That would be the work of centuries, if it could ever be completed. But they had learned about as much as anyone hoped for—a scattering of facts, some fragments of patterns—when shortly afterward they must leave.

First they returned their nonhuman members. As *Dagmar* ran from Gargantua toward a point high enough in the gravitational well to allow a hyperjump across light-years, Lissa stood in the saloon, watching the planet recede. She could have done so in her cabin, but it was cramped and the viewscreen here was bigger.

Never mind how familiar, she never wearied of such a sight. On its daylit half, the globe shone white, swirled with a hundred shades of blue, drowning out vision of the multitudinous stars. Nightside glimmered in the light of three moons, small golden crescents. More atmosphere than lay around Asborg or Earth, more clouds. But they opened enough for Karl's people to have seen those stars and at last sought a way to them; and he himself was a mountaineer, used to her thin air.

She smiled as she remembered him. Might they meet again, often. Now the course was for Xanadu. The three little beings from there, with their extraordinary senses adapted to cold and darkness, had been as valuable in studying Jonna's long night as his strength, woodcraft, and biological knowledge had been under its sun.

The leap after that would indeed be to home.

Dagmar murmured around her, like the great organism that in a sense the ship was. Air passed by in a cool breeze, currently bearing a slight piney fragrance. One standard gravity of acceleration gave a lightness welcome after Jonna. No matter how far they fared, the children of Earth brought along their remembrances.

A step on the deck made her turn her head. Romon Kaspersson Seafell had come in. She suppressed a grimace, suddenly realizing that she wanted to be alone.

Not that the man was horrible. Medium-tall, slender, with sharp features, sharp dark eyes. and curly black hair, he wore a plain coverall like hers; but his bore the badge of his House on the shoulder, as if defiantly. Well, he was the only Seafell aboard, and only here because the Seafells had, surprisingly, contributed to the cost of this expedition and, reasonably enough, wanted at least one of their own along. He'd given no particular offense, and been a competent interpreter of geographical data.

"Good daywatch," he greeted, adding after a moment's hesitation, "milady."

Why suddenly so formal? she wondered. Not that they'd been what you'd call close friends. In fact, she had confessed to herself, she didn't quite like him—or, at any rate, she disliked what he stood for. However, relationships all around had been amicable enough, as they'd better be on a foreign planet.

"Likewise, Romon Kaspersson," she answered carefully.

He drew alongside her and stopped, glanced at the screen, then regarded her. "Are we the only two idle ones aboard just now?" It sounded as though he wanted to make conversation.

"I daresay everybody else has their own activities," she said—science, games, sports, sleep, whatever, while the ship conned herself through space.

He did not let the curtness put him off, but smiled a bit. "And I daresay you've been musing about your trailmate back yonder?"

It was easiest to reply, "Yes. Karl's good people." Actually, Hebo had been adrift in her mind. How was he doing? How would he fare, on an Earth that had become the strangest of all the known worlds?

"Agreed." Romon laughed. "A little too much so perhaps. He made me feel less than saintly."

Ah, well, Lissa thought, if he's reaching for a touch of human warmth, why not? He never said much, but he must have felt rather lonely among the Windholms. Mostly he stayed with his computer and readouts, his reports from robots and landsats. She made a smile. "Why, you were perfectly well-behaved."

Jesting was not natural to him. "I tried to be." He bent his lips upward. "My thoughts, however, were often unruly."

Was he probing for intimacy? She wasn't interested, even though it had been a pretty long while. "That's your business."

He lifted a hand. "Please don't get me wrong. I didn't mean it in the usual way. I mean from—m-m-m—your standpoint, and probably your fellows'."

"What, then?" Not to seem naive: "You want to tell me, don't you?"

"Frankly, yes. I've been watching for a chance to talk with you like this."

"Why me?"

He must have rehearsed his answer. "Because you're Lissa Davysdaughter, and your father has the major voice in House Windholm's space operations."

She felt almost relieved. "Your House has its own."

"But we're basically commercial. Investors, developers, and our space operations are interplanetary and minor."

She turned cold. "True."

He allowed himself a hint of anger. "You know Seafell's never had anything like Windholm's landholdings. We're latecomers on Asborg. We can't afford aristocratic attitudes."

"You could by now."

"But traditions, institutions—" Yes, he was in earnest. "Can't you believe we have ours, our ways of thinking and living, the same as you have yours?"

"Of course you do." Every House does, she thought. And we

all live on the same planet, and share in its governance, and what's he leading up to?

"You don't like ours, do you?"

"I don't hate it. A matter of taste. The communal versus the corporate style?" Lissa shrugged. "They say diversity makes for a healthy society."

"Is it so absolute a difference? We did help finance this expedition. We have our human share of curiosity. We're not Shylocks, not in any sense." Romon paused a moment. "Though he too had his ideals, didn't he? And the haughty Christians scorned them."

She almost caught the reference. Something literary, wasn't it, and ancient? Yes, she'd noticed him screening old texts. He was not entirely a money machine. Maybe not even mostly.

It softened her mood a little. She'd better lighten it anyway. "I'm afraid we've all of us had our curiosity more aroused than satisfied."

But he didn't take her hint. "Yes. The Forerunner artifact—It changes everything."

"A remarkable find," she parried.

His tone accused. "You don't seem to care that those vagabonds only intended to make money off it."

Lissa lost whatever small kindliness she had begun to feel. She stiffened. That's different, she almost said. They're private parties, entrepreneurs of the classic sort—adventurers—who had no idea of grabbing a monopoly and couldn't have if they'd wanted to.

Why do I think so, and so strongly?

"Well," she decided to respond, "they found it and did the preliminary work. They deserve some reward."

"Yes, yes. Beside the point. Which is, what shall *we* do with it?"

"Why, I expect there'll be quite a swarm of investigators. Planetologists and biologists will piggyback. What else?"

"That's the obvious outcome. All too obvious. But ask yourself: To whose profit? In the long run?"

"Everybody's."

His gaze never left her. "That's not necessarily true, milady. It isn't even likely. Look at history. Human history, and what little we know about nonhuman ones. Whatever there is to learn, science, technology, is going to give power. To do what? For whom?"

"Scarcely overwhelming power."

"Are you certain? If nothing else, more clues to the Forerunners, and everything that may mean—" Romon drew breath. "Profit, gain, is power in itself. Your spendthrift friends don't seem to have understood that. Or else it's simply that there are just the two of them. A House, though, a world, a race has to think further ahead."

Taken aback by the intensity, Lissa rallied to demand, "What are you getting at?"

"My superiors and I, we honestly thought we were joining the pure-science game. We have been venturing into it now and then, you know. Yes, I was to keep an eye out for possible commercial values, but that was a sideline. An idea absolutely absent from you Windholms."

No, Lissa didn't say, not really. We're human too.

"Now this," Romon pursued. "Milady, it needs to be kept in responsible hands. People who won't recklessly let the knowledge run wild across the galaxy, but keep it under control, *think* hard about everything they learn, use the knowledge and the power wisely."

"And keep the power for themselves," Lissa said half automatically.

"You believe you, you Windholms, can afford idealism. I say you can't. Nobody can."

"What is realism?" she retorted. "How far can the races trust a—a set of interlocking corporate directorates?"

Romon sighed. "Let's not get into a quarrel, milady. There's no basic secret anymore. The news has been hyperbeamed to Asborg and by now has gone everywhere." He tautened. "But discretion, control of access, caution about making any findings public—I agree, probably the artifact in itself can't show us the way to more than some harmless technological progress. But it may have further clues—as I said, even to the Forerunners—and what might that mean?

"It's not too late. I'm proposing cooperation between the leaders of all our Houses. And, yes, for the time being at least, working out diplomatic ways to keep nonhumans off. They're still less predictable than we are. Not so?

"Milady, I simply wish to persuade you to help persuade your father to listen to the case I'm trying to make."

And that the Seafell directors will be trying to make, Lissa thought. How much of this is genuine, how much is in hopes of gaining power? Control. And how much does a desire for control spring from common sense, how much from fear of the universe?

This man seems halfway honest. Maybe more than halfway. An ideologue? A fanatic? I can't tell. Nor am I qualified to probe his psyche, nor do I want to.

Besides, why? It isn't important. What matters is what he maybe represents.

She shivered.

It was a faint surprise how cool her voice remained. "You exaggerate my influence, Romon Kaspersson. As well as the meaning of that artifact. You're always free to contact my father, or anybody else."

He scowled, "Oh, yes. Theoretically. But I want him to listen, seriously listen, and then talk to his peers. You can get him to do that much, can't you?"

"If he finds merit in the idea."

"It'd help, it might be critical. Can you and I talk further? Soon?" His tone softened. Did she hear a sigh? "The voyage won't last much longer."

Thanks be, Lissa thought.

And yet— She was a Windholm. That carried an obligation to do what she could whenever it seemed needful. A small enough return for the wealth and privilege to which she was born. Not that this business looked sunshaking. But it could be an early sign of something larger.

Be that as it might—"If you want. Within reason. Not right now, please. I'd like to rest a while." She escaped to her cabin.

Actually, the encounters afterward weren't so bad. They were only occasional, and only in the course of a few ship-days. He spoke mildly, often smiling, and indeed tried to shift them into more personal conversation. She found she could divert that by asking him to explain the classical quotations he threw in, whether or not she recognized them. They were apt to be lyrical, even tender. Their authors, historical backgrounds, and whatever else she could get him to tell her about them used up time. He wasn't a scholar or anything like that; however, his tastes surprised her a little by their depth and frequent delicacy.

What waited for her when she came home scattered all of it into the far corners of her mind.

IX

Coming out of hyperjump and moving inward through the Solar System, Torsten Hebo's little ship chanced to pass near enough to the Enigma that it showed as a star-twinkle in a viewscreen. He'd heard about this construct, orbited in the asteroid belt a couple of centuries ago. Curious, he magnified the image and amplified the light, until the thing should have been plain to his eyes. It still wasn't. A bewildering geometry of—what, slender girders and braces, complexly curved?—surrounded a core of ever-changeable, softly opalescent glow. No more identifiable now than it was in pictures he'd seen, taken by other visitors and released on the interstellar communication webs.

Not a secret. Merely incomprehensible. Earth didn't issue news releases, but the questions of outsiders got polite, if rather brief and formal, answers. This was an instrumentality for fundamental research. That alone had, at first, been startling enough. Weren't the basic equations of physics written down several hundred years ago? Well, maybe there really was more to be discovered. Unfortunately, said the responses, the principles behind this thing were not explainable, in any meaningful sense of the word, to any organic brain—including unreinforced Earth-human—or any artificial intelligence developed on any other planet. Whatever the results of its investigations, they would be made as public as possible.

The rest was silence.

Well, Hebo thought, I suppose they're working on it yet, and maybe getting nowhere. And maybe I ought to resent the claim that I and every organic being, human or nonhuman, haven't the brains to understand what's going on. But, hell, the universe is full of things I can't understand, like women or affine geometry or Arzethian politics, and so what? My ego isn't tied that hard to my intellect.

It is kind of eerie, though, that Earth seems to be the only planet that everybody thinks of as speaking with a single voice, like a single entity.

The Enigma passed from view, and soon into the bottom of his mind. After all, knocking about in space, he'd encountered plenty of different weirdnesses. And ahead of him was no threat but, he hoped, release and renewal.

He turned his attention to the waxing radiance ahead and presently its silvery companion. It seemed to take a long while, and then it seemed to have taken almost no time, before he was there.

Seen from the outside, Earth had changed little since the last few of his visits. The same white-marbled blue beauty shone athwart crystalline darkness, bearing the same heraldry of continents. The polar caps kept their same modest size, a few dun spots of desert remained, no city lights clustered and sprawled across the nighted side. Fewer solar-power collection fields glimmered on the moon, but he'd known about that change. Information did diffuse starward, news, images, borne more by transients than by direct communication, and less and less often, but apparently nothing kept deliberately secret. Apparently. Maybe, he thought again, it was just that nothing much was going on anymore that his kind of people could follow.

Procedures for approach, orbiting, descent, and such-like matters had certainly gotten streamlined. He especially appreciated not having to lie several hours abed while nanoprobes swarmed through him checking for pathogens; now a scanner did the job in about one minute. Nevertheless, the feeling of being moved along in a huge, smooth-running machine was unexpectedly lonesome.

A robotic flitter set him and his meager baggage down at one of the two hostels kept for humans from outside. The rest had gradually been shut down as demand for them dwindled. He'd picked the one on Oahu, mostly because he'd been recalling youthful days—his first youth—sailing a knockabout around among the Islands and beachcombing on them with a delightful young woman.

Whatever became of her? Had he been a fool to lose touch? Or, he wondered, had wistful memory colored those days brighter than they'd really been and put in happenings that never really happened? He couldn't bring her name to mind.

From the air, he'd seen that Honolulu and the other cities were completely gone. A few low, sleek buildings lay scattered amidst gardens and stands of tropical wildwood. But beyond Diamond Head, Hanauma Bay was about the same as ever and the diving was, if anything, better now when he had it to himself and the coral had been so well rehabilitated. Some congenial company would have been nice, though. He walked back up to the hostel in a mood less happy than the scenery deserved.

It affected an ancient style. That made sense. What its guests chiefly had in common was the history of this world before their forbears—or, in a few cases like his, they themselves—departed. When Hebo came down from his room casually dressed for a drink before dinner, he was shown to a covered deck open to the breezes and the sight of sea and cliffs. A bewildering richness of birds soared, dipped, and cried. He'd heard that some were of native species long extinct, recreated on the basis of records equally old.

The drink was served by an unobtrusive machine. The food, when it came, was good but nothing he recognized; a really first-chop wine came with it. Still, he was glad when another man appeared, and invited him to his table.

Seiichi Okuma spoke no language Hebo could handle. The servitor brought a translator and they were soon in conversation. The other man turned out to be from Akiko, in the Beta Centauri region, which was somewhat off Hebo's usual beat. He was here as part of a small team of—anthropologists? His fellows were currently scattered over the globe. Their sponsors hoped they could gain a somewhat better understanding of present-day Earth, experiencing its life in more detail and with less predictability than verbals, visuals, and virtuals offered.

"And how've you been doing?" Hebo asked.

"None of us are sure yet," Okuma admitted, "but already it's rather discouraging. We knew, of course, the human population is down to only about fifty million. That's anomalous enough. But I, at least, I had not guessed how remote that population has become."

"People aren't friendly?"

The question was of more than academic interest to Hebo. He hadn't yet spoken at any length with anyone but a space traffic control officer, and that was by beamphone and she was modified-human—not ugly, but not his type. Her words had been polite, no more. He'd wondered why she cared to do something so routine, when it could easily and more efficiently be cybered. Maybe fleeting encounters with yokels like him amused her. As for the utility of it, he supposed a live person was meant as a courtesy to newcomers.

Unless, of course, she too was a virtual.

"Oh, those I have sought out have been ready enough to talk, if not very forthcoming," Okuma said. "Some have actually extended hospitality of an austere sort. But I have never felt their attention was really on me."

"Most of their awareness in linkage." A slight shiver passed through Hebo. "The world-mind. Yeah."

Okuma shook his head. "That is a misnomer. It is—forgive me, sir—a common misconception. My group had learned that much beforehand. Consciousness on Earth—human, parahuman, quantum-net—is not joined in one entity. Relationships are more subtle and changeable than that."

"I know, I know. Sort of, anyway. I'm just not sure how far the business has, uh, evolved."

"That is a major part of what we are trying to discover. I suspect increasingly that we'll get answers we cannot quite comprehend."

Okuma paused. Surf beyond the reefs murmured, wind whispered, bird-cries began to die away as the sun went low.

"In a sense," he mused, "we who live among the stars, we whose ancestors moved there and founded what they imagined were new societies, are the relics, the archaic life-forms. We remain in our old human ways because we are suited to them. Longevity, rejuvenation, reinforces this basic conservatism, but our children grow into it likewise. Ours is, after all, a rich, infinitely diverse and exciting environment—from the old human viewpoint. But so, no doubt, is yonder sea to the sharks in it. They have scarcely changed for many millions of years. Yet for the past millennium, they have survived on human sufferance."

"Hey!" exclaimed Hebo. "You don't mean we're in that situation?"

"No, no, not precisely. Earth poses no threat to us. The life on it, including the synthetic and machine life, has passed us by. It has other interests than spreading out into a material universe."

Hebo relaxed. "Well, maybe that's how *it* sees the matter. But look, why hasn't the same development overtaken—or transfigured, or whatever word you want—any nonhumans?"

"They are too unlike us. You probably know better than I how vastly their psychologies, instincts, drives, capabilities differ from ours, and from each other's. Please correct me if I'm mistaken, but I think we interact with them, and they with us, only on a rather superficial level. Partnership is possible between human and alien, yes. Sometimes even what the human feels as friendship. But how does the alien feel it? That may be ultimately unknowable, on either side."

Hebo rubbed his chin. "M-m, yes, in a way I have to agree. Kind of like a—a falcon and a dog. Men used to hunt with them."

Okuma's eyes widened. "Indeed? When?"

"Before my time. But I do go far enough back to've read about it and seen historical shows."

"Fascinating," the scientist breathed. "As, I am sure, is all of your long experience."

Hebo sighed. "Too long, maybe."

"I would be glad to hear something about it," said Okuma eagerly.

Talk went on while clouds crossed the horizon. When Hebo explained why he had come back, Okuma assured him, "I am certain you will be well treated at the clinic, not merely with competence but with consideration, sympathy, and, yes, warmth. Good practice calls for it."

"Sure, they've got excellent interactive programs," Hebo said cynically.

Okuma shook his head. "True, but I expect that you will deal with living humans, too, if only because you will interest them as you do me. And their feelings for you will be perfectly genuine. A person on Earth today can at any instant attain any chosen emotional state." After a moment: "I have an idea that this is a major factor in making them foreign to us."

When at last Hebo said goodnight and returned to his room, he could have had whatever virtual surroundings he wanted; but his wish was only for sleep.

He didn't drift off at once, though. For a while he lay wondering whether maybe the Forerunners had gone the way of Earth and that was why they were no longer around and what they might have become by now.

Oh, sure, strictly speaking, there was no such thing as simultaneity when you looked at interstellar distances. He'd heard about experiments with sending a hyperbeam signal into the past. But nobody had managed to boost a spacecraft to speeds high enough that the effect amounted to anything you didn't need ultrasensitive instruments to detect. Energy considerations and friction with the interstellar medium seemed to forbid. Besides, didn't theory say the effect was necessarily limited? A causal loop . . .

you can't rewrite what God's already written. . . . Leave the philosophy to the physicists. For practical purposes, when he got home he'd have lived just about as many seconds, minutes, days, months as the folks who'd stayed there. Meanwhile, he could call them on a hyperbeam if he had some reason for taking the trouble to arrange it. He might as well think of them as they were at "this moment."

Forerunners reminded him . . . how was Lissa Windholm getting along? Quite a girl, that. . . .

X

Inga never quite slept. After dark the towers and slipways of its centrum flared with light, pulsed with traffic, life that the free city, largest on Asborg, drew unto itself from the whole planet and beyond. The harbor district lay quiet, though, watercraft and machines waiting for sunrise. Walls along the docks lifted sheer, their darknesses blocking off all but sky-glow. Thus eyes found stars above the bay. Past full, the bigger moon was nonetheless rising bright enough to throw a bridge over the waves, which they broke into shivers and sparkles. Their *lap-lap* against the piers sounded clear through the throbbing westward. Smells of salt, engines, cargoes drifted cool.

Gerward Valen stopped before his apartment building. "Here we are," he said needlessly. Was it shyness that thickened his accent? Ordinarly he spoke fluent Anglay. The vague illumination showed him tensed within the gray tunic and breeks of a Comet Line officer. "The hour's gotten later than I expected. If you'd rather postpone the, the conference—"

Lissa considered him. He stood a head taller than her, with the slenderness, sharp features, fair complexion of his Brusan people. As was common these days on Asborg, he went beardless and kept his hair short. Those blond locks had thinned and dulled, furrows ran through brow and cheeks, he must be well overdue for a rejuvenation. She hadn't ventured to ask why. The eyes, in their deep sockets amidst the crow's-feet, remained clear. "No," she said, "I think we had best get to our business," putting a slight emphasis on the last word, lest he misunderstand.

It had, after all, been a pleasant evening, dinner at the Baltica, liqueurs, animated conversation throughout, that continued while they walked the three kilometers to this place. They discovered a shared passion for Asborg's wildernesses; he resorted especially to the Hallan Alps, and had had some colorful experiences there. Otherwise he said little about himself, nothing about his past. However, she felt she had come to know him well enough for her purposes. Several personal meetings, after her agents had compiled a report on him, should suffice. They'd better. Time was growing short.

"Very well," he agreed. "If you please, milady." The door identified him and retracted. He let her precede him into a drab lobby and onto the up spiral. It carried them to the fourth floor.

Admitted to his lodging, she glanced about, hoping for more clues to his personality, and found disappointment. The living room was small, aseptically clean, sparsely furnished. While she had gathered he was an omnivorous reader, it seemed he owned nothing printed but drew entirely on the public database. Well, maybe he'd picked these quarters because a transparency offered what must be a spectacular daylight view of bay, headlands, and ocean.

"Please be seated," he urged. "Can I offer you a drink?"

Lissa took a chair. Like the rest, it was rigid. "Just coffee," she said. "No sweetener."

Valen raised his brows. "Nor brandy? As you wish. I'll have a snifter myself, if you don't mind." The dossier related that he drank rather heavily, though not to the point of impairment and never in space. He shunned psychotropes. His occasional visits to Calie's Bower hardly counted as a vice in a man unmarried. The girls there found him likeable, yet none of them had really gotten to know him, any more than his shipmates and groundside acquaintances had.

He stepped into the cuisinette. She heard a pot whirr. He came back carrying a goblet half full of amber liquid. "Yours will be ready in a couple of minutes," he said, and sipped. The motion was jerky. "Would you care for some music? Only name it."

"No, thank you," she replied. "Nice in the restaurant, but pointless now. Neither of us would hear, I think."

He tautened further. "What do you want with me, Milady Windholm?"

Her hazel gaze met his blue. "First and foremost," she told him, "your pledge to keep everything secret. I've satisfied myself that you can. Will you?"

"I take for granted this is . . . honorable," he said slowly.

She stiffened her tone. "You know my father is Davy, Head of our House."

"Indeed. And I've heard about you." A lopsided smile creased the gaunt face. "When a member of one of this world's ruling families seeks me out, talking about a possible service but not specifying it, I do a bit of inquiry on my own. I found a couple of men who've gone exploring with you. They spoke highly." He drew breath. "You have my promise. Absolute confidentiality until you release me from it. What do you want me to do?"

Despite herself, she felt her pulse quicken. "Don't you think you're wasted as mate on a wretched ore freighter?"

His expression blanked. He shrugged. "It's the best berth available. At that, you remember, I had to work up to it. There isn't much space trade hereabouts."

The thought flitted unbidden: No, there isn't, as isolated as we are, on this far fringe of human settlement. Not that distance matters when you hyperjump. But after two centuries, we are still not so many on Asborg, and most of us are preoccupied with our local affairs. The other planets of Sunniva suffice us. Even I and my comrades find exploration ample for lifetimes among the immediate neighbor stars.

Is that what called you to us, Gerward Valen? Our loneliness?

"Once you had a command," she threw at him. "It was a fully robotic vessel. How would you like it again?"

He stood unstirring.

"That was long ago," she pursued, "but we, my associates in this enterprise and I, we don't believe you've lost the skills. A little practice should restore them completely. If anything, to be an officer with a live crew, as you are these days, is more demanding, and your record is good.

He kept his countenance locked, but she barely heard his question, and it trembled. "What ship do you mean?"

"The *Dagmar*, of course. Windholm only has one of that kind." Few Houses possessed any; they cost. "We sponsor scientific expeditions, you see. I'm lately back from one on her. No cosmonaut myself, but I can assure you she's a lovely, capable craft."

"I know." He stared beyond her, drank, and asked in an almost normal voice, "Why do you want me? You have your qualified people."

"Three," stated Lissa. "Fallon Windholm is currently undergoing rejuvenation. The other two are from client families, perfectly fine except that—Chand Mikelsson is a blabbermouth. You can trust him with anything except a secret. Sara Tomasdaughter's husband is one Rion Stellamont. I don't say she would betray our confidence to him and his House, but . . . best not subject her to a conflict of loyalties, right?"

He seemed to have quite regained his balance. "Since we're being so frank, what about me? The Comet Line belongs to the Eastlands, after all, and the Windholms have been at loggerheads with them as often as the Stellamonts or any others."

"You're a resident foreigner. You owe them no fealty and they've had no oaths from you. Take an unpaid leave, and you're a free agent. Afterward, I expect we'll offer you something permanent." Lissa softened her words. "Not that we ask any betrayal. We simply don't want outsiders thrusting in—at least not till we understand the situation ourselves."

His glance went to the transparency and the stars that the lighting hid from him. "Does that include everybody? Human and nonhuman?"

She nodded. "Aside from the Susaians, those of them that already know, and are concealing the truth. Whatever it is. Something tremendous, we believe. Potentially—explosive? For good or ill, not anything we want irresponsibly released."

His dryness was a challenge: "Especially not to rival Houses."

Anger flickered. "We're no saints in Windholm. But I don't think you, either, would like this planet if the balance of power lay with a religious fanatic like Arnus Eastland or a clutch of reckless commercialists like the Seafell."

He cocked a brow. She practically heard him refrain from saying: So you deem them.

"And as for the galaxy at large," she continued, striving for calm, "simply think what an uproar that Forerunner artifact on Jonna is already raising. And it probably doesn't hold a fraction of the potentials that this new thing may. I repeat, may. There's no foretelling what equilibriums it could upset. Perhaps none, but it'd be irresponsible not to proceed with every possible precaution. There may well be danger anyway, danger enough to suit the rashest rattlebrain."

He smiled. "Which you assume I am not."

The abrupt lightness of his manner eased her. He can handle people pretty well when he wants to, she thought. Excellent. She laughed. "Explorers have an old, old saying, that adventure is what happens to the incompetent. What we intend is simply an investigation. Once we know more, we'll decide what to do next." Sobering, she finished, "My father has been the Head of his House, with as strong a voice in the World Council as any, for nearly two hundred years. Ask yourself, hasn't he proven out? A hardheaded realist, yes, but concerned with the welfare of Asborg more than of his kin or clients, and with civilization as a whole over and above that. Will you put your faith in him, or in a coven of lizards?"

Valen frowned the least bit. She suspected he found her language objectionable, as a person might who had fared widely about and dealt with many different beings. "Oh, I'm not parochial," she said quickly. "Contrariwise. In fact, we were alerted to this by a Susaian, and he'll travel with us."

"Us?" he murmured.

Blood heated her face. "If you accept the mission."

"I rather think I will." He inhaled a fragrance from the cuisinette. "Your coffee's ready, milady. I'll bring it."

XI

Taking a datacard out of her sleeve pocket, she put it in his terminal. "This has been edited, but only to bring time-separate parts together and cut out nonessentials," she explained. "It's our basic record of the encounter."

A woman appeared in the screen, seated at a desk. She was a sister of Lissa's, but well-nigh a stranger, born eighty years earlier and, newly rejuvenated, looking girlishly younger. The image showed date and time in one corner. Behind her, a viewscreen displayed the mining camp she superintended. Beyond it, rock and ice lay in a jumble to the near horizon. The moon's gas giant primary hung as a crescent in the darkness above. Another satellite, shrunken by remoteness till the disc was barely perceptible, gleamed near the edge of its ring system.

"Evana Davysdaughter Windholm, wedded to Olavi Jonsson, calling from Gunvor," she proclaimed. The name of her present husband wasn't necessary to identify her, but she always made a point of using it. He was among the House's most prominent clients, chief engineer at the base and, at home, grown wealthy from his investments. "I have immediate need to speak with the Head, communications enciphered."

The screen blinked, the time indicated was half an hour later, and she was saying as crisply: "A strange spacecraft has arrived unheralded and taken up orbit about us. The pilot, who claims to be alone, sent a request for tight-beam laser contact. I obliged. It is a Susaian, asking urgently to be put in touch with the leadership of our House. Yes, it seems to understand Asborgan sociopolitics fairly well and to be aware that operations on Gunvor are Windholm's. That may be why it sought us instead of somebody else, this chance for secrecy. It doesn't want anything made public." She hesitated. "I have no experience in dealing with nonhumans. Nobody here does. Pending your orders, I've restricted news of its arrival to those few who already know, and have activated the censor program in all transmitters. Rumors are flying. I have no idea how long the Susaian will wait. Please advise me."

The scene cut to a magnified image of the outsider vessel, a black blade athwart stars and Milky Way. Valen whistled. "Susaian, for sure," he said. "Scout type, small, high-boost, maneuverable. However, if one of them single-handed her, it was pretty desperate. The best of their automatic systems don't compare to the average of ours, you know."

"Daring more than desperate, I'd say," Lissa murmured. "You'll see. Watch."

Davy Windholm's fine-boned visage took over the screen, against a backdrop of his study, swirl-grained wainscot, an antique table, shelves of codex books and memorabilia that had been in the family for generations. She thrilled to the steadiness of his voice. "The Susaian doesn't want to talk through hyperspace. Fears the beam being tapped. Well, it could be, and our ciphers aren't absolutely secure." Not for the first time, Lissa wished quantum encryption had been made to work for transluminal communication. "So we require a personal representative of the House, and time is lacking for consultation. Therefore I am appointing Lissa Windholm envoy plenipotentiary. Her part in explorations of planets in this galactic vicinity has given her as much knowledge of nonhumans as anyone on Asborg seems likely to possess. She has also demonstrated self-control and sound judgment, alike in emergencies and in ordinary difficulties. I have every confidence in her."

Dad thinks that of me!

The screen showed Lissa in the command cabin of a courier boat. In Valen's apartment, she observed herself observing herself as if another person were yonder, and thought, Why? Do I want to know how he sees me?

The rush to make ready and be off had told on her. Instead of tonight's glittery flowrobe, she wore a coverall, smudged here and there. The auburn hair wasn't netted in gold but, under low acceleration, hung sweat-lank past her ears. Still, she thought, she didn't look hideous. A fair-sized number of men found her attractive. . . . Stop that! she silently snapped.

The pilot gazed into the pickup and said: "I record my understanding of my assignment just prior to medicating, getting into the flotation tank, and ordering top boost for the passage.

"I've never met a Susaian before, and only talked casually with people who have, but naturally I've been interested and studied up on them. Now I've brought along a database and will be accessing it en route. Transit time, about sixty hours, should let me learn something, though I'd better arrive reasonably rested and fresh. Better try to avoid preconceptions, too. However, I can't help guessing. Since that may influence my actions, I'll enter my thoughts at this point.

"I doubt we've got any subtle scheme under way. We're as alien to the Susaians as they are to us. What buttons could they single out to push? Oh, they do have that curious sensitivity to emotional states, but on an indvidual basis. It doesn't tell them how groups of us will react to something.

"I also doubt we've got a criminal trying for a haven. Not that we can be very sure what constitutes a crime among them. But anybody smart enough to make it here must know we won't risk provoking an interstellar incident for nothing. We'll need to be convinced it's worth our while to help.

"Nevertheless, this isn't exactly a usual way for a stranger to show up. My guess is that our visitor has come on behalf of some faction. The Susaians are no more united than us humans."

The image smiled. "Don't worry, I won't embroil us in a civil war of theirs. I couldn't if I wanted to. I'm really only empowered to ask questions and make suggestions. Believe me, I'll think hard before I do either."

The screen blinked. The time displayed was two and a half standard days later. Lissa floated weightless. She had spruced herself up. "I've proposed to the Susaian that we rendezvous elsewhere," she said, and projected the coordinates and orbital elements, a million kilometers from the giant planet. "It has agreed. That should enable Evana to damp out rumors and gossip on Gunvor. Please inform her. She can tell the troops this is probably some minor matter."

Valen chuckled.

He leaned tensely forward when the other ship swelled in view. Running commentary described the matching of velocities and the extension of a gang tube. Lissa appeared, spacesuited, an automatic camera on either shoulder.

"I'm crossing over like this," said her voice. "Not that the air or the temperature or anything would kill me, but . . . well, just in case. The suit is reinforced, and I've got a blaster in my oddments pouch."

"That much was beamed back to my father," she said in the city. "The rest had to wait till I had returned to my boat— No, I misspoke. All I sent then was word that I was safe and things looked interesting. The real information I wasn't about to trust to any transmitter."

An interior flashed before her and the man. Its cramped plainness seemed almost familiar, until one noticed the details. The Susaian poised free-fall at the center. The sinuous body, dull red, as long as a man's, was tautly curved about the four stubby legs. The tail, half that length, coiled to complete the ring. Two hands, each with three spidery fingers, at the end of supple arms, held a standard model translator. Just "above" them swayed the neck. Behind the blunt snout of the head, which lacked earflaps, the eyes glowed quite beautiful, like twin agates. The trans rendered purring, rustling sounds into flat Anglay. "Well be you come,

Earthblood. Have you immediate desires I might perchance fulfill?"

Lissa's helmet included a sonic unit. "Can we get straight to business? I don't want to be discourteous, but I don't know what's polite in your society. My database told me that if we both belonged to the Thornflower nation,"—the trans turned that human name into the appropriate buzz—"we'd spend the next hour exchanging compliments. I'm willing, but not sure how."

Again Valen chuckled.

"I am not a member of it myself," the Susaian said. Did the vocal tone carry wrath, or sorrow, or eagerness? "And I will gladly go by the straightest tunnel, the more so when I sense that, beneath a natural wariness, your intentions are honest."

Listening on Asborg, Lissa wondered anew about that race's ability to read emotional states, apparently among each other and, to some uncertain degree, in her species. Whether they could do it or not in more sentients than that was unknown, at least to any observers whose writing she'd consulted; but those were all human, of course. Could there be some exhalations of pheromones or whatever to smell—not impossible, as basically similar as the biochemistries were—or even the faint, faint radiations of brains to sense?

Both implausible here, when she was encased in a spacesuit. Body language, facial expression, tone of voice? She'd thought the best guess was that the Susaians used a suite of clues, and a highly-developed innate capability of interpretation. Very likely this one had had direct experience of her kind, or else had spent considerable time studying virtuals.

The question slipped out of her mind as she heard the being continue: "Names first? I designate myself—" the trans hesitated for an instant, tried "Mountain Copper," and settled on "Orichalc. At present I function as male."

"Lissa Windholm," she had answered. "Female. I . . . imagine you know what my name signifies."

"Yes. You belong to that one of Asborg's dominant consanguinities." It was the best rendition the program could make of a phrase in that particular Susaian language, which attempted to describe a concept perhaps unknown to any Susaian culture. "The one that I sought."

"Then you know more about us than I do about you."

"I was here briefly, three rejuvenations ago. That was as a crew member of a ship conveying an expedition sent to gather information about what was then a new colony."

"Yes. I've studied the accounts. Your people's only visit, wasn't it?" Xanaduans, Rikhans, Sklerans, and Grib had also come for a look, found no threat nor any particular promise to them, and gone away again. Later contacts had been between individuals or crews or other small groups.

"Correct. Since then, of course, much has evolved. I have striven to bring my information up to date. Travelers often take along databases about their homes. A copy is an appreciated gift or a trade item of some value."

"I know. But why did you care about us especially?"

The tail slithered back, whispering along the glabrous hide. "The second planet of this sun would be quite hospitable to my species."

"Freydis?" Lissa's image registered surprise. That hot, cloudy world of swamps and deserts? "Well, yes . . . I suppose so . . . but there must be plenty more in the galaxy, some of them better, that you haven't settled yet, or even found."

"True, However, I pray you, consider *who* will take them. S-s-s-s—" Orichalc's head struck at air, to and fro.

"House Windholm doesn't own all Freydis," Lissa said. "Nobody does."

"Correct." The head grew large in sight, drawing near her helmet. Fangs glistened, eyes smoldered. "But your consanguinity is uniquely qualified. First, it does own the large island on the planet that you call New Halla." He must have put a special entry in the trans's program. "Territory of scant or no use to you, originally claimed for prestige and on the chance of mineral resources, retained merely because of inertia and, s-s-s, pride. Second, as of recent years, you have maintained exclusive operations on the moon Gunvor. This gave opportunity for a discreet approach. I realize my plan is hopeless unless we, your people and I, can suddenly present the Galaxy with an accomplished fact."

Lissa's tone grew strained. "What do you want?"

"The island. What else? I have considered how the transaction may be done. Pay me a sum equal to the agreed-on price for the land, with an option to buy it. Leave the sum in escrow until I have fulfilled my part of the bargain. I will know whether your chieftans intend to abide by this and, afterward, whether I have truly met the terms as they understand them. My researches lead me to expect they will be honest."

"You're asking . . . a great deal."

"I offer much more."

"What?"

Orichalc hooked his tail around a stanchion. The long body swayed. "I cannot precisely tell you, for I myself do not know. But it is of the utmost."

"Get to reality, will you?" Lissa snapped, impatient.

The undulations went hypnotic, the words sank to a breath. "Hearken. I am a cosmonaut of the Great Confederacy. It embraces four of the seven Susaian-inhabited planets, about seventeen hundred light-years from here. You have heard? Yes-s-s.

"During the last several of your calendrical years, its Dominance has repeatedly dispatched expeditions elsewhere. They are totally secret. Nothing whatsoever is said about them. Key personnel return to live sequestered in a special compound. I have gathered that they enjoy every attention and luxury there, and are well satisfied. Ordinary crewfolk of the several ships go more freely about on their leaves, but may not speak to anyone, no, not nestmates or clones or even each other, of what they have done and seen.

"That is easy to obey, for we know well-nigh nothing. Our vessels leap through hyperspace to someplace else. We lie there for varying times while the scientists use their instruments and send out their probes, operations in which we do not partake. All we perceive is that we float in empty, unfamiliar interstellar space until we go back. Ah, but the feelings of those officers and scientists! They flame, they freeze, they strike, recoil, exult, shudder; the glory and the dread of Almightiness are upon them.

"And at home, I have once in a while come near enough to certain of the Dominators that I sense the same in them. Not the awe, no, for they do not venture thither themselves, to yonder remote part of the galaxy; but their inward dreams grasp a pride and a hope that are demonic." (What did that last word really mean in the Susaian tongue?)

In free fall, there is no true over or under. Nonetheless Orichalc loomed. "Is this not a sufficient sign that something vast writhes toward birth?" he demanded.

"I, I can't say," Lissa stammered. "You, how and why did you—"

"They knew I was unhappy, until presently, slowly, I went aquiver," Orichalc said. "Well, my race has learned dissimulations. I led them to believe that I suffered private difficulties, hostilities, until I began seeing ways whereby I might cope. They expected little of a humble crew member, therefore suspected little. Meanwhile I took my surreptitious stellar sightings and made my calculations.

"And at home, I plotted with others. Jointly, they raised the means to obtain this spacecraft and send me off in it, all under false pretenses. Our need is that great.

"Here I am. I know, quite closely, where and when the monster thing is to happen. It will be soon. What is this worth to you and your kindred, Earthblood?"

XII

Lissa spent the day before departure with her parents.

They were at the original family home, on Windholm itself. A stronghold as much as a dwelling, Ernhurst offered few of the comforts, none of the sensualities in mansions and apartments everywhere else. Yet Davy and Maren had refrained from enlarging it, and often returned there. It held so many memories.

From the top of a lookout tower Lissa saw immensely far. Southward the downs rolled summer-golden to the sea, which was a line of gleaming argent on that horizon. Wind sent long ripples through the herbage; cloud shadows swept mightily over heights and hollows. It boomed and bit, did the wind, but odors of growth, soil, water, sunlight brought life to its sharpness. Northward the land climbed toward hills darkling with forest. Other than the estate, its gardens and beast park, the sole traces of man lay to the west, toylike at their remove, a power station, a synthesis plant, and the village clustered around them.

"Oh, it's good to be here again," she sighed.

"Then why are you so seldom?" her father asked quietly.

She looked away from him. "You know why. Too much to do, too little time."

His laugh sounded wistful. "Too little patience, you mean. You're trying to experience the whole universe. Relax. It won't go away."

"I've heard that aplenty from you, when Mother hasn't been after me to settle down, get married, present you with another batch of grandchildren. You relax, you two. *That* won't go away. My next cycle, or the next after that, I'll be ready to start experimenting with domesticity." Assuming I find the right man, she thought—as how often before? One I could really partner with. None so far. In all these years, none. Unless maybe now—

"If you live till then." She sensed how he must force the words out. "We were content to let you enjoy your first time around in freedom, like most people. But your enthusiasms are never just intellectual or artistic or athletic, and your idea of a truly grand time is still to hare off and hazard your life on some weird planet. . . . I'm sorry, my dear. I don't want to nag you again, on this day of all days." Her right hand rested on the parapet. He laid his left over it. "We're afraid, though, Maren and I. How I rue the hour I asked you to go meet that Susaian. Ever since, you've charged breakneck forward."

She bit her lip. "You could have taken me off the project. You can still."

Aquiline against the sky, his head shook. "And have you hate me? No, I'm too weak."

"What? You?" She stared.

He turned to smile at her. "Where you are concerned, I am. Always have been, for whatever reason."

"Dad—" She clung to his hand.

He grew grave. "I do need to talk with you, seriously and privately. This seems to be my chance."

She released herself, stepped back a meter, and confronted him. He had now put the well-worn importunities aside, she knew. Doubtless he had only used them as a way into what he really had to utter. Her heart knocked. "Clearance granted," she said, and realized that today this was no longer one of their shared jokes.

"You're bound into an unforeseeable but certainly dangerous situation—"

"No, no, no!" she protested automatically. "Must I explain for the, it feels like the fiftieth time? The environment's safe. Orichalc saw no extraordinary precautions being taken."

"But Orichalc did learn that an extraordinary event will occur there in the near future. Who knows what it will involve? If nothing else, the Susaians won't be overjoyed when outsiders break in on their ultra-secret undertaking. Their resentment might . . . express itself forcibly."

"Oh, Dad, that's ridiculous. They're *civilized.*"

"There are Susaians and Susaians," he declared, "just as there are humans and humans. The rulers of the Great Confederacy are not the amiable, helpful sorts who lead most of their nations. It isn't general knowledge, because we don't want to compromise our sources, but some of our intelligence about them makes me wonder what we may have to face, a century or two from now."

She didn't care to pursue that. The immediate argument was what mattered. "Anyhow, we'll be in clear space. If anything looks threatening, we'll hyperjump off in a second. No, a millisecond. *Dagmar* computes and reacts faster than any organic brain."

"Understood. Otherwise I'd never have authorized the venture. But you in turn understand—don't you?—you can't depend on the ship to handle everything, especially make the basic decisions. If she could do that to our satisfaction, she wouldn't need a master, nor even a scientific team aboard. Lissa, the more I've considered your choice of personnel, the more I've discovered about them, the less happy I've become."

She clenched her fists. "Orichalc? He's got to come along. Guide, advisor, and, well, hostage for his own truthfulness. Yes, we know very little about him, but that's hardly his fault."

"Orichalc worries me the least," Davy replied. "Why did you co-opt Esker Harolsson?"

"Huh? You know. He's an able physicist, specializing in astronomical problems. Bachelor, no particular attachments, easily persuaded to join an expedition whose purpose he won't learn till we're in space. If anybody should be loyal to us, that's Esker." You made him what he is, Dad, recognized the talent in a ragged patronless kid, sponsored him, funded him through school, got him his position at the Institute.

Davy frowned. "Yes, I assumed as much myself, till it occurred to me to order an inquiry. I'd lost touch with him. Well, it turns out he's not popular—"

"Abrasive, yes. I've generally gotten along with him. Consulted him about stuff relating to various explorations, you remember."

Davy's lips quirked a bit. "You don't feel his arrogance, as his inferiors do." Earnestly: "Also, I suspect that— Never mind. The fact is, he is . . . no gentleman. Less than perfectly honest, in spite of that raspy tongue. And I daresay an impoverished childhood like his would leave many people somewhat embittered, but most wouldn't make it an excuse for chronic ill behavior."

"As long as he can do the job—"

Lissa broke off, went back to the parapet, gazed over the vast billows of land. After a moment she said, "I think I know where part of his trouble stems from. He's a scientist born. Nature meant him to make brilliant discoveries. But there aren't any to make anymore, not in fundamental physics. Nothing new for—centuries, isn't it? The most he can do is study a star or a nebula or whatever that's acting in some not quite standard way. Then he puts the data through his computer, and it explains everything in conventional terms, slightly unusual parameters and that's all. When I hinted we might be on the trail of something truly strange—you should have seen his face."

"Scientific idealism, or personal ambition?" Once more, Davy sighed. "No matter. Too late now in any event. I'm simply warning you. Be careful. Keep on the watch for . . . instability. If he proves out, fine, then I've misjudged him; no harm done."

Lissa turned to face him again. "Have you anything against the rest of the team?"

"Noel, Elif, Tessa? Well, you told me he nominated them to you, but otherwise— No, they appear sound enough, except that they lack deep space experience."

"*Dagmar* and Captain Valen supply that."

She saw the change in him. It was as if the wind reached in under her coat. "All right, what is it, Dad? Speak out."

"Gerward Valen," he said bleakly. "Seemed to me, too, as good a choice as any, better than most. But why did he abandon his career, drift away, finally bury himself among us? That's what it's amounted to. If he's certificated for robotic ship command, he was near the top of his profession. Here, the best he might ever get was a captaincy on some scow of an interplanetary freighter—until you approached him. What happened, those many years ago?"

Lissa stood braced against the stones. Their hardness gave strength. "None of our business," she replied. "A tragedy he doesn't want to talk about, probably not think about. My guess—a few words that slipped loose a couple of times, when we were sitting over drinks—he does drink pretty fast—I think he lost his wife. If they'd been married a long time, maybe since his first cycle, her death would hit hard, wouldn't it?"

"Not that hard, that permanently, if his spirit was healthy," Davy said. "Why has he postponed his next rejuvenation so long? Another two or three decades at most, and it will be too late, you know. I wondered, and got background information on him. He's making no provision for it, financial or otherwise. How much does he want to live?" He raised a palm. "Yes, of course I had no legal or ethical right to pry. To destruction with that. My daughter's life will be in his hands."

"Not really."

"By now he's integrated with the ship. Her skipper. His orders will override anyone else's."

Defense: "Yes, down underneath, he is a sad man. I think this voyage, this fresh beginning may rouse him out of that. But mainly—Dad, I haven't survived so far by entrusting myself to incompetents. Look at Gerward—at Valen's record, just in this system. The *Woodstead Castle* wreck, the Alanport riot. Both times he earned a commendation. No, whatever his emotions are, they don't cloud his judgment or dull his sense of duty." Lissa felt the blood in her face. She turned into the cooling wind. It tossed her hair.

"I took that for granted, given the facts," Davy pursued. "But were they sufficient? Finally I sent an agent to Brusa, Valen's home planet."

She gasped. "You did? Why, the—the cost—"

"It was your life."

She flared. "And you didn't see fit to tell me."

"I did not," he replied. "You'd object. Even if you promised to keep silent, I feared you'd let something escape to him."

We know each other too well, Dad and I, she thought.

"Well," Davy continued, "the spoor was cold, and it led off Brusa, and the upshot is that I only got the report yesterday. I think you'd better hear what it said."

Her neck had stiffened till it was painful to nod. "Go ahead."

He regarded her with a pain of his own behind his eyes before he asked low, "Do you remember the Naia disaster?"

The foreboding in her grew colder. "Yes, of course I've read about it. But it was long ago and far away. Who on Asborg has given it any thought for decades? I've almost forgotten."

Remorselessly: "Let me refresh your memory, then. Human-colonized planet. A large asteroid was perturbed into a collision orbit. It happened suddenly and unpredictably. A recently settled planet, the system not yet properly charted, no adequate skywatch yet established. The asteroid passed near a gas giant with many moons. Chaotic events occur sometimes in celestial mechanics, as well as on smaller scales. Factors are so precariously balanced that an immeasurably small force can make them go one way rather than another. This asteroid was flung almost straight at Naia.

"Almost. It plowed through the atmosphere. That would have been catastrophe enough, the shock wave, a continent ignited, but friction slowed it into capture. An eccentric, decaying orbit, bringing it back again and again. At each approach, more broke off, huge chunks crashing down on unforeseeable spots. They touched off quakes and volcanoes. The tsunamis from ocean strikes were nearly as bad. A war passing over the planet would have done less harm than that asteroid did, before the last fragment of it came to rest.

"Meanwhile, naturally, as many people as possible were evacuated. Temporary shelters were established on the Naian moon, to hold the refugees till they could be transported outsystem. Spacecraft shuttled between planet and moon. An appeal went out, and ships arrived from far and wide to help. Yes, some of them were nonhuman.

"Your friend Valen was among the newcomers. He commanded a robotic vessel chartered by the Cooperative Stellar Survey. Her owners put her at the disposal of the rescue effort. For a short while, Valen was a busy ferryman.

"Then the asteroid returned. The next bombardment began. He got in his ship and fled. Raced out of the gravity well, sprang through hyperspace, slunk home to Brusa.

"He could offer no excuse. The owners fired him. His wife left him. He went on the bum, drifting about, living hand to mouth off odd, unsavory jobs, now and then wangling a berth in a ship that'd take him to some different system. Finally, when he reached Sunniva, he pulled himself together and got steady employment. But his promotions—I've verified this for myself—they haven't been due to any particular ambition on his part. He's merely moved up the seniority ladder.

"That is your captain, Lissa," Davy finished.

She stood a long while mute. The wind skirled, the cloud shadows hunted each other across the downs.

"I'm afraid it's too late in this case, also," she said finally, dully.

"No, we can replace him. Chand or Sara aren't really totally unsuitable. Or I can look outside our House."

She shook her head. "Any replacement would take too long. Ship-captain integration. Orichalc keeps reminding us that the climax will come soon. Any day now, perhaps. If we showed up afterward, could we discover what the Susaians did? Besides, it's a cosmic-scale thing. The environment later may be lethal."

She attempted a grin. "Anyhow," she said, "aren't you glad we've got a cautious man in charge?"

Schooled in public impassivity, he still could not entirely hide from her what he felt. It was well-nigh more than she could bear.

"Come on," she proposed, "let's go down and say silly things at Mother, the way we used to, till lunch."

XIII

Forest had overgrown the ruins of the town, pine and hemlock murky against gray heaven, roaring in the wind. The church had stood near its eastern edge, on a headland where surf clashed and burst. Only bushes, bayberry, blueberry, sumac, and harsh grass grew there. Hebo thought he could trace the foundation; and nearby a few gravestones remained, fallen, lichenous, the names long since weathered away.

Here he had married Julie.

It was as if he could see the white clapboard and high steeple, hear the minister say the words, feel her hand in his. He wondered whether anything survived other than his memories, and whether those weren't imagination. Nature was what Earthfolk today cared about, living Earth, Gaia Gloriatrix, and that—he supposed—mainly as something to explore and enjoy with the senses, like sex, a pause in their communion with the machine gurus. Should somebody take an interest in something left behind by merely human history, the database could immediately present it in full virtuality: or, better yet, reveal it as it originally was, the Parthenon fresh from the hand of Phidias, Columbus's ships under sail, Broadway ablaze with lights, Cape Canaveral with a Saturn rocket blasting off for the moon.

And that would be half imagination, too, he thought, guesswork, though by intellects colossally greater and more systematic than his.

"Hey, Julie, girl," he whispered, "how're you doing? Where are you now?"

No sense asking, after so many centuries. If she lived, which he hoped, and was still on Earth, she must have been taken up into its oneness, little by little, each renewed youth making her able to learn those new things, think and feel in those new ways, that had been evolving around her. It would have been willingly. Refusal would have left her mighty lonesome.

Or did she also at last say, "Enough" and depart for the stars? Now and then he'd tried to find out, but the galaxy was too vast. Even this fragment of its outer reaches that humans and their fellow spacefarers had some slight knowledge of was.

Each time he came to Earth and found it more strange than before, Hebo had wondered if he might already have been escaping, way back then. The change hadn't gone very far, but he'd had a sense of walls closing in. Or was it plain restlessness, yes, boredom that drove him yonder? He recalled how, after their first rejuvenations, which were among the first ever, he and Julie had fallen head over heels back in love. For a while it'd been a fire fountain. The kids were grown and off their hands, they had ample money, strength and beauty—her beauty—were theirs already. . . . He began to chafe and play around, she did, the parting was reasonably amicable. Since, he'd only heard of two or three marriages that lasted more than two or three cycles. Maybe nothing human could be forever.

Fare you well, Julie, always well, and thanks.

The gratitude felt ghostly.

A few gulls wheeled. He couldn't hear them mewing above the wind they rode. Once upon a time they'd been many, but that was when people lived here, squanderous man, scattering his wastes for the scavengers.

Wolves and bears ruled the woods. They kept the deer down.

Hebo shivered a bit and turned from the sea and the graves toward the little airflitter waiting for him. He ought to stop these sentimental zigzags around the globe and get down to the business of hard thinking.

Face it, his earliest memories, the clearest and most enduring, had left no more behind them than the wind did. It wasn't just that this church had crumbled away, or the gentle Danish landscape of his childhood was mostly beech forest, or the energy-focusing climate-control satellites he'd helped construct had plunged to their meteoric deaths hundreds of years ago, Earth needing them no more than a recovered invalid needs medicine, or—or any such touchable things.

It was his father lifting him up on a shoulder, he squealing with delight at how suddenly and immensely high above the ground he had risen. It was a hummingbird, a living bit of jewelry, soon after the family moved to America. It was a fiddler in an Irish pub in Santa Fe, of all places, a mug of Guinness, a pretty waitress impulsively joining him in a jig on the sawdust floor. It was tramping through the misty Irish countryside itself, or backpacking in the Rockies, or campfire talk with friends lost when he left the Solar System.

Most of his life was traceless, he realized. Artemis abided, but tamed into almost a New Earth; and maybe Kayleigh, too, lived there yet. That marriage, however, those children, the house in the wilderness, the hunting of the dracosaur—well, yes, some fossils of it were doubtless retrievable if he cared to search them out, but why?

And the other women, more than he could count up—in some cases, had wished for but never won—the times he'd been in love—which did he truly want to keep?

An encounter in a distant spaceyard with his son by Julie? After four hundred Earth years, they discovered they had practically nothing to say to one another. Yet something of her lingered in his face and eyes. Was this a valuable lesson?

The later years, the later enterprises, alien planets, alien beings, those were the memories most apt to blur or drop out of awareness, and those were the ones he most needed. For survival's sake, they must be recalled, reconstructed, reordered. That was necessarily at the cost of the older. His brain lacked the storage and correlation capabilities of a quantum-net intelligence.

Oh, sure, the kindly mind in the clinic would record everything that it deleted—everything that wasn't hopelessly garbled or decayed—and turn the crystal over to him, for playback whenever he chose. Some parts of it might be suitable for virtuality; most would doubtless just be words and patchy images. All of it would be abstract to him, narration of events that might as well have happened to somebody else. In fact, the stories would be more vivid if he'd come upon them in a piece of fiction.

How much of the old half-reality must he give up?

How much could he find it in his heart to give up?

Hebo walked slowly back to the flitter.

XIV

The ship accelerated outward, seeking free space for her leap across light-years. Aft, Sunniva dwindled. Forward and everywhere around, night glittered with stars, the Milky Way was a white torrent of them, nebulae glowed or reared dark across brilliance, sister galaxies beckoned from across gulfs that imagination itself could not bridge.

In her saloon, revelation. The physicists—Esker Harolsson, Elif Mortensson, Noel Jimsson, Tessa Samsdaughter—stared over the table at Orichalc. After a moment their eyes swung toward each other's, as if for comfort or comradeship. Watching in a corner, Lissa saw lips move silently and caught Esker's muttered, amazed obscenity.

He, the team chief, recovered his wits first. But then, he had always kept his associates dependent on him. "Have you no clues to what the object may be? he demanded.

Curled on the opposite bench, head uplifted, the Susaian considered before responding. "None that appear significant. We common crew were seldom allowed as much as a look out; viewscreens were kept blank most of the time. I obtained my star sightings, from which I later calculated the location, when I went forth in a work party to retrieve a probe that had failed to dock properly with our ship."

Esker's dark, hooknosed features drew into a scowl. "How did you take measurements, anyway?"

"I had fashioned an instrument while home on leave, and smuggled it aboard in my personal kit. On a prior trip, despite the unfamiliar shape of the Galactic Belt, I had recognized certain navigational objects, such as the Magellanic Clouds. When this opportunity came, I withdrew from my gang, telling them I had spied what might be a loose object, missing from the probe. When out of sight, I quickly made my observations and discarded the instrument. The numbers I stored in my mind. I had been confident such a chance would come, because the probes frequently had difficulty with rendezvous."

"Yah, your Susaian robotics aren't worth scrap. And we're supposed to proceed on your memories of your amateur star shooting?"

"We've satisfied ourselves that the data are adequate," Lissa declared.

Esker glanced her way. "Uh, sure. Sorry, milady." Half ferociously, he turned back to Orichalc. "But did you never see or overhear anything? Did you never *think* what this might all be about?"

"The Dominance knows well how to keep secrets. Given our species' ability to sense emotional states, perhaps it has developed a few methods slightly better than you conceptualize."

A shame, Lissa thought, that the trans just gives out unemphatic Anglay. What's Orichalc really saying with overtones and body language?

"But you must have speculated," exclaimed Tessa.

Esker threw her a glower. "I'll handle this discussion," he said.

Well, Lissa thought, everybody babbling at once would make for confusion and wasted time. Nevertheless—

She admired how Orichalc remained dignified. Or did he not care whether the bipeds were polite? "Since the location is in interstellar space, the phenomenon is presumably astronomical," the Susaian said. "The probability of someone having come upon it by accident is nil, considering the volume of space involved."

Was that a studied insult? Certainly Esker flushed. "Doubtless something was noticed from afar. Most likely this was in the course of a general astrographic survey. The Great Confederacy, like most nations that can afford to, has mounted several during its history. They do not significantly overlap, as huge as the galaxy is. One of these ships detected some anomaly, such as a peculiar spectrum, and went for a closer look. The report that it brought back caused the Dominance to make this a state secret and mount its own intensive investigation."

Esker tugged his chin. "Well, yes, your reasoning is, uh, reasonable. Have you any further thoughts?"

"Mainly this. Given the character of the Dominance, I am sure that its members hope for some outcome, some discovery, that will greatly strengthen the Confederacy and therefore themselves. It may be military, it may be economic, it may be something else. I do not know, and doubt that they know, yet. But in their minds, the possibility justifies the effort—which is, actually, a modest investment, a small gamble for a perhaps cosmically large stake."

Esker straightened on his bench, as if he were a judge. "And you're betraying your people?"

"They are not my people," Orichalc replied, his natural voice gone soft.

Lissa stirred. "That will do," she ordered. Things looked like getting nasty. The expedition could ill afford quarrels.

Esker shifted his glare to her. "Milady, I've had a hard life," he said. "I've learned lessons a patron like you is spared. A traitor once is apt to be a traitor twice."

"Our comrade's motives are honorable," she clipped. "Watch your language. Remember, it's going into the log."

Embarrassment yielded visibly to relief among the subordinates when Esker hunched his shoulders and growled, "As milady wishes. No offense meant." And maybe, she thought, that's true. Maybe he does not perceive his own boorishness.

Noel plucked up courage to say, "I beg milady's pardon, but what's this about a log?"

"A robotic ship records everything that happens on a voyage, inboard as well as outboard, unless directed not to," Lissa explained. "It isn't normally a violation of privacy. We have very little of that anyway, while we travel. As a general rule, at journey's end, the ship edits everything irrelevant to the mission out of the database. But we can't foresee what may teach us something that may be valuable in future operations. Psychological stresses are as real as physical, and as dangerous, when you're bound into places never meant for humans."

Had Valen been listening outside, or did he chance to enter at that moment? His body filled the doorframe vertically, though its jambs stood well apart from him. "Pardon me," he said in his usual mannerly style. "I know this has been a big surprise sprung on you four and you have a sunful of questions; but we're just a couple of hours from hyperjump, and I need to make a certain decision first. Would you come confer with me in my cabin, Orichalc?"

"Indeed." The Susaian flowed off his bench and stumped to the captain. They departed.

The rest gaped after them. "Well," said Esker. "Isn't he the important one? What might this decision be that we commoners mustn't hear about?"

Why does that irritate me? wondered Lissa. Aloud, curtly: "I daresay he wants to consider possible hazards, without groundsiders butting in. You, sir, might best be preparing yourself and your team for your job, once we've arrived."

And what will mine be? she thought, not for the first time. What's waiting in space for me? I'm only a planetarist. And even that title is a fake. I don't do geology, oceanography, atmospherics, chemistry, biology, ethology, or xenology. I dabble in them all, and then dare call myself a scientist.

She rose to her feet. I help get the specialists together, and keep them together, and sometimes keep them alive. That's *my* work. That justifies my being here, though I had to force it every centimeter of the way.

Esker got up too and approached her. His squatness barely reached above her chin. As he neared, he made a dismissing gesture at the others. They didn't leave, but they sat where they were, very silently.

"Maybe I could put a few of our questions to you, Milady Windholm," he said.

"Certainly," she replied. After all, it was she who had co-opted him into this, and for justifiable reasons. She knew him for able, quick-witted, fearless. That she sympathized with him, felt sorry, would like to give him a shot at his dreams—these things were beside the point. Weren't they? "I'll answer as best I can. This isn't a military mission."

He cocked his head. "But we are under confidentiality. There might be some advantage to our House."

She picked her words with care. "Possibly. Still, you know Windholm isn't interested in conquering anybody. We simply want to . . . stay on top of whatever wave we'll be riding. Keep the power to make our own fate."

"Of course. But then why are you willing to cede New Halla to that creature?"

"We won't necessarily. An assembly of the House will judge how much Orichalc's help was worth to us." I never felt more proud of what I am than when he agreed to trust our honor, he who can feel our feelings. "We will take good faith for granted and into account. The island would be no great loss to us."

"But why does it, uh, he want the place?"

"Well, you see, Orichalc is a . . . a crypto-dissident in his nation. I don't entirely understand the situation. Maybe no human can. But it seems—we've verified—there's been a movement among the Susaians, starting several centuries ago. The trans calls it the 'Old Truth.' A religion, a way of life, or what?" Lissa spread her hands. "Something that means everything to its believers. And that doesn't fit well into most Susaian societies. It's been generally persecuted, especially in the Great Confederacy, where it was finally forbidden altogether. Orichalc's lineage is one of those that pretended to convert back to orthodoxy, but has maintained the rites and practices as best it can in secret, always hoping for some kind of liberation."

Esker gazed at a bulkhead. "I see. . . ."

"New Halla would be a haven for the Old Truthers," Lissa proceeded. "They aren't so many that they need more, and probably quite a few couldn't manage to leave their planets anyhow. But Orichalc does have this idea of a refuge for them."

"Yes." The black eyes caught at hers. "They'll be under Asborgan sovereignty. We'll be their protectors. And they'll multiply, and move into other parts, and eventually our evening star will be full of them, won't it?"

"How would that harm us?" she retorted. "They'd acquire any further land legitimately. We've made sure that their principles are decent. I should think there'd be pretty wonderful potentials in having beings that different for our friends and neighbors."

"Well—" The hostility dropped away. He shivered. "Maybe. Who knows? You understand, milady, don't you, I'm concerned about our House. It's mine, too. I'm only a client, adopted at that, but I belong with Windholm."

Pushy, she thought; and then: No, that's unfair. Isn't it?

Encourage him. "Leave politics to the patrons, Esker. Look to your personal future. Why would the Dominance be so interested in this thing ahead of us, if they didn't believe it may lead them to something really new? Something maybe as revolutionary as, oh, quantum mechanics or nuclear fission and fusion or the unifying equation."

She saw the pallor come and go in the blue cheeks, the hair stir on the backs of his hands. "Yes," he said, "yes, that's possible, isn't it? Thank you, milady."

The upward blazing wish to discover, to know, briefly transfigured the ugly face.

XV

"Stand by for hyperjump." The ship's voice filled her cabins and corridors with melody. Lissa had a moment's envisionment of her as the stars might see, a golden torpedo soaring amidst their myriads.

"Ten, nine, eight—" sang the countdown. It wasn't necessary, only a custom followed when time allowed. That sense of oneness with history, clear back to the rockets of old, gave heart on the rim of mystery. *"—five, four—"* Lissa tensed in her safety harness. The console before her seemed abruptly alien. She, the fire control officer? A jape, a sop. *Dagmar* alone could direct the weapons she carried. *"—two—"* Well, but somebody had to decide whether to shoot and at what, and Valen would have plenty else occupying his attention. *"—one—"* Besides, Valen was a coward.

"—zero."

And the viewscreens that englobed Lissa showed a sky gone strange.

Inexperienced, she lost a second or two before she saw the differences. Stars in space were so many, unwinking diamond-bright; constellations became hard to trace. Moreover, the distances she had hitherto traveled, to suns near hers, changed them but little. Now she had skipped over—how many light years had Orichalc said? Seven hundred and some.

Acceleration had terminated shortly before transit through hyperspace. The ship fell free, at whatever velocity her kinetic and potential energies determined. It couldn't be high, for an instrument revealed that she had not generated an exterior force-field to screen off interstellar atoms. Nor did there seem to be any other radiation hazard. Weightless, Lissa revolved her chair three-dimensionally and studied her new heavens.

Odd, she thought, how familiar the Milky Way looks. Some differences, this bend, that bay, yonder silhouette of the Sagittarian dust clouds; but I expected it to be quite altered. And Orichalc didn't mention red stars. How many? A score at least, strewn all around us—"Damn! I clean forgot." Sweat prickled her skin. "Any trace of Susaians?"

"None," replied the ship.

Her muscles eased. "Well," she said redundantly, "our navigation data aren't what you'd call precise. We'll have to cast around a sizeable region till we find what we're after, close enough to identify it."

Valen's command over the intercom was otherwise. "Captain to science team. Start your studies."

"What?" responded Esker. "We can't be anywhere near our goal. Commence your search pattern."

"I'll give the orders, if you please. We're not going to hyperjump about at random till we have some idea of what this part of space is like. I want at least a preliminary report within an hour. Get busy."

Captain Caution, Lissa thought. But it does make sense, I guess. She touched her own intercom switchplate. "Fire control," she said. "I'm obviously no use here. May I be relieved? I could give a hand elsewhere."

"Perhaps." Valen sounded skeptical, as well he might. "Stay aft of the command sector."

Why, what will you be doing that nobody else should interrupt? "Aye, aye." Lissa unsecured, shoved with a foot, and arrowed toward the exit. A dim circle of light marked it, for it was part of the simulacrum system. When it retracted for her, she passed as if through the galactic band into a prosaic companionway.

Motion in zero gravity was fun, but now she sped on business—to find Orichalc and put certain questions to him. The Susaian occupied one of the crew cubicles. It was unlocked. Entering, she found it empty, save for the few curious objects that were personal possessions.

Hm. Would the wight scuttle around idly under these conditions? No, he was a cosmonaut and knew better. Just the same, Lissa searched everywhere she was permitted to go. It took a while to establish that the Susaian must be forward with Valen.

Why? Well, he did go reticent after that private talk of theirs. What are they hatching? Let's try the physics lab, she decided. I barely glanced in earlier.

There Lissa found confusion, Esker's three assistants struggling with apparatus that wandered perversely from them. The chief was shouting at the intercom: "—weight! These people can't work in free fall!"

"Then they'd better learn," Valen's voice snapped.

"Destruction curse it, do you want a quick report or don't you? Nobody else is here to detect us, unless you've brought along some phantoms of your own."

After a moment during which the whirr of the ventilators seemed loud: "Very well. One-half gee in five minutes."

Esker switched off. "Treats us like offal. What's he think he is, a patron?" He noticed Lissa. "Oh. Milady."

"I'll help you get your stuff together before the boost," she said. "Not to let it crash down helter-skelter." Skillfully, she moved about, plucking things from the air. "I didn't know you three lack this training," she told them angrily. "I took for granted you had it. What possessed you to chose them, Esker?"

The man's tone went sullen. "I made sure they aren't subject to spacesickness. That'd have been adequate, if our dear captain showed some common sense. Why should we conduct these studies? Elementary, routine procedures. The ship can perfectly well do them. Bring up one or two robot bodies from the hold, if necessary."

"This tests how well you'll perform when we need procedures that are not routine," Lissa replied. "Well, I'll give you three some basic drill as soon as may be, and hope for the best. But Esker, I'm very disappointed in you."

She wondered how much rage he must suppress in order to mumble, "I'm sorry, milady." The wondering was brief. A thought came to the fore, instead. Test—

Countdown gave warning, power coursed silent through the engine, the deck was once more downward and feet pressed lightly against it. Having nothing better to do, Lissa sat in a corner and watched the physicists work. She confessed to herself that Esker got things organized fast and thereafter efficiency prevailed. Spectroscopes, radio receivers, mass detectors she recognized; others she did not, but they spoke to those who understood.

Excitement waxed. "Yes, got to be masered— Three hundred twenty kiloherz— This'n's nearly twice that— And another—" Minute by minute, suspicion gathered in her.

Valen: "You've had your hour. What can you tell me?"

Esker muttered an oath and raised his shock head from the instrument over which he had stood crouched. "We don't need interruptions!" he called.

"I didn't say you must stop work. I only want to know what you've found out so far. You can keep on as long as needful."

Esker straightened. "That may be some while." His tone gentled, with a tinge of awe. This is certainly . . . a very peculiar region. Radio emissions from—a number of sources, we haven't established how many but they're in every direction. Mostly coherent waves. Frequencies and intensities vary by several orders of magnitude. We've only checked two Doppler shifts as yet, but they show motions of kilometers per second, which I suspect are orbital. Many graviton sources are also present. I can't state positively that they are invisible accelerated masses. . . . Oh, we'll be busy here. Is this a natural phenomenon, or could there be artifacts of the Forerunners, still operating after how many millions of years—?"

"What do you propose to do?"

"Keep studying of course. Examine everything. We haven't

even begun to search for matter particles, for instance. Neutrino spectra, perhaps? Captain, I don't want to make any hypotheses before we know a muckload more."

"Very well. Carry on." Valen laughed. "Don't forget to fix yourselves a bite to eat now and then." He switched off.

He wouldn't crack a joke here, would he? Unless—

It shivered through Lissa. She rose. "Esker," she said, "would you analyze one or two of those red stars?"

The physicist blinked. "Huh? Why, they're just dim red dwarfs, late M types, milady. You'd need amplification to see any that are more than three or four light-years off."

"Please. I have a notion about them."

"But—"

Lissa put command in her voice. "I have a notion. You can do it quickly, can't you?"

"Well, yes. Automated spectroscopy." With visible resentment, Esker squinted into a finder and operated controls on a box.

"Hasn't it struck you odd that we've got this many around us?" Lissa asked. "Not that I've seen any except the closest, as you said, but they imply plenty more."

"Red dwarfs are much the commonest kind of star, milady," Tessa ventured. "They often occur together."

"I know," Lissa answered. "These, though, aren't enough to be a proper cluster, are they?" Of the usual sort, that is.

She saw how Esker stiffened where he stood. Did he see what she was driving at? He stuck to his task regardless, until he could look up and announce: "This specimen is extremely metal-poor. As much so as any I've ever seen described. Ancient—" His features congealed. "Shall we survey the rest?"

"I don't think that will be necessary." Lissa touched the intercom. "Captain Valen, I can tell you what we have found."

An astonished-sounding hiss bespoke Orichalc's presence at the other end. "Then do," the man said slowly.

Victory responded. "This is the remains of a globular cluster.

Old, old, formed almost at the beginning, first-generation stars, when hardly any atoms heavier than lithium existed. Probably drifted in here from the galactic halo. All the big suns in it went supernova ages ago. The lesser ones evolved into red giants, sank down to white dwarfs, radiated away that energy too. Only the smallest and feeblest are still on the main sequence. Everything else is clinkers, cold and black, or at most emitting so little it's well-nigh lost in the cosmic background. Maybe a few neutron stars give off pulsar beams yet, but weak, and none happen to be pointed at us. More likely, I'd guess, they're also dead. Cinders, embers, ashes; let's get out of here."

Air whispered.

"The radio waves?" Valen asked. She heard the strain.

"Beacons," she said. "What else? You'd need them to find your way around in this gloom. The debris may not be closely packed by planetside standards, but the risk of collision would be appreciable, especially when you hyperjump, if you didn't know where objects are. A higher risk would be coming out of a jump too deep in a gravity well, and blowing your engine.

"Somebody finds it worthwhile to mine the cluster. The ancient supernovae must have plated certain smaller bodies with a rich layer of rare isotopes. I daresay it's a Skleron enterprise. This sort of thing fits what I've read about them."

Lissa glanced around. The three assistants had retreated toward the bulkheads. They looked alarmed. Esker stood his ground, legs wide apart, shoulders forward, hands flexing at his sides. Lips had drawn away from teeth. Word by word, he spat, "You knew about this. You did not take us to our goal."

"I will, when your team is ready to cope," Valen replied coldly. "Congratulations, Milady Windholm. I didn't expect my little puzzle would be solved this fast. Maybe I should arrange another practice session. Though it won't be as informative when you've been forewarned, will it?"

"You swinesucker," Esker said. "You smug, white-bellied

snotfink. If you think you and your lizard bedmate are fit to command *men*—"

"Enough. Silence, or I'll order up the robots and put you in confinement. Go back to your duties."

Her exultation had vanished from Lissa. It was as if the frozen darkness outboard reached in to touch her. "Captain," she said, "you and I had better hold a conference."

He hesitated. "Immediately," she said.

The response came flat. "Very well. The ship has things under control." Aside from the people, she thought.

She turned the intercom off. "That's right, milady," Esker snarled. "Give him his bucketful right back in his mouth. You've got the rank to do it."

"Have a care," she said into the smoldering eyes. "Without discipline, we're done for."

Striding the corridors, she worked off some tension and arranged some words. At the back of awareness, she was glad of the acceleration. Weightlessness made faces go puffy and unattractive.

XVI

Given *Dagmar*'s omnipresence, the captain need seldom occupy his own viewglobe. Lissa found him in his cabin. The ship must have announced her arrival to him, for the door retracted as she approached it and stood waiting. "Come in, please," he invited. She heard the tension in his voice, saw it in visage and stance.

Orichalc uncurled on the deck. "Best I betake myself elsewhere," he said.

"No, I want to speak with you too," Lissa answered.

The head shook, solemnly imitating a human negation. "Not at present, honored one. Later, if you still wish. I shall be in my quarters." Holding the trans in delicate hands, the long body slipped past her. The door closed behind it.

Lissa stared after. "Why?" she asked. "If he meets Esker along the way, there'll likely be an unpleasant scene."

"Susaians read emotions," Valen reminded her. "Orichalc must deem we'll do better alone." His tone sharpened. "As for Esker, I'm bloody sick of his insolence. Maybe you can warn him. If he pushes me further, I just might give him twenty-four hours of sensory deprivation, and hope to teach him some manners."

Yes, she thought, his type is bound to grate on yours. I should have foreseen. Well, it's up to me to set matters right—or, at any rate, make them endurable.

Returning to him, her glance traversed the cabin. It was larger than the sleeping cubicles, but mainly because it contained a desk, a four-screen terminal with associated keyboards, and access to a tiny bathroom. Otherwise it was monkishly austere, the bunk made up drumhead tight. His garb was a plain white coverall and slipshoes.

"Be seated, milady." He gestured at the single chair. When she took it, he half settled on the desk. His smile was forced. "Seated because I suppose we'd better allow our groundlubbers another thirty minutes or so of weight to get their stuff properly stowed."

Nor did she sit at ease. She compelled herself to meet his gaze and say, "I know Esker can be difficult, but he is able. On balance, I judged him the best person readily available for his tasks. I did not anticipate—Valen, I must insist you show the understanding, the, the kind of leadership I thought you would."

His reply was low, almost subdued, but stubborn. "What have I done wrong?"

"This trick you played on us, with Orichalc's connivance. I mean to reprimand him as well. Frankly, I feel insulted. But it's the scientists whom you've wronged most."

"Milady, did you really think we'd be wise to plunge straight to an unknown destination without a single trial run? Now it's proven that we need a training period, if not a complete shakedown cruise."

"You know perfectly well, doctrine is that the moment we spot something we're not sure we can handle, we hyperjump away."

"We may not be able to, on half a second's notice."

"Yes, and strolling through Riverside Park at home, we may be struck by lightning. One can't provide against every conceivable contingency, not even by huddling forever in a hole." Lissa drew breath. "This is getting beside the point." It is getting closer to the basic truth that I want. "We will have no more such incidents. Is that clear?"

Valen frowned. "Milady, I am the captain. My duty is to follow my best judgment."

Davy might have uttered those words, with the same gravity. Yes, and as Valen did, he looked much like the Head. For an instant, Lissa's eyes stung, her heart stumbled. She pulled herself straight and replied, recognizing that she spoke too loud and fast, "You're in command of the spacecraft while she's under way. She and her robots obey you. The rest of us must not obstruct, nor refuse a legitimate order. However, it is the House of Windholm that sponsors this expedition and its policies that you are to execute. I speak for it. I have authority to direct us to any lawful destination, including directly back home; and upon our return, you are answerable to the House for all actions."

He folded his arms and leaned back a little. "Let's not fight," he said quietly. "Just what is your complaint?"

"I told you. Your distrust of us is bad enough. Don't you know how important morale is, élan, on every exploratory mission? The way you showed your attitude was downright humiliating. I can swallow it for the sake of peace; but then, it didn't touch me in my honor. Esker is a proud man. He has a right to be infuriated."

"Proud? 'Overbearing' would be a better word; and he doesn't have the genuine worth that might excuse it. He's too small, in psyche still more than body. He can't stand having his superiority called into question. Most of his tantrum was because you, the amateur, reached the truth before he did."

You see cruelly well, Lissa thought, but your vision is narrow. "You don't understand. And you've got to. Esker's had to fight for everything, all his life. His parents weren't only poor, they were lowly, despised—patronless. As a boy he needed unlimited brashness, first to keep hope alive, then to bring himself to the attention of those high and mightinesses who could help him. In spite of his adoption, his scholarships, his accomplishments, he continued suffering scorn and discrimination. Professionally, too, he was always thwarted. He was born too late to become the great scientist he could have been, centuries ago. Unless this voyage of ours— That's a reason I picked him, Gerward. Don't ruin his dream!"

"Must everybody indulge him forever?" Valen retorted. "Is he the single being alive that's had troubles and frustrations? A real man puts such things behind him, acknowledges his mistakes, and goes on."

"Like you?" escaped from her.

"What do you mean?" he cried.

He jerked to his feet and swayed above her. She must needs rise too. He had gone appallingly white. "D-don't be so self-righteous," she stammered. "You've made y-your mistakes. Everybody has."

"Mine?" It sounded as if he were being garrotted.

I've got to retrieve this, oh, God, I didn't realize how woundable he still is. "Your, well, your record shows you gave up an excellent position once. You must have . . . had reasons."

His head sank. He turned from her. A hand dropped to the desktop and lay helpless. "You know them, then." The words fell empty.

I could bite out my tongue, she thought. Or should I? May it not be better to bring this forth, between the two of us, and I try to gauge how trustworthy *he* is? If I can. If I can. Dad, be with me, lend me your wisdom and strength.

"About Naia, yes," she said.

He stared at whatever rose before him. "And still you kept me on?"

"We didn't find out till almost departure time, and Orichalc thinks the hour is late for us. Which is one reason this . . . delay . . . upset me. But I, I was willing to have you anyway, Gerward. We'd gotten to know each other, at least a little. I'd like to hear your side of the story."

"Nobody else ever did . . . Ha-a-ah!" he cawed. "Now I'm sounding like Esker. Self-pity. No. There was no excuse. I ran away because I was weak. Couldn't stand it. How many might I have saved?"

She reached toward his back, but withdrew. "It was terrible, I'm sure."

"Blackened land, ash blowing on acid winds. Craters, trees

strewn around them like jackstraws, kilometer after kilometer after kilometer, snags of wall above toppled ruins, a burnt-out city. The dead in their thousands—millions, we knew—animal, human, sprawled bloated and stinking till they fell apart and the bones grinned through—" Valen checked the shrillness that had arisen in his voice. After a moment, he went on in a monotone: "But it was good when we helped survivors. Planetside vehicles, ground and air, located them and brought them to the spacecraft. Many were ragged, filthy, starved, sick, but they would live. I lifted my share of them to the moon, and came back for more."

He stopped. When the silence had lasted too long for her, she touched the hand that dangled at his side and whispered, "What happened then?"

He turned around. She looked upon despair. "The next lot of stones arrived," he said harshly. "They were strung out along the whole orbit, of course, so that the night sky was always full of shooting stars, except where dust or storms hid them. We'd get a major strike somewhere almost daily. But the bulk of them stayed clustered together. When that returned, the real barrage began again.

"The orbit was perturbed and the planet rotated, so new areas were hit worst at every such time. Now Ranz's turn came, a big, beautiful, heavily populated island off in an ocean that from above looked like blued silver. I was ordered to a certain town, unharmed as yet. Night had fallen when I landed. Another ship was already there. An awkward, crewed hulk, she was. But much bigger than mine, with a belly that could take a hundred. They were streaming out toward her. It was chaos. Not quite a mob scene, everybody seemed brave, struggled to maintain order, but nevertheless the mass swirled and eddied, yelled and moaned, mothers tried to pass small children along over the heads of people in front—the rescue operation always was badly confused, you see. There had been so little warning, and then volunteer vessels like mine kept appearing unannounced—do you see? Nobody here had heard I was coming. At least, nobody appeared to know. I wondered if anyone had even seen me land; it was some distance off, naturally. I debarked, hoping I could do something toward straightening matters out. I was shaken and sickened by what I'd seen earlier, but I did debark. I shouted and waved. 'Over here! This way!' "

He fought for air. She could not but take both his hands in hers and ask, "What then? What was it like?"

"Like the, the end of the world, the wreck of the gods, in, in some ancient myth," he groaned. "I was in a brushy meadow, near a road, several kilometers from the town. Its roofs, spires, domes stood black against the sky. The sky was afire, you see. Flames streaked over it, out of the west, from horizon to horizon. Hundreds of flames—the great fireballs, blue-white, tailing off in red and yellow, that left me half blinded, till I didn't know what was after-image and what was rock booming in at kilometers per second—and the little devils, countless, zip-zip-zip, wicked for an instant across the dark, gone, but more were there at once, more and more. Only the night wasn't really dark. Not with all those thunderbolts splitting and shaking it, and a forest burning to the south, and— They roared, screamed, whistled. When a big one struck somewhere, I'd see a flash over the horizon. A second or two later the ground shivered under my feet, up through my bones and teeth; and then the airborne noise reached me, sometimes like a cannon, sometimes like an avalanche that went on and on, below that uproar overhead. The air reeked of smoke and lightning. And I knew I was defenseless. If anything hit anywhere near, by the sheerest blind chance, that ended my universe."

His hands were cold between her fingers. "You could face that," she foreknew.

"Yes." The tears broke forth. "Barely."

"But what happened next?"

"I—I—" He wrenched free of her. "No."

"Tell me."

He slumped onto the chair, covered his eyes, and shuddered.

"I hurried toward the crowd," she made out. "I waved and

shouted. Several on the fringes, they saw, they moved my way. A girl ran ahead of them. She was maybe six or seven years old, light on her feet. I've wondered why she went alone. Got separated from her family in the scramble? There I was, as terrified as her, but she didn't know that. I was a man, holding out my arms to her under that horrible sky, and at my back the ship that was life. She held a kitten to her breast—"

He wept, long, racking gulps and rattles, into his hands. "The strike— The town went up, a crash that deafened and staggered me, a blaze that rose and lost itself in a black tree of smoke and dust—fragments—they tore through the crowd like sleet. Those people that were making for me, they, they became . . . rags flung right and left. The little girl rolled over. She flopped into a bush. It caught fire. I ran to her and stamped out the flames. It'd been such a pretty dress. Her hair— 'Please, oh please!' I think she screamed. The chunk had ripped through her. Guts slurped out. Her kitten was burned too. I put my heel down on its skull. It crunched. That was all I could do for her. Wasn't it? By then she was dead. A bolide trundled and rumbled overhead. Its light brought her face out of the shadows, in fits and starts, fallen jaw and staring eyes. She looked very like my daughter the same age, my daughter who'd died the year before.

"I don't remember much else, till I was back in space, outbound."

Valen raised his head, pawed at the tears, caught a breath, and said, saw-edged, "No excuses. I never made any. I had that much self-respect left me."

We are none of us infinitely strong, Davy Windholm had told his own daughter. *Always the universe can break us. If we go on afterward, scars and all, it's because luck made us brave.* She knelt to enfold the man who had opened himself to her.

XVII

The ship sprang to a known part of space. There she coasted while Noel, Elif, and Tessa practiced in free fall. Violet and rose, a nebula phosphoresced across a fourth of heaven. Through its laciness gleamed fierce points of light, new-born giant suns, and the coals that were stars still forming. Oh, no lack of wonders whereon to sharpen skills!

Given intelligence and healthy reflexes, most people soon learned how to handle their weightless bodies. Precision work was the hard thing to master. It began with always, automatically, making sure that objects would stay where you left them. Over and over and over, Lissa put her pupils through the drill, explained, chided, encouraged, demonstrated, guided. Then followed assignments in partnership with the three robots. Who knew but that the multiple manipulators and ship-linked but individual intelligences of Uno, Dos, and Tres would be needed?

"Time for lunch," she said wearily. "Meet again in half an hour. You're doing quite well. In fact, you no longer require me to hector you."

"Why, Sergeant Major, you sound downright human," Elif japed.

Lissa laughed. "I have reason. *I* won't be here, next session. Seriously, I am pleased. Keep on as hard as you have been, get your efforts a little better coordinated, and we'll be in shape to fight mad tax collectors."

Their friendship felt like a warmth at her back as she left. Yes, she had driven them hard, but they realized why. House Windholm's clients knew that it traditionally expected more of its patrons than it did of them.

The whole cosmos was warm and bright. Flying down the corridors, Lissa whistled that bawdy old ballad "Two Lovers in Two Spacesuits."

She assumed Esker would be at a rec screen, whether to play three-dimensional *go* against the ship or watch one of the loud, flashy musical shows he'd put in the library database. He wasn't, though. She inquired. "He is in the electronics shop," *Dagmar* told her.

"What's he want there?" Lissa wondered aloud.

Hitherto, she wouldn't have gotten a reply. The ship's capabilities weren't for crewfolk to spy on each other. Valen had lately directed that she have the same full access as himself. It was just a gesture, impulsive, scarcely significant, but endearing. She'd forgotten, and felt surprise at first when *Dagmar* said, "He appears to be writing a program. I cannot tell for certain, because he is using a personal computer he brought along, unconnected to my systems, and his body blocks the keyboard and display from my sensors. Do you wish a visual?"

"No, no. I only have to talk with him. I'll go in person." Lissa set off.

Already competent in zero gravity, he hunched at the middle of the compartment, legs wrapped around a stanchion, machine geckofooted to his lap. It was a mini, useful enough when something more powerful wasn't available. He started when she entered and slammed the cover shut. She smiled. "Hullo," she greeted. "What are you up to?"

He swallowed. "An, uh, experimental procedure. I don't want to show it to anybody till it's finished."

"Why not use *Dagmar*'s systems? You'd finish in a tenth the time, not counting blind alleys that that gimcrack may let you wander into."

He flushed, then paled. How haggard he had grown, these past several watches. And solitary, silent. She almost missed his waspishness. "I don't choose to! When my program's ready, when I'm satisfied, I'll put it in the network."

And if it's a failure, there'll be no record of it. Nobody will ever know, not even the ship. You poor, forlorn devil.

Best avoid the subject. "As you like. I'm afraid you'll have to set it aside and rejoin your team, at 1230 hours."

He glared. "Why?"

"They're ready to practice with you."

"And where will you be?" After a pause: "Milady."

"Elsewhere." It tingled through her skin. "I've given them their basic instruction. Now I should not be underfoot. It's your team. Get them into unison with you."

"I see," he said. "And you will be elsewhere."

"Look," she pointed out, as mildly as possible, "it shouldn't take long. I hope not. We don't want to come late for the big event. However, when you're prepared, we'll take two extra watches and rest before we proceed to destination. We'll do it under boost, so everybody can feel at ease while regaining some muscle tone. Captain Valen thinks, and I agree, we'd better reach the scene in optimum condition. That'll give you time to complete this project of yours, if you want." And you will. You don't sleep much or well, do you?

"Captain Valen." Esker's attention went back to his computer. "Very well, milady. Now, if you will excuse me, I may be able to write this subroutine before assuming my duties."

"Of course." If only I could share happiness with you who hardly know what it is. Impossible. So why mar mine? "Good luck." Lissa left him.

Elif, Noel, and Tessa were fixing their meal, but the Susaian was evidently through eating. By tacit accommodation, he did so alone. Communality would have been awkward, given the differences in shape. "Will you not join your fellows?" he hailed her.

Courtesy demanded she press palm against bulkhead and brake herself. "Later," she said. "I must report to the skipper."

The luminous eyes searched her. "You are hungry."

She laughed. It sounded the least bit nervous to her. "Does

your emotion-reading extend to that? Yes, I would like a sandwich, but it can wait."

The artificial voice lowered together with the sibilant purring. "Honored one, let me suggest you be more . . . circumspect. Feelings toward you have intensified."

Blood throbbed in her throat. "What do you mean?"

A ripple down the long body might correspond to a shrug. "I detect emotions, not thoughts, and with an alien race my perceptions are basic; nuances are lost on me. Still, I can identify joy, and rageful bitterness, and even amicable, slightly prurient curiosity. This enables me to make deductions that as yet are probably mere speculations in the minds of the rest." Those lips could not smile, and the speech was synthetic. Yet did she sense benevolence, concern, perhaps a kind of love? "None of my business, as your saying goes, especially when I am a total outsider. But I do pray leave to counsel discretion. We are embarking into mystery. We must remain united.

"Sufficient."

Orichalc departed. She looked after him till he disappeared around a corner, before she continued forward.

He's right, she knew. We have been careless, Gerward and I. Well, it happened so suddenly, overwhelmingly. . . . No justification. We're not freed from our responsibility for crew and mission.

On earlier expeditions she had stayed prudent, celibate except on the two she made in company with Tomas Whiteriver, and there it was known beforehand that they would be together. (They had dreamed of forging one more marriage bond between their Houses. That faded out with the relationship, in wistful but not unpleasant wise. He was too immature.) Planetside, you could be as private as you wanted, and in any event jealousy wouldn't create a hazard.

But damn it, Gerward's the best lover I've ever had or hoped to have. Knowing, considerate, ardent. As fine a human being as I'll ever meet. Wise, gentle, resolute. He's come back out of the night—I raised him from it, he says—with a strength, a knowledge, beyond my imagining, I who have never been there. Dad and Mother won't be happy at first, but they'll learn, they too.

Meanwhile, yes, of course, we'd better see to our masks. If we can. How do you appear in public not radiating gladness?

XVIII

Jump.

Brilliance.

Slowly, she eased. Nothing had happened. She floated before the weapons console in silence and the ocean of stars. Well, she thought, we knew Orichalc's fix was rough, and the smallest difference in astronomical distances is big beyond our conceiving.

She gazed about her, searching the strangeness for anything she might identify, as the Susaian had done. Magellanic Clouds, Andromeda galaxy, a few naked-eye sisters—clotted darkness shielded her from the blaze at the heart of her own galaxy and marked it for her—an obvious blue giant, ten or twenty light-years away, might be in some survey catalogue—

"What do you detect?" Valen breathed through the night.

"No radiations such as spacecraft emit," *Dagmar* reported. "An anomalous source at 1926 hours planar, sixty-two degrees south. Radio, optical, X-ray; possible neutrino component."

Excitement pulsed in Valen's voice: "That's got to be *it*. All right, let's aim the array."

"Request permission to leave my post," Lissa said.

"Granted," Valen answered. "Come join me. We may want to swap ideas off the intercom, not to disturb the scientists."

You transparent innocent! Lissa thought. We could talk directly, cubicle to cabin. . . . Well, but if I know Esker, he's now too engaged in his work to notice. . . . Never mind him. What better time to be at your side, darling?

She hastened. Glorious though the sight was, he had abandoned it for his quarters. The kiss lasted long. "Hold, hold," he mumbled when her hands began to move. "We'd better wait a while. The team should have word for us in a few minutes."

"I know," she said in his ear. "Make some arrangements for later, though, will you? And not much later, either. Have I told you you're as good in zero gee as you are under boost?"

He chuckled, low in his throat. "The feeling's mutual. Uh, the ship—"

"Oh, *Dagmar* knows too, the way we kept forgetting she existed. And if we cut her off now, we might delay an emergency call. You won't tell on us, will you, *Dagmar* dear?"

"I am programmed not to reveal mission-irrelevant matters to others than the captain upon command, and yourself," replied the sweet tones. "Those will be wiped upon our return, prior to logging the permanent record."

"Yes, yes. But it's nice of you to, well, care." Did the robotic brain? A philosophical question, never really answered. Certainly *Dagmar* was not, could not be voyeuristic. Still, her consciousness didn't seem completely impersonal and aloof. And—Lissa felt a blush—that unseen presence did add a little extra spice.

As if any were needed! She nuzzled. "You smell good," she murmured. "Clean but male. Or should that be male but clean?"

Half an hour passed. They required something to discuss if they were to stay chaste and alert. Valen declined their search as a subject. "It is a capital mistake to theorize before one has data," he said. She got the impression he was quoting, perhaps a translation from an ancient writer; like her father, or like Romon Kesperson, or like Torben Hebo, she supposed . . . How was he doing? . . . he read widely.

Well, she and Gerward had their future to imagine, and to plan soberly. They were quite aware that much in it would be difficult, especially at first, before he had once more fully proven himself.

The intercom chimed. They accepted. Esker sounded almost friendly, or was that sheer exuberance? Whichever, Lissa was delighted to hear it. "We've got our preliminary data, Captain, milady. Something peculiar, for certain. I'd rather keep my ideas in reserve for the moment."

Valen, too, showed pleasure. "What can you tell, in layman's language?"

"Well, actually there are two radiation sources. Radial velocities seem to indicate galactic orbits, but highly eccentric. Spectra indicate mostly hydrogen, some helium, traces of metals. In short, interstellar medium, but at sunlike temperatures. Each source appears to be rotating differentially, the inner parts at speeds approaching *c*, but we aren't sure of that yet. Nor of much else, aside from— It is extraordinary, Captain."

"Good work. I hereby become your errand boy. What do you want us to do?"

"Skip around. Get parallaxes so we can determine the location in space, transverse component of velocity, intrinsic brightness. Observing from various distances, over a range of a hundred parsecs or so, we can follow any evolution that's been taking place. That should let us figure out the nature of the beast."

Valen frowned. Esker's reply had been scoffingly obvious. Valen's brow cleared. Lissa saw he was willing to overlook the matter. As keyed up as he was, Esker doubtless bypassed tact without noticing. "Fine. Give me your plan."

"I'll develop it as we go along and collect more information. For the present, hm, I must do some figuring. I'll get back to you with the coordinates of the next observation point in about an hour." The physicist cut the connection.

"An hour," Lissa said. "That'll serve."

Valen blinked. "What?"

"An hour of our own. Let's take advantage. We may not have more for some time to come."

XIX

Fifty hours of leap, study, leap were unendurably long and unbelievably few. At the end, the travelers met in the saloon. Word like this should be face to face, where hand could seize hand. For it, they gave themselves boost, weight, that they might sit around the table at ease, perhaps the last ease they would ever know.

Esker rose. Pride swelled his stumpy form. "I am ready to tell you what I have found," he said.

"After the Great Confederacy." Orichalc murmured the words, but forgot to keep the trans equally quiet. Well, Lissa thought beneath her heart-thumping, Children's Day morning expectancy, of course all beings want their races given all due honor, whether or not they like the governments.

Esker surprised her with a mild answer: "True. And your people scarcely came upon this by last-minute accident. I imagine a survey ship found it ten or twenty years ago. They—the rulers, that is—saw the potentialities, but bided their time till the climactic moment neared. Humans couldn't have kept a secret like that."

Has his triumph made him gentler? wondered Lissa. I'm glad for you, Esker.

"What are the potentialities, then?" Valen demanded.

"I don't know," the physicist replied. "Neither do the Susaians, or they wouldn't be making such an effort." He paused. Something mystical entered his speech, his whole manner. "An unprecedented event, rare if not totally unique in the universe. Who can say what it will unleash? Quite possibly, phenomena never suspected by us. Conceivably, laws of nature unknown even to the Forerunners."

And what technologies, what powers might spring from those discoveries? went chill through Lissa. For good or ill, salvation or damnation. I can't blame the Susaians or the Domination for wanting to keep it to themselves. I wish we humans could.

"Tell us what it is!" she blurted.

The three assistants shifted on their bench. They knew. Their master had laid silence on them. This was to be his moment.

He looked at her and measured out his words. "I can give you the basic fact in a single sentence, milady. Two black holes are on a collision course."

Orichalc hissed and Valen softly whistled.

Black holes, Lissa evoked from memory. Stars two—or was it three?—or more times greater than Sunniva, ragingly luminous, consuming their cores with nuclear fire until after mere millions of years they exploded as supernovae, briefly rivaling their whole galaxy; then the remnant collapsing, but not into the stability of a neutron star. No, the mass was still huge, gravitation overcame quantum repulsion, shrinkage went on and on toward zero size and infinite density, though to an outside observer it soon slowed almost to a halt and would take all eternity to reach its end point. The force of gravity rose until light itself could not escape. . . .

She had seen pictures of a few, taken from spacecraft at a distance and by probes venturing closer. No more than that; their kind was surely numbered in the billions, but explorers were still ranging only this one tiny segment of a thinly populated outer fringe of the galaxy.

Wonder and terror enough, just the same. The event horizon, the sphere of ultimate darkness, was asteroid size, sometimes visible as a tiny round blot in heaven, sometimes not. For it captured matter from space, and if there happened to be enough of that nearby, a nebula or, still more so, a companion sun from which the hole sucked mass, then fire wheeled around it, the accretion disc, spiraling ever faster into the maw, giving off a blaze of energy as it fell. The stupendous gravity dragged at light waves, reddened them, twisted their paths. Its tidal pull stretched a probe asunder and whirled the fragments off into the disc. . . . Most of the knowledge was to Lissa little more than words, quantum tunneling, Hawking radiation, space and time interchangeably distorted. . . .

I'm not badly informed for a layman, she thought. I remember Professor Artur remarking how much remains unknown to any of the spacefaring races. He felt that in the nature of the case it would always be unknown too, because there is no possible way for information to reach us through the event horizon. But if a pair of them crash together—

"That must be rare indeed," Orichalc said low.

"Unless at galactic center?" Valen mused.

"Conjecture," Esker snorted. "Yes, perhaps lesser black holes are among the stars that the Monster engulfs. That might help account for some of the things we have glimpsed there, such as short-lived trails of radiation. They may be from matter that it somehow accelerates almost to light speed, soon slowed down again by interaction with the interstellar medium. We don't know. I tell you, in spite of all proud pretensions to having a final theory, *we don't know.*"

The Monster, Lissa remembered. The truly gigantic black hole at the galactic heart, hidden from sight behind the dust clouds gathered around there, barred from exploration by unloosed energies that would almost instantly kill any organic being and wreck the circuits of any robot.

How did the conventional scientists dare imagine that no fundamental mysteries remained in the universe?

Esker's voice lifted as if in triumph. "Here such an event is out where we can watch it."

Again the academic tone took over. "Also, this is not a simple linear collision, such as we believe we have some theoretical understanding of. That would be vanishingly improbable, two singularities aimed straight at each other. This will be a grazing encounter, the convergence of two eccentric galactic orbits.

"From our observation of orbits and accelerations, we've obtained the masses of the bodies with considerable accuracy. They are approximately nine and ten Sols. That means the event horizons are about sixty kilometers in diameter. Calculation of closest approach—that involves some frank guesswork. We have good figures for the orbital elements. If these were Newtonian point masses, they'd swing by on hyperbolic paths at a distance of about thirty kilometers and a speed of about one-third light's. But they aren't, and it'd be a waste of breath to give you exact figures, when all I'm sure of is that the event horizons will intersect. The ship has programs taking relativistic and quantum effects into account. I've used them. However, certain key answers come out as essentially nonsense. The matrices blow up in a mess of infinities. We simply don't know enough. We shall have to observe.

"Observe," he whispered. *"See."*

"Can we get that near, and live?" Valen asked.

"As near as the Susaians, I daresay." Now Esker sounded boyishly bold and careless.

"How near is that, do you suppose?"

"Probably closer than humans would venture, if this were their project from the beginning. We'd send in sophisticated robotic vessels. The Susaians will do their best with probes, but that best isn't very good. No nonhuman race's is. They all keep trying to copy from us, and never get it right."

"Every species has its special talents," Lissa interjected for shame's sake. She wondered if Orichalc cared, either way.

"Give me a figure, will you?" Valen snapped.

"An estimate," Esker replied. "To start with, the collision will produce a stupendous gamma burst, detectable across the width of the universe. Nobody and nothing could survive anywhere near that. However, it's known from theory and remote observation that this doesn't happen at once. It results from the recollapse of matter hurled outward by the electromagnetic and other forces released in the encounter. The recollapse to critical density takes two or three days. Meanwhile, yes, radiation background and gas temperatures will be high and increasing.

"However, our advanced protective systems can fend off more than most ships. The Susaians must have some that are equally shieldable. Integrating the expected radiation over time around the event, and throwing in a reasonable safety factor, I'd undertake to keep on station at a distance of two hundred million kilometers, for two hundred and fifty hours before the impact and maybe as much as thirty hours after it, depending on what the actual intensities turn out to be. That's far too deep in the gravity well for a hyperjump escape, of course, but I'd call the odds acceptable."

He spread his hands. "Granted," he went on, "the whole reason for the exercise is that nobody can predict what will happen. I make no promises. All I say is, if I were the Susaian in charge, I'd post four live crews at approximately that distance. One each 'above' and 'below' the point of contact, the other two 180° apart in the impact-orbital plane. I'd put others elsewhere, naturally, but these four should have the best positions, if our theories correspond to any part of reality.

"And if I were that Susaian, I'd join one of those crews."

Lissa leaned forward. She shivered. "When will the encounter be?" she asked.

"If we jumped now to the vicinity," Esker told them in carefully academic style, "we would observe it in a little more than eleven standard days."

"That soon," Valen murmured into stillness renewed. "We barely made it, didn't we?"

He shook himself, straightened where he sat, and clipped, "Very well. Thank you, Dr. Harolsson. If you haven't already, please put your data and conclusions in proper form for transmission. We've got to notify headquarters. What we've learned thus far mustn't be lost with us. Besides, I'll be interested in the exact information, the actual numbers, too." His smile was crooked. "Personally interested."

Lissa saw doubt on Elif; Noel swallowed; Tessa laughed aloud. They foreknew. It was Orichalc who said, "Thereafter, do you intend that we shall see the event?"

Valen's head lifted. "What else? On Asborg, they'd never outfit and scramble another ship in time."

"Humans won't get another chance," Esker agreed, "and I doubt the Susaians will share what they learn."

Lissa paid him no heed. She caught Valen's arm. "Yes, certainly," rang from her. "It's up to us. That's how you were bound to think, Gerward."

The glee drained out of Esker, as if somehow gravity had reached from the lightless masses yonder. Sexual frustration, Lissa thought. We shouldn't flaunt what we have, that he can't.

XX

A hyperbeam bypassed light years, carrying the findings made aboard *Dagmar*. Lissa wished she could talk with her father when they were done, but haste forbade. The instruments gathered information at rates hugely greater than the transmitter could send it. Conveying all they had took several irrecoverable hours. For the same reason, the expedition would dispatch nothing but the new data from each stop along its course henceforward—and nothing whatsoever, once it was close to the black holes, until it was outward bound again.

Esker spent the waiting period in the electronics shop. Lissa supposed he tinkered with something in hopes that it would ease his tension and . . . unhappiness? Or did the magnificence ahead of him drive out mortal wishes?

Noel monitored the reporting. Valen studied the facts, with Tessa and Elif on hand to answer questions. In the saloon, Lissa and Orichalc played round upon round of Integer until, at length, they fell into conversation. It turned to private hopes, fears, loves. You could confide to a sympathetic alien what you could not to any of your own species. "I look forward to your Freydis colony," Lissa said finally, sincerely.

The summons resounded. Crew took their posts. Countdown. Jump. A light-year from their destination, they poised.

Words reached Lissa in her globe as if from across an equal gulf. She had instantly established that no other vessel was in the neighborhood. Absurd to imagine that any would be, those few score motes strewn through the abyss. Why, for starters, consider that the light-year is a human unit, a memory of Old Earth like the standard year and day, the meter, the gram, the gee. Nobody else uses them. . . . The view was, as always, glorious with stars. One outshone all the rest, a dazzling brilliance. Wonderstruck, she asked what that might be. The ship replied that it was a type B giant, about four and a half parsecs off, passing through this vicinity at this time. She dropped it out of sight and mind as she set the console viewscreen to the predicted coordinates of the search object. Her fingers trembled a little. She turned up the optics.

The breath caught in her throat. Magnified, amplified, two comets flamed before her. From their shining brows, flattened blue-white manes streamed toward each other, shading through fierce gold to a red like newly spilled blood. Where they met, they roiled, and she imagined the turbulence within, great waves and tides, lightning-like discharges, atoms ripped into plasma, roaring to their doom.

The gas was thin, she knew; on Asborg it would have seemed well-nigh a vacuum. But the totality was monstrous, drawn out of the interstellar medium as the black holes hurtled through, spinning down into them with a blaze of radiation. And now, when they had drawn close, their pulls coacted to redouble that infall. The accretion discs had just begun to interact. The shock was mostly generating visible light. Later it would shift—it had shifted—toward X-rays, harder and harder.

"Next jump," Esker called.

"Already?" Valen asked.

The reply screeched. "Chaos take you, we haven't got a second to waste! Nothing registers here that we can't account for in principle. I've programmed everything for maximum data input and processing. Make use of it, you clotbrain!"

Hoy, that's far too strong, Esker, thought Lissa, half dismayed. Gerward has every right to put you in confinement. Are you off your beam? Now, in these last, supreme days?

Relief washed through her when Valen rapped, "Watch your language. The next offense, I will penalize."

She had a sense of deliverance when she heard his grudging "Sorry, . . . Captain. May we proceed?"

Dagmar knew how she was to approach. "Ten," she sang. Valen must have given her a signal, not quite trusting himself to speak. "Nine. Eight. Seven—"

At half a light-year, the comets burned naked-eye bright. Optics showed a diamond pattern in the shock front, and intricate strands that looped around as if seeking forward to the hungry furnaces of the comas. Elif's voice was full of awe and puzzlement: "Sir, that looks almighty strange, doesn't it? I can't think how you'd get curvatures like that in the gas, at this stage of things."

"Nor can I," Esker admitted eagerly. Rapture had eclipsed wrath. "The cosmos is running an experiment like none we've ever seen before or likely ever will again. I'd guess that mutual attraction is—was—appreciably distorting the event horizons. That'd be bound to affect magnetic fields and charge distributions. But we need more information."

Not that it would soon reveal the truth, Lissa realized. Understanding must wait upon months or years of analysis, hypothesis, tests in laboratories and observatory ships and brains, back at Asborg and no doubt elsewhere. The task here set Esker's genius was to decide what sorts of data, out of the impossibly many his team might try for, would likely bear such fruit. "The polarizing synchrometer should—" The conversation over the intercom went out of Lissa's reach.

She tuned it low and made a direct connection with Orichalc in the saloon. Her yearning was for Valen's words, since she could not have his presence. The skipper shouldn't be distracted, though, nor should the others be given grounds to suspect he was. Besides, she felt sorry for the Susaian, become functionless, restricted to whatever view *Dagmar* got a chance to project on a rec screen for him.

"How're you doing?" she inquired softly.

"We fare among splendors," she heard. "Is this not worth an island?"

"Yes, oh, yes." A thought she had not wanted to think pushed to the forefront. "Will your—will the Dominator ships really let us carry it home?"

"We have considered this before, honored one. The vessels on which I served were unarmed. The Dominators have no cause to expect us. The fleet come for the climax may include a few naval units of models suitable for rescue and salvage operations, should those prove necessary; but they are probably not formidable."

"I know. I remember. However, it's occurred to me—it didn't before, because on Asborg we don't think that way—in a number of human societies, the military would insist on having a big presence, if only for the prestige."

"They do not think like that in the Confederacy either, honored one. There is no distinction between organizations serving the Dominance; they are simply specialized branches of the same growth. This means that commanders can act decisively, without having to consult high officials first. You see, their intelligence and emotional stability have been verified beforehand. I warned your father that I do not know what the doctrine is with respect to preserving this secret. But I doubt that orders read 'at all costs.' Additional combat vessels will scarcely be sent from afar, under any but desperate circumstances. That would mean leakage of the truth, from crewfolk not predisciplined to closeness about it. Besides, the Confederacy is as desirous of maintaining stability as any other nation is." Orichalc hesitated. "I do counsel that we avoid undue provocation."

"Well, you can advise the captain. Can't you?"

"I can try. Perhaps I shall bring you into conference, if possible. Your rapport with both him and me may enable you to make ourselves clear to one another."

It thrilled in her. "I can't imagine any better service. Thank you, old dear, thank you."

Jump went the ship in a while. And again, presently, *jump*. And hour after hour, *jump,* to a different point of view, to a new distance, but always nearer, *jump, jump, jump.*

XXI

Jump.

At one light-hour, the incandescence around the black holes made them even brighter than the giant star. You could have read by that livid radiance. Their closeness was deceptive; *Dagmar* had emerged well off any normal to their paths. Yet even as Lissa watched, her unaided eyes saw them creep nearer. Chill went through her, marrow-deep. Second by second, those colossal accelerations were mounting.

And what when they met? Esker believed the masses would fuse. If nothing else could leave such a gravity well, how could the thing itself? But this was no simple, head-on crash, it would be a grazing blow. He said the case had been considered theoretically, centuries ago, but not as fully as it might have been, and had since lain obscure—probably in the archives of other races too—for nobody awaited it in reality. He spoke of problems with linear and angular momentum, potential fields, quantum tunneling by photons, leptons, baryons, gravitons. The event horizons should undergo convulsive changes of shape. Still more should the static limits, below which everything from outside was ineluctably hauled into orbit in the same sense as a black hole's rotation. This pair had opposite spins with distinct orientations. What wavelike distortions might their meeting send out through the continuum? Already, space-time around each was warped. In a black hole's own frame, the collapse to singularity was swift. To a safely distant observer, it took forever; what she saw was not a completed *being* but an eternal *becoming*. Yet if somehow the inside of it should be bared, however briefly, to her universe, there was no way even to guess what would follow.

"Emissions from spacecraft powerplant detected," said *Dagmar*. "I estimate the nearest at fifteen million kilometers."

No surprise, here. Nevertheless Lissa knew guiltily that for a pulsebeat she had let her attention stray from her guns. Valen remained cool: "Any indications that they've noticed us?"

"None. They may well fail to. The background is high because of emissions from the search objects, and the Susaians have no reason to be watchful for new arrivals."

"Uh-huh. Hard to see how they can think about anything but . . . that."

Lissa allowed herself a magnified view. The optics must adjust brightness pixel by pixel before she could see any detail against the glare at either forefront. The comet tails had fused, while changeable light seethed in a ring around each flattened fire-globe. She thought she could make out fountains and geysers within it, brief saw-teeth on the rims. Dopplering shaded it clearly toward violet on the one edge, red on the other, a whirling rainbow.

"Emissions indeed!" Esker shouted. "What readings!"

Nothing dangerous to ship or crew. This puny radius, which would not have touched the Oort cloud of a typical planetary system, was still beyond mortal comprehension. You could give it a name and hang numbers on it; that was all.

"Yes, event horizons distinctly deformed," Esker crooned.

Lissa knew that his instruments saw what she could not. The sight before her, like every such earlier, must in at least some part be illusion. Gravity sucked matter in from every direction, while its colliding atoms gave off radiation that grew the more furious the deeper it fell; but as it neared the static limit, bent space-time compelled it into the maelstrom. Yonder comas were no more than its last clotting and sparking before it entered the accretion disc; the ring was no more than the verge of an inward-rushing cataract. Esker's devices looked past them, through the ergosphere, to the ultimate blindness itself. And they had not the eyes of gods wherewith to do this. They took spectra, traced particles, measured mutable fields; from what they gathered, computers drew long mathematical chains of inference.

That process would not end for years, perhaps not for rejuvenations. The readouts and graphics that Esker saw flash before him were the barest preliminary theorizing. They might be dead wrong. It was a powerful mind that could, regardless, immediately grasp something of what went on.

Time went timelessly past, but in retrospect astonishingly short, until he said, "We're clear to move on, Captain."

Praise him, Lissa thought. He needs it. He's earned it. "Fast work," she chimed in.

His laugh rattled. "Oh, we could spend weeks here and not exhaust the material. But we haven't got them."

No, she thought, we now have days to reap a share of the harvest for which the Susaians spent years or decades preparing.

"Right," Valen agreed. "I take it you want to go on to your next planned point?" Same distance, but directly confronting the impact to be.

"No. I've changed my mind, on the basis of what I've learned in the last few stops. The latest input seems to confirm my ideas. We're going straight in."

"What? Immediately? You know we're close to the boundary for hyperjump, given masses like those."

Once inside it, we run strictly on plasma drive, till we've gotten remote enough again, Lissa knew. We're committed.

"Yes, yes, yes." Lissa heard how Esker barely controlled his temper. "But *you* know, or should, contact will take place in a hundred and seventy-six hours. I want to be at the two hundred million kilometer radius I calculated was safe, before that happens, in time to set up experiments I've devised. How fast can you get us there, ship?"

"At one gravity acceleration, with turnover, considering our present velocity, that will require eighty-eight hours, plus maneuvering time," *Dagmar* told him.

Lissa visualized him shaking fists in air. "You can boost higher than that. A lot higher! We've got medications against excess weight. We could even go into the flotation tank."

"Such a delta vee would seriously deplete our reserve. Does the captain order it?"

"No," Valen decided at once. "One gee it is. You can still observe as we go, Harolsson."

"But—" The physicist gasped in a breath. "Can't you understand? We've got to be close in, and prepared, for the main event. I expect fluctuations in the metric, short-lived superparticles, polarized gravitons, superstrings— Aargh! Time's grown so scant as is. If you hadn't farted it away, everywhere else in space—"

"Most of what we lost was because the people you chose turned out to require training," Valen interrupted stiffly. "Prudence demands we don't squander so much mass that we can't get onto emergency trajectories."

"Yes, you'll keep your hide safe, won't you, whatever else may be sacrificed?"

"That will do. If your considered judgment as a scientist is that we should head directly inward, I assume you don't want to dawdle here arguing. Give the ship the coordinates you have in mind. Crew, stand by for boost at one gravity."

XXII

Lissa and Valen were in his cabin when the message came. "To the captain," *Dagmar* said. "Incoming audio signal on the fifth standard band. Radar touched us sixty seconds ago and is now locked on. Code: 'Acknowledge and respond.' Shall I?"

Valen disentangled himself and rose from the bunk. "Do, and relay to me, with translation. Surely a Susaian." To Lissa, wryly: "I knew this couldn't last. We're picking up more powerplant emissions every hour. Somebody was bound to notice ours, and wonder."

She needed a moment more to swim up from the sweet aftermath of lovemaking. The warmth and odor of him still lingered as she heard "Ship *Amethyst,* Dominator Ironbright commanding and speaking, to vessel accelerating through Sector Eighty-seven dash eighteen dash zero-one." That must be *Dagmar*'s best attempt to render the coordinate system established for this locality, she thought. "You do not conform to the plan. Identify yourself."

"Captain Gerward Valen, from Asborg, Sunniva III, with crew on a scientific mission," the man stated. "We intend no interference or other harm, and will be glad to cooperate in any reasonable way."

The last drowsiness fled from Lissa. She glanced at her watch. Silence murmured. She got up too. The deck felt sensuously resilient beneath her bare feet, but remote, no longer quite real.

Twenty-eight seconds before response. If Ironbright hadn't hesitated, his(?) craft was four million-plus kilometers away. "Your presence is inadmissable. This region is closed. Remove yourselves."

Lissa bent over the intercom control and pushed for Orichalc's cubicle. "We are not aware of any such interdiction," Valen was saying. "By what right do you declare it? It seems to be in violation both of treaty agreements and general custom."

"Orichalc," Lissa whispered. "They're on to us. At least one ship. They command we turn back. Listen in, and tell us what you think."

"S-s-s," the fugitive breathed.

"The Dominance of the Great Confederacy has taken sovereignty," Ironbright said. "Under its policy and in its name, I order you to return to clear space immediately and hyperjump hence. Else you are subject to detention and penalties. I warn you, we have weapons. If necessary, we will use them, with regret but without hesitation."

"I should hope no civilized being would make a threat like that, without even having discussed the matter first," Valen answered. "Certainly we require more authority than yours. What are your reasons for this demand?"

"He bluffs, I believe," Orichalc murmured. Given his instinctive sensitivities to his own species, yes, he'd be able to hear that Ironbright, too, was currently in male phase. Valen also leaned close to hear, flank to flank with Lissa. She laid an arm around his waist. "Tell him that the Houses of Asborg would have known if any such claim were registered under the Covenant of Space."

She noticed the time lag had grown. *Dagmar* was outrunning *Amethyst*, if "run" made sense when you spoke of coordinates, vectors, fields, and their derivatives in three-space. Evidently Ironbright thought that switching over to hypertransmission would be more trouble than it was worth. Or did he welcome these moments, to consider what to say? "The Dominance is concerned about safety." Was he trying to wheedle? "A cosmic cataclysm will soon take place. You are not prepared for it."

Valen straightened and grinned. "Oh, but we are. That's why we're here." He went on as Orichalc had advised, finishing with: "Since no claim has been assented to, we have as much right as anybody. They know on Asborg where we are, and that you are here. I don't imagine your colleagues want an interstellar incident."

Dismay and rage hissed under the incongruous mellowness of *Dagmar*'s translating voice. "How do you know? What spies have you set on our sacred Nestmother?"

"To the best of my knowledge, none. And I wouldn't call the concealment of a scientific treasure trove a friendly act. Nor do I suppose other spacefaring societies, including the other Susaian nations, will so regard it. I repeat, we mean no harm or interference. We hope your chief of operations will contact us when your officers have conferred and decided on a proposal intended to be mutually satisfactory. I respectfully suggest, and ask you to convey the suggestion, that they start thinking at once."

"Good," oozed from Orichalc's cubicle. "Firmness and correctness, after Ironbright faltered in both. The grand commander should well evaluate the playback of this conversation."

"Signing off, then," the Susaian captain grimly. "You shall receive more soon." Lissa heard an abrupt absence of background sounds she had not noticed before.

"You did it! Whee, you did!" She leaped at Valen, threw her arms around his neck, kicked heels in air. "I love you!"

"We've just begun, and God knows what'll happen next." She let go and he activated the general intercom. "Attention. Urgent news."

"We're busy, for Founder's sake!" Esker exclaimed, obviously from the main lab.

"Too busy for the Susaians?"

"Huh? Oh. Carry on, you," to the assistants. "A minute. . . . All right. Tell me."

Valen did. "We're leaving them behind, you say," the physicist answered. "They're doubtless unarmed anyway."

"Unless that fellow was lying, they do have some combat-worthy units. And messages must be flying from end to end of their fleet."

"The farther in we go," *Dagmar* reminded, "the smaller the

volume of ambient space and therefore the more difficult evasion becomes. It is certainly incompatible with keeping station."

"I'll bet you're better armed than anything they've got here," Esker said. "Stand up to the stinking lizards. Make them crawl."

"Orichalc," Valen sighed, "may we have your opinion, and your pardon for that language?"

"My guess is that naval strength is small and incidental, confined to two or three craft whose real task is to help out in emergencies," replied calmness—or steely self-control? "Granted, the command will consider our advent an emergency. If they do possess superior force, they will probably threaten us with it."

"They don't," Esker said. "I swear they don't. Fight. Blow 'em out of the universe."

Lissa remembered violent deaths she had witnessed. It was like a benediction when Valen responded, "Only in self-defense, and only as an absolute last resort. I don't want to hear any more such talk. Go back to your studies. Let me know if a worthwhile thought occurs to you." He switched off.

Turning to Lissa, he took her hands in his. "I'm afraid that henceforward we're on twenty-four-hour duty." He smiled the smile that was like Davy's. "Well, we did luck out on this watch." He drew her close. The kiss was brief and wistful.

"Memories to look at, whenever we get a moment to pull them out of our pockets," Lissa agreed. "We'll enlarge the collection in future." Abruptly she giggled. "Speaking of pockets, we'd better grab a quick shower and get dressed. It doesn't make any difference to the Susaians, but we'd scarcely overawe our human shipmates as we are, would we?"

XXIII

Ahead, the envelopes of the black holes burned hell-bright, drowning naked-eye vision of everything else in the dark around them. Without magnification, they were still little more than star-points. Incredible, that the masses of whole suns and the energies to annihilate them were rammed down into volumes so tiny. But the gases around the ergospheres were now mingling in an incandescent storm cloud. Sparks blew off, glared and guttered out.

Elsewhere in heaven, from her control globe, Lissa saw the Susaian ships. They and *Dagmar* had matched velocities and now orbited unpowered, those three in linear formation, she some thousand kilometers from them, a separation that would increase only slowly for the next hour or two. Much enlarged, their images remained minuscule, spindle shapes lost in the star-swarm beyond.

Just the same, she felt very alone. Valen was in his own globe. He had linked his communicator to hers, but no other human was in the circuit, nor was Orichalc. This connection would be audiovisual, and he had counseled against letting the other Susaians know of one whom they must regard as a traitor. Yonder midges could spit lightnings and missiles. Her heart beat quickly.

The screen before her flickered. Its projection split into a pair. Valen's head confronted that of a Susaian, whose skin was yellow with black zigzags down the sides. Was the same strain upon both faces? She couldn't read the alien's. Nor could she know what feelings were in the tones that went underneath *Dagmar*'s methodical running translation. But then, the opposite applied too. Didn't it?

"Hail, Captain Gerward Valen," she heard. "I am Moonhorn,

Dominator, in ultimate command of the Great Confederacy's astrophysical quest."

"Your presence honors us, madam." How does he know that creature's quasisex? she wondered. Well, in the past he dealt with members of many races, and he's intelligent, observing—he cares.

"Ts-s-s." A laugh? "You show us curious courtesy, sir. In total contempt of authority, you have continued on your way, forcing us to divert these craft from important duties. That makes hypocrisy of your assertion that you mean to create no disturbance."

"No, madam." Valen spoke levelly, patiently. "As soon as your representative called for rendezvous at a point we agreed was reasonable, we commenced maneuvers toward it. I cannot see any need for you to send three vessels. One would have served, surely; or we could have talked by radio. Are you trying to intimidate us? Quite unnecessary. We're the same peaceful scientists we took you to be."

Now there's hypocrisy for you! whooped Lissa. A fraction of the sweat-cold tension slacked off within her.

Hairless head lifted on sinuous neck. "Police need weapons against contumacious lawbreakers. Indications were that your ship is of a heavily armed type."

"That is true, madam, but it doesn't mean that we want to menace anybody or throw our weight around." No more than we've got to. "You have had a good look at us. If your databanks are complete, you've recognized the model and know more or less what firepower we carry. You should also know why. This vessel is for exploration, where unpredictable demands on her can always come out of nowhere."

"You do not need nucleonics against primitive natives, sir, and when have starfarers attacked you?"

"Never, madam. And we devoutly hope none ever will. Certainly the owners, the House of Windholm, have no such intention. But an expedition just might run into, ah, parties willing to violate civilized canons. Far more likely, of course, nature may suddenly turn hostile. Antimissile magnetohydronamics deflect solar flare particles. A warhead excavates where a shelter is to be built. An energy beam drills a hole through ice, for geologists and prospectors to reach the minerals beneath. Besides work like that, this ship took a large investment. People protect their investments."

"Your best protection is to depart, sir. This vicinity will soon be unpredictably dangerous." Does she have a dry sense of humor? wondered Lissa. Well, Orichalc does.

"We're prepared for that as fully as I'd guess you are, madam. This situation is unique. We can't abandon our mission without betraying our race." Valen raised his brows and smiled—for Lissa. "Unless the Dominance plans to share everything you discover with the rest of the civilizations."

Moonhorn's head struck back and forth at emptiness. "How did you learn of us?"

"I'm not at liberty to tell you, madam, assuming for argument's sake that I know. But we've transmitted home the data we acquired along the way. You'd expect us to, wouldn't you? The basic secret is out. Why not let us carry on our observations in peace—or, better yet, join you in making them? Think of the goodwill the Confederacy will earn throughout space."

Silence seethed. Had the black holes moved perceptibly closer? Less than two days remained before the crash.

"No," fell from Moonhorn. "I . . . have no right . . . to grant such permission. This was our discovery. We staked our efforts, our lives, for cycle after cycle. Yes, you have stolen something from us, but the great revelations you shall not have. Turn about, sir, or we must destroy you."

"Can you?" Valen challenged. "And firing on us would be an act of war, madam."

"Sir, it would not. Asborg would feel aggrieved, but be a single planet against the Confederacy. No other nation would be so lunatic as to fight about an incident so remote in every sense of the concept. Arbitrators would offer their services, an indemnity might be paid, and that would be that."

She understands politics, Lissa thought. And . . . I wouldn't spend lives and treasure myself, over something like this. Maybe, in a hundred years, when the Dominance has powers nobody else does, maybe then I'd be sorry. But today I'd just hope that things will work out somehow.

"Therefore," Moonhorn continued, "I urge you, sir, I implore you, not to compel us. Be satisfied with what you have. Go home."

Valen made her wait for an entire minute before he replied, "Madam, with due respect, your demand is unlawful, unreasonable, and unacceptable. The right of innocent passage and access to unclaimed celestial bodies is recognized by every spacefaring nation. I have no intention of heeding your demand, and do not believe you have the power to enforce it."

"They are small units," Dagmar *had said. "Their combined firepower barely approximates mine; and I am a single vessel, self-integrated, with stronger defenses and more acceleration capability. They could perhaps take me in a well coordinated attack, but I estimate the probability of that as no more than forty percent."*

"And supposing they did wipe us, you'd get one or two of them first, most likely, wouldn't you?" Lissa had pointed out. "That'd be a big setback to their whole operation. I'm sure those three are all the armed craft they have here. They aren't meant for guardians, they're for possible rescue or salvage work, and they must have scientific assignments of their own as well."

"Right," Valen had said. "They'll be making the same calculations."

The image of Moonhorn's head leaned forward, as if trying to meet the man's eyes. "Would you truly be so barbarous as to initiate deadly violence?" she asked low.

"We'll go about our business, and defend ourselves if assaulted," Valen declared. "After all, madam, a government that really upheld civilized ideals would not have kept a discovery like this hidden. It would have invited general cooperation, for everybody's benefit. Please don't speak to me about barbarity."

Silence and stars. Is Moonhorn ashamed? Poor being. But dangerous, because dutiful.

"We don't want to disrupt your work, or anything like that," Valen continued. "We absolutely don't want a battle. Nor do you, madam. In spite of everything, you are civilized too."—no matter those aspects of your society that drove Orichalc to seek refuge, and caused you to conceal these wonders. "Can't we compromise?"

Silence again. Lissa's knuckles whitened above the weapons console.

"It appears we must," said Moonhorn, and Lissa's hands lifted through weightlessness to catch at tears.

XXIV

Again *Dagmar* decelerated toward her destination.

Valen, Lissa, and Orichalc entered the saloon together. The physicists were already there, aquiver. Esker leaped to his feet. "Well?" he cried.

"We have leave to proceed." Valen told them.

Elif gusted out a breath. Noel and Tessa raised a cheer. "Marvelous!" Esker jubilated. "Oh, milady—" He saw her face more closely and broke off.

Valen moved to the head of the table. His companions flanked him. "It was a tough bargaining session," the woman said.

"I know," Tessa mumbled. "It went on and on. And when boost came back, and we didn't know where we were bound—"

"You'll have your shot at our target," said Valen. He sat down. The rest who were standing did likewise. Orichalc crouched on the bench. The captain's gaze sought Esker.

"I couldn't push my opposite number, Dominator Moonhorn, too hard," he went on. "She must have been given considerable discretion and choice. That's usual for Confederacy officers in the field. And mainly, no reinforcements could reach her in time. Even if somebody withdrew to hyperbeam distance and called, and they jumped at once, it'd take them too long to cross the normal-drive distance. The black holes would already have met, and meanwhile we could be playing hob with the Susaians on the scene. And in fact, *Dagmar* hasn't detected any new arrivals, which she could do. Still, Moonhorn surely received orders not to give away the store."

"An officer of the Confederacy who shows cowardice is strangled," Orichalc said. "One who shows poor judgment is ruined. Over and above these considerations is nest-honor."

"So I mustn't leave her with no choice but to attack," Valen continued. "That would mean a certainty of heavy loss to the Susaians and a better than fifty percent chance of losing everything; though if we won, we might still be crippled. And while the political repercussions wouldn't be catastrophic, they'd be troublesome. On the other hand, Moonhorn couldn't, wouldn't meekly stand aside and let us take all the forbidden fruit we might.

"The fact that we had already taken a good deal, and passed it on to Asborg, weighed heavily. What I had to do was give Moonhorn a way to cut her side's losses. We dickered—"

Esker's fist smote the table. "Will you get to the point?" he yelled. "What did you agree to?"

Valen squared his shoulders. "No cooperation, no information exchange," he said. "That was too much to hope for. But we may take station at the minimum safe distance you want. Congratulations; they'd arrived at almost the identical figure, and had more and better numbers to work with. They have four live-crewed ships there, on the two orthogonal axes you described.

"We must not come any nearer to either axis than—the Susaian units equal about one million kilometers. We must not enter the orbital plane of the black holes at all."

"What?" Esker sprang back to his feet. He leaned across the table, shuddering. "Why, you— That plane's where the most vital observations— You clotbrain! Didn't you ever listen to me? A rotating black hole drags the inertial frame with it. Those two have opposite spins, differently oriented. Cancellations, additions—the whole tendency will be for things to happen, unprecedented things, exactly in that mutual plane—and you threw this away for us!"

"Quiet!" Valen shouted. Into the rage that choked and sputtered at him, he explained in a voice gone flat: "I did know. So did Moonhorn. I asked for a place farther out on the axis in the plane, or at least somewhere in it. She refused. We went around and around, with me offering different versions, and always it ended in refusal. I couldn't stop to consult with you, if I'd wanted to. Frankly, I was amazed to get what I did. The minimum radius, only a million kilometers north of the plane. Not quite twenty minutes of arc to sight down along. Does it make any serious difference?"

"Yes," Esker said as if through a noose. "Plane polarization of generated gravitons is likely, and who can foresee what else? It—it—Captain, you've got to renegotiate. You must."

"No," Valen stated. "I can't risk it."

"The balance in Moonhorn's mind is certain to be fragile," Orichalc added. "She may well decide that an attempt to alter the agreement shows bad faith, and feel compelled to give us an ultimatum, that we depart or fight."

"Then, by God, you give the ultimatum yourself!" Esker flung forth. "They'll back down. You admit you were surprised at what they did concede. They *are* weaker than us. We can destroy them, do our research, and be safely homeward bound before they can bring any real warship to bear. And they know it."

"If I knew for sure we'd win any fight without damage to ourselves," Valen said, "I still would not risk killing sentient beings for as little as this."

"Little, you call it? Little? You idiot, you idiot, you—traitor to your race—"

Wrath flashed up in Lissa. She slapped the table. "That will do, client," she called. "Hold your tongue, or else if the captain doesn't confine you, I will."

The eyes into which she looked seemed glazed, blind. "Yes, you would," Esker raved, "you, his slut. Do you imagine we haven't seen you two smirk, sneak off, and come back smarmy enough to gag a disposal?"

It isn't the loss to his science that's driven him over the edge, she understood, appalled.

Worse came after: "Oh, you've got fine taste in men, you do. You pick the great Gerward Valen, the one who ran away at Naia.

Have you heard, shipmates? They were evacuating people from a meteoroid bombardment. He lost his nerve and bolted. Now he's so very tender of lives. How many did you leave to die on Naia, Valen?"

He stopped, stared past them all. A convulsion went through him. He fell back on the bench and buried face in hands.

Silence lasted. His breathing hacked at it. Nobody else moved. Valen's features had stiffened and bleached, like a dead man's.

At last, hearing it as if a stranger spoke far away from her, Lissa said, "That's what you did in your spare time. Worked out a program to slip into the ship's network. To listen to us, what we discussed in private. And to watch? Isn't that correct, *Dagmar*?"

"I have been unaware of it," the robot brain answered. "I would be, if the program was cleverly designed. Let me search. . . . There is a new file. Access is blocked to me."

"I would kill you," Lissa said. How calm she sounded. "But it isn't worth the trouble it would cause. And my hands would always be soiled. The authorities will deal with you when you return. Go to your cubicle. Rations will be brought you. You may visit the lavatory at need. Otherwise you are quarantined for the duration of this voyage."

Esker raised his head. Tears whipped down the coarse cheeks. Sobs went raw. "Milady, I crave pardon, I did evil, scourge me but—but don't deny me—"

"I told you to go."

"Wait." No robot spoke as mechanically as Valen did. "We do need him. For scientific purposes. Without him, we could not learn half as much. Can you continue in the laboratory, Harrolson? If your performance is satisfactory, we will consider entering no charges against you."

Does a tiny, evil joy flicker? A trial would bring everything out in public. "Y-yes, sir," Esker hiccoughed. "I'll do my best. My humble apologies, sir."

I may have to let you go free, Lissa thought. You'll have your professional triumph. But never a place on my world. You'll dwell elsewhere, anywhere else. Aloud: "*Dagmar,* knowing about the illicit program you can screen it off, can't you?"

"Certainly," said the ship. "I will take precautions against further tampering."

"Not needed, I swear, not needed," Esker mouthed.

Lissa ignored him. "Good, *Dagmar,*" she said. "Save the program itself. We might want it for evidence." Her glance swept around the table. "Shipmates, I'll be grateful for your silence after we return. Meanwhile, I trust you will carry on, setting this deplorable business aside as much as possible. Now I think Captain Valen and I deserve some privacy. It's still several hours to destination. We aren't likely to meet trouble en route." She rose. "Come, Gerward."

She must pluck at his sleeve before he got up and followed her.

In his cabin she turned about to cast herself against him. "Oh, darling, darling. Don't let it hurt you. You mustn't. That horrible little animal. Can't gnaw you down. You're too big."

He stood moveless, looking past her. She stepped back. "Gerward," she pleaded, "what does it matter if they know? They also know what you *are,* what you've made of yourself s-s-since then. I do. That's what counts. Isn't it?"

He hugged himself and, momentarily, shivered.

"You didn't run because you were afraid," she said. "You couldn't stand seeing the pain, the death. Isn't that right?"

The reply came rusty. "Is it?"

"And, and you've lived it down, whatever it was. You've become strong and brave. A man for my pride, Gerward."

"Have I?"

"I'll show you!" Again she embraced him, arms, hands, lips, tongue, body. After a while he began to respond.

She led him to the bunk. Nothing happened.

"It's all right." She held his head to her breasts. "I understand.

Don't worry. It's only natural. Come on, boy, cheer up. We've got a job waiting for us. The two of us."

Oh, damn Esker Harrolsson. Damn him down into the bottom of a black hole.

XXV

The ship took station. Maintaining it was a delicate, intricate balancing act, when the ambient gravitational field constantly changed as the two masses hurtled inward. Those ever-shifting linear accelerations gave no weight that flesh and blood noticed, but sometimes you felt it a bit when the hull rotated.

Oddly enough, or perhaps not, her people worked on in almost normal fashion. Esker spoke softly and avoided Lissa's eyes on the rare occasions when they met in a corridor. An assistant fetched food and drink for him to take among his instruments. Those three persons likewise were seldom away from the laboratory, never for long. What they did, what unfolded before them, was all-absorbing, overwhelming. She blessed it.

Mostly she, Valen, and Orichalc watched the drama roll onward. *Dagmar* supplied not only exterior views, modified as desired, but graphics and commentary to the rec screens, adapted from the ongoing analysis of the computers. Lissa was soon wholly caught up. Valen continued generally silent. But what can you say in the presence of inhuman might and majesty? She saw his tension lessen, until at last he smiled once in a while or his fingers responded when she caught his hand.

She had taken an opportunity to draw Orichalc aside. "How is he doing?" she asked, and trembled.

"He approaches calm," the Susaian said. "The shock was savage, like a half-healed physical wound torn open. However, he is not shattered. Given peace, inner peace, he should regain his sense of worth. It may be the stronger for this." The long body flowed through the air and curled lightly around her. "Until then, his strength comes from you."

She hugged him and laid her cheek against the dry, cablelike suppleness. "Thank you," she whispered.

With detectors and optics she found the scientific vessel occupying the fluctuant point that Esker had desired. Valen beamed a greeting—"out of curiosity," he said. How wonderful that he began again taking some interest in things. The craft turned out to be Ironbright's *Amethyst.* Amusing coincidence. No, not unduly improbable. The Susaians couldn't have dispatched a large fleet if they wanted to preserve secrecy. Traders, diplomats, outsiders of every kind would inevitably have noticed something afoot and started inquiring. Besides, if each vessel had half *Dagmar*'s capabilities, ten or fifteen should be ample. They must be that many, however, to contain the large scientific teams—twenty to fifty individuals per hull, she guessed—that made up for the relatively primitive robotics and automation.

If only we'd come with more of our own, Lissa thought. Well, we'll bring home enough knowledge that the Confederacy never will spring a surprise on the galaxy. . . . She grimaced. "We" in that context meant Esker. She must admit it. She need not like it.

Amethyst had a partner, or guardian, or both. Moonhorn's flagship, whose name *Dagmar* rendered *Supremacy,* maintained at a few kilometers from her. Probably specialists aboard conducted experiments of their own. Certainly she was where she was, after a rapid reshuffle of plans, to make sure that the humans observed the terms of the truce. Alone, she couldn't stop them, but by harassment she could make a breach pointless.

All vessels hovered isolated. Because it would interfere with various delicate instruments, transmission through hyperspace was stopped; and what did anybody have to say over the lasers? Paradoxically, the muteness made Lissa feel closer to yonder beings. Her folk would keep their promises. So would the Susaians. As the judgment instant neared, you forgot your merely mortal quarrels.

XXVI

Shrouded in fire, the black holes sped to their destiny. Minute by minute, second by second, they swelled in sight, blazed more wildly brilliant, roared the louder throughout every spectrum of radiance. The discs were whirling storms, riven, aflare with eerie lightnings. Vast tatters broke off, exploded into flame, torrented back down or threw red spindrift across heaven before vanishing into vacuum. It was as if the stars, their light rays bent, scattered terrified from around those masses. Afloat in the captain's globe, Lissa heard the blood thunder in her ears like the hoofs of galloping war horses. And yet this was only a shadow show. To have seen with your bare eyes would have been to be stricken blind, and afterward die.

She gripped Valen's hand. It was cold. His breath went harsh. The sky had burned over Naia too; but not like this, not like this.

The black holes met.

Nobody in real time saw that. It was too swift. At one heartbeat they were well apart, at the next they blurred into streaks, and then light erupted. White it was at the center, raw sun-stuff; thence it became night-violet, dusk-violet, day-blue, steel-blue, gold-yellow, brass-yellow, blood-red, sunset-red. Outward and outward it bloomed. The fringes were streams, fountains, lace in a wind. They arced over and began to return in a million different, pure mathematical curves.

"I didn't know it would be beautiful!" Lissa cried.

Force crammed her against her harness. Her head tossed. With no weight for protection, dizziness swept black across vision and mind. Another, opposite blow slammed, and another. The metal of the ship toned.

"Graviton surges," she dimly heard Valen gasp. "Predicted—uneven—hang on—"

The waves passed. He floated. The noise and giddy dark drained from her head. He, in his chair, strained toward her. "How are you, darling?" The words quavered. "Are you hurt?"

"No. No. I . . . came through . . . intact, I think. You?"

"Yes. If you hadn't—" He mastered himself. "But you did. It was a, a wave of force. The physicists didn't expect it'd be this strong, with this short a wavelength. Most of it was supposed to spread out in the orbital plane— Look. Look."

The fire geysers rained back toward what had become a single fierce, flickery star. As they fell, their lovely chaos drew together and made rivers of many-hued splendor. The flows twisted, braided, formed flat spirals that rushed inward, trailing sparks. A new accretion disc was forming. Elsewhere, though, half a dozen blobs of dancing, spitting luridness fled from them.

The light played unrestful over Valen's face, as if he were a hunter on ancient Earth, crouched above his campfire in a night where tigers and ghosts prowled. "Report," he said at the general intercom. "Everybody. *Dagmar*?"

"All well," the ship said. Her serenity was balm. "Minor damage, mostly due to a blast of lasered gamma rays that struck well aft. Nothing disabling or not soon repairable. Interior background count went high for half a second, but the dose was within safe limits and the count is down to a level acceptable for twenty watches."

"We'll be gone well before then," Valen promised. "Uh, crew?"

The replies babbled, joyous, one (never mind whose) half hysterical. No harm sustained.

"How'd the observations go?" Valen asked tartly.

"We won't know for weeks," Esker answered. "That flood of input— But it seems like every system functioned. I do believe we . . . we have a scientific revolution at birth."

Lissa's attention had stayed with the mystery. "It seems to be dimming," she ventured.

"It's receding fast," Esker said. "The resultant momentum. But, I'm not sure yet, but I think the tensors aren't quite what relativity would predict. Something we don't understand came into play. Certainly that gravitational effect exceeded my top estimate by orders of magnitude. Captain, we will follow the star. Won't we?"

"Of course," Valen replied. "For as long as feasible. Taking due precautions. Positioning ourselves here, we took a bigger gamble than we knew. I don't want to push our luck further."

"Nor I, sir." Esker laughed like a boy. "Not with everything we've got to carry home!"

They've forgotten their feud, Lissa thought. I have too. At least, it doesn't matter anymore. Probably it will again, when we are again among human things. But today it's of no importance whatsoever.

Carry home. . . . Yes, this precious freight of knowledge. There must be more data aboard now than we could transmit back in days, maybe in tens of days. We have more in our care than just our lives.

"Those fiery clouds that got ejected," she asked, "why weren't they recaptured?"

"The energies released caused them to exceed escape velocity from the vicinity of the ergosphere," Esker said. "I'm half afraid to calculate how much energy that was. However, it seems to have expended itself mostly on that escape. They're not giving off much hard radiation. The ergospheres themselves, like the event horizons, went through contortions as they met and fused. Spacetime did. I don't know what happened in those microseconds. Maybe we never will." Awe shook his words. "For an instant, the gates stood open between entire universes."

"The hints alone should reveal a new cosmos to your minds," Orichalc murmured.

Lissa nodded, dazed more than comprehending. "But what,

now, holds the clouds together? Why don't they whiff away, evaporate?"

Esker laughed afresh. "Do you take me for an oracle, milady? At this stage, we can only guess. Magnetic bottle effects, conceivably. Or maybe each is the, the atmosphere around a new-formed mass. Yes, I think that's a bit more likely. But we'll find out."

"Those masses would need to be planet-sized," Valen said low. "That gas is incandescent hot. It'd never stay around anything less. As if . . . this union tried to beget worlds—"

"Signal received," *Dagmar* broke in. "Audio on the fifth standard laser band. Code: 'Distress. Please respond immediately.' "

A dream-hand caught Lissa around the throat.

"You know where it's from?" she heard Valen snap.

"Yes. The Susaian ships just south of us. One of them." If *Dagmar* has to correct herself, is she frightened?

"Acknowledge and translate, for God's sake!"

Lissa had an impression that the hisses and whistles beneath the impersonal robotic voice were equally calm. "Moonhorn, commanding *Supremacy*, beaming to Asborgan vessel *Dagmar*. We request information as to your condition after the event."

"We're in good shape," Valen said. "You?"

"Not so," came after seconds of time lag. "We and *Amethyst* were tossed together, too fast for effective preventative action. Both ships are disabled. Casualties are severe."

"A gravitational vortex," Esker said raggedly. "A potential well, an abnormal local metric, expanding principally in the main inertial plane. It didn't flatten to the ordinary curvature of spacetime till it had passed you." Lissa thought he found refuge in theory. Did he utter mere guesses? Belike he did. Who was sure of anything, here?

Her eyes tracked the dwindling star that was not a star. It gleamed exquisite, like a ringed planet seen from a distance, save that it was also like a galaxy with a single spiral arm. There passed through her: If Gerward hadn't settled for less than we wanted,

Dagmar too would be drifting helpless, a wreck. I might be dead. Oh, he might be!

"We're sorry to hear that, madam," Valen said. "Can we help?"

"I do not know," Moonhorn answered, "but you are our single hope. We have contacted our nearer fellows. Ordinarily we could wait for them. However, observation and calculation show we are on a collision trajectory with one of those gaseous objects spewed from the fusion. We shall enter it in approximately four hours and pass through the center. At its speed, that will go very fast. But radiometric measurements show temperatures near the core that even in so brief a passage will be lethal. No Susaian craft is close enough, with sufficient boost capability, to arrive before then."

Stillness descended. The time felt long until Valen asked, slowly, "You have no escape? No auxiliaries, anything like that?"

"Nothing in working order," said Moonhorn. "Else I would not have troubled you. We realize that for you, too, a rescue may well be impossible."

"We can cross the distance between at maximum boost, ten Terran gravities, with turnover," *Dagmar* said, "in approximately one hundred and fifty minutes. To escape afterward, we should accelerate orthogonally to the thing's path, but at no more than five gravities, since you have injured persons with you and the hale will have no opportunity to prepare themselves either. This acceleration must begin no later than half an hour before predicted impact, if we are to avoid the hottest zone. Before we start, my crew must make ready; otherwise, at the end of the first boost, they will be disabled, perhaps dead. Allowing time for that also, we should have half an hour, or slightly less, for the transfer of crews from your vessels to me."

In short, Lissa thought, the operation is crazily dicey. No. We can't. The odds are too big against us.

Her gaze went to the clouds. She didn't know which of them was the murderer on its way, but they seemed much alike. Faerie nebulosity reached out around a glowing pink that must be gas overlying the white-hot, ultraviolet-hot, X-ray-hot middle. As she watched, small light-streaks flashed from it and vanished. Meteors. No, they must in reality be monstrous gouts of fire.

"I see," Moonhorn was saying gravely. "Our hope was slight at best. Since those are the actual parameters, the risk is unacceptable. I would make that judgment myself, were situations reversed. Thank you and farewell."

"No, wait!" Valen clawed at the locks on his harness. "We're coming. Crew, prepare for ten gee acceleration."

Is this possible? "Gerward, you can't mean that," Lissa protested.

His look upon her was metallic. "You heard me," he said. "All of you did. Get into the tank. That's an order."

XXVII

The chamber was completely filled and closed off; should a sudden change of vector occur, slosh could be fatal. The salt water was at body temperature; apart from their sanitary units, skinsuits served only modesty. Afloat, loosely tethered, breathing through air tube and mask, you might soon have drowsed, were your faring peaceful. Not that comfort was complete. The liquid took weight off bones and muscles, it helped keep body fluids where they belonged. Yet heaviness dragged at interior organs, while nothing but medication held pain and weariness at bay. Eventually you must pay what your vigor was costing you, with interest.

A low, nearly subliminal pulse throbbed through Lissa. *Dagmar* could not hurl herself along at full power without a little of that immense energy escaping to sing in her structure. Hands and the miniature control panel on which they rested were enlarged in vision, seemed closer than they were. Yet shipmates on every side had gone dim, half unreal, in a greenish twilight.

Talk went by conduction from a diaphragm in the mask. After the scramble and profanity of getting positioned were done and boost had commenced, silence replaced a privacy that no longer existed.

Lissa broke it first. "Captain," she said stiffly.

Valen never took his eyes off the single viewscreen, before which he was. "Yes?"

"Captain, I petition you to reconsider. I believe the others will join me in this."

"I do, sir!" She had not expected shy Noel to speak up. "The science we're losing, that we might do every minute if we weren't idled here."

"The science we *will* lose, sir, if we don't survive," Tessa chimed in. "That all the human race will."

"The chances of our survival are poor, you know," Lissa said.

"A crazy gamble," Elif felt emboldened to add, "and for what? For some lizards that did their best to keep us away."

"Mind your language," Valen reprimanded in an automatic fashion. "Esker, have you any comment?"

"Well, Captain, uh, well," the physicist replied, "of course, when you commanded, we obeyed. We're no mutineers. But it's not too late for you to reconsider and turn back, sir. Your impulse was generous—fearless, yes—but thinking it over, wouldn't you agree we have a higher duty?"

He's actually desperate enough to behave reasonably, Lissa thought in amazement.

"Orichalc? . . . No, I forgot, your trans wouldn't work here." Lissa thought fleetingly how lonesome that must feel. Valen turned his head. "But you have picked up a little Anglay, I believe. Nod if you vote for us going on, wave your tail if you vote for us going back."

After seconds had mounted, it was the tail that moved.

Valen barked a laugh. "Unanimous, eh? Except for me." He stared again at the viewscreen. From her post, Lissa saw it full of night; but he must be watching the flames. "However, I am the captain."

She summoned her will. "Sir," she said, "I have the authority to set our destination. It is in safe space."

"I have the authority to overrule you if I see a pre-emptive necessity."

"Crew may lawfully protest unreasonable orders."

"If the protest is denied, they must obey."

"This will mean a board of inquiry after the voyage."

"Yes. After the voyage."

"If the captain shows . . . dangerous incompetence, the crew may relieve him of his duties. The board of inquiry will decide whether or not they were justified."

"How do you propose to do it? This ship is programmed to me." Valen raised his voice, though it remained as cold as before. "*Dagmar,* would you remove me from command of you?"

"No," came the level answer. "What you attempt is exceedingly difficult and may fail, but success is possible, and it is not for me to make value judgments."

"Values," Valen murmured. "Everybody always told me what value sentient life has. The old, old saying, 'Greater love has no man than this, that he lay down his life for his friends.' Don't you agree any longer? Have your beliefs suddenly changed? We are seven. There must be ten or twenty times that many aboard those ships. Civilized spacefarers go to the aid of the distressed. We shall."

Sharply: "My judgment is that we can do it, provided we keep our heads and work together. Otherwise we doubtless are doomed. I assume you are all able, self-controlled people when you choose to be. Very well, we'll now develop a basic plan of action. As we approach, I'll contact Moonhorn again, learn in detail what the situation is as of that time, and assign tasks."

"No, please, sir," Esker stammered.

Lissa unclenched her jaws. "You heard the captain," she said. "Let's get cracking."

XXVIII

The sky burned.

A fireball glared lightning-colored. It would have been blinding to behold, were it not shrouded in a vast nimbus that glowed blue, yellow, red with its own heat. Smoke streaked the vapors, ragged, hasty as the thing whirled. Currents twisted themselves into maelstroms. The limb of the flattened disc faded toward darkness. Tongues of flame leaped from it, arced over, streamed sparks behind their deluge. At the equator, many broke off and sprang free, cometary incandesences. Those that were aimed forward ran ahead of the mass that birthed them. Right, left, above, below, they passed blazing around the ships. They would not gutter out for thousands of kilometers more.

If any of those thunderbolts hits us, we're done, Lissa knew.

Spacesuited, she clung to a handhold near the portside forward airlock and waited. A viewscreen showed a pale ghost of what lay ahead. *Dagmar* maneuvered now at fractions of a gravity. Magnetic fields must be crazily twisting her plasma jets as they left the ejectors. Shifts in direction brought momentary dizziness, as if chaos reached in to grab at her. The Susaian craft were outlined black across the oncoming lightstorm. Their impact had driven plates and ribs together, formed a single grotesque mass, two boughs reaching from a stump. It wobbled and tumbled. Shards danced around.

A fire-tongue streaked, swelled, was gone. It had missed *Dagmar* by a few hundred meters. At Lissa's side, Valen caught a breath, half a cry. In her audio receiver it sounded almost like the scream of a bullet. Through their helmets she saw sweat runnel down the creases in his face. "You shouldn't be here," she told him. "You belong in the command globe."

He shook his head. "The ship c-can cope. We need . . . every hand."

At least, she thought, he has enough sense left to refrain from boasting he won't send crew into any danger he won't meet himself. The hazards are much the same wherever we may be, with that ogre booming down on us. But if he stayed behind, he wouldn't be out *among* the meteors. And he'd have an overall view; he might make the snap decision a robot brain wouldn't, that saves us.

No use. I've tried. He's determined. And, true, we're ghastly undermanned as is.

Lissa swallowed fear, anger, bitterness, and braced herself. They were about to make contact.

Weight ended. She floated free. Silence pressed inward, save for noises of breath and her slugging heart. Voices went back and forth, she knew, *Dagmar*'s and Moonhorn's or Ironbright's or whoever was in charge over there; but she wasn't in that circuit. The screen showed her the silhouette of an extruded gang tube, groping for an airlock. Wormlike, obscene, amidst the terrible beauty of the flames. To hang here passive was to lie in nightmare. How long? Seconds, minutes, years? It had better be less than half an hour. That was about as much time as they had before death became inescapable. Could she choke down her shriek that long?

How had anybody stayed sane at Naia?

Contact. Linkage. Weight returned, low but crazily, sickeningly shifty as *Dagmar* matched the gyrations of the other hulls. The airlock valve moved aside. The mouth beyond gaped. Lissa pushed into the chamber before she should lose her last nerve. Valen followed. They collided, whirled about in clownish embrace, caromed off the side. The valve shut. For a moment they were adrift in blindness, and she wanted to hold him close.

The inner valve opened. Air brawled down the gang tube. The

compartment beyond lay bared to vacuum. Lissa let the wind help her along. Frost formed briefly on dust, little streamers that glittered in the beams from wristlights.

She and Valen came forth into a cavern. Air fled and light fell undiffused, hard-edged. Things sprang solitary out of shadow that otherwise engulfed sight—save where the hull was rent and stars marched manifold past.

The rotations of the conjoined wrecks caught at your blood and balance, cast you about. Space was too confined for safe use of a jetpack. You must somehow recover, compensate, be a master juggler; and the ball you kept going was yourself.

Yourself and others. Susaians in their long, many-jointed spacesuits waited for deliverance. Most tumbled helpless. A number were violently nauseated, their helmets smeared with spew on which they choked. A handful of trained personnel were there to shepherd them as well as might be. The task was too much for so few. Victims, especially the injured, kept flopping and drifting away. The humans went after them.

Things couldn't be so bad at the waist lock. It was joined to an unruptured section. Clumsy though they might be, Esker and his scientists could give the Susaian marshals some help. And elsewhere, *Dagmar*'s three robots flitted to a part torn entirely loose. They would break in and tow back those whom they found.

But this half of *Amethyst* had been barred from the rest. Damaged servos didn't allow personnel trapped in it to transfer to the middle and await rescue. Instead, crewfolk from *Supremacy* must bring extra spacesuits and, as rendezvous neared, herd, drag, manhandle the people into this ripped compartment, the only one that *Dagmar*'s forward gang tube could reach when the middle one was engaged.

Lissa's light picked out a thrashing, drifting shape. She went for it. Spin changed its path. She kicked against a crumpled plate, intercepted, clutched. Panicky, the Susaian struggled in her arms. "Hold still, you idiot," she groaned.

Noises she could neither understand nor imitate gibbered in her ears. Some that were calm and steady came to damp them. The Susaian didn't relax, but stiffened, became a load Lissa could manage. She heard the Anglay: "Honored one, I am informed that several victims are near the breach in the hull." Back aboard *Dagmar,* translator active, Orichalc was the living message switchboard.

Lissa bore her burden to the tube mouth and gave it an impetus. The passage was already half filled with bodies. A Susaian officer at either end clung by the tail to a handhold and issued orders. Several at a time, the fugitives were passing into the lock and thus to the Asborgan ship. Lissa kicked off toward the gap where the stars danced.

Hoo! Nearly went through it! She clutched a piece of metal in time and cast light rays about. The reptile-like forms appeared in the gloom, suits ashimmer. They had clung fast to whatever they found, lest they be cast adrift into space.

"Orichalc," Lissa called, "tell them to link hands or tails or whatever and let go when I take the lead. I'll guide them to the tube—"

Heaven vanished in a burst of brilliance. For a moment there was no more night. Throughout the cavern, each being, body, bit of wreckage sprang forth into sight. They had no color; that radiance showed them molten white. Thunder crashed in Lissa's skull. The doomsday blow sent her off, end over end, barely aware. She heard a man howl and knew it was Valen. Dazzlement blew in rags. As if she dreamt, there passed across her: Very near miss. Electric field. Discharge. How close by now are we to the volcano?

Then a solidity captured her, and brought her to rest, and she heard, "Lissa, are you all right, oh, Lissa."

Slowly, she looked about her. The fire-splash after-images began to fade; she glimpsed stars. The ringing in her ears diminished. I'm alive, she knew.

"Get into the tube," Valen chattered. "Back aboard *Dagmar*. I'll finish here."

"No," she said hoarsely. "You go on. Back to your work. We've damn little time left. I'll join you in a couple of minutes."

A sob caught in his throat. He released her and sped off.

XXIX

Stars, Milky Way, sister galaxies shone in majesty. The black hole was lost to naked-eye sight. Even the cloud from which *Dagmar* fled was now scarcely more than another gleam in the brightness-crowded dark. The crimson that for minutes had raged and roared about her was become a memory. She had radiated its heat into space. The brutality of five-gee boost lingered only in aches, bruises, exhaustion, nothing that a good rest wouldn't heal; she flew at gentle half-gee weight.

Memory still echoed. Nor had the ship yet relinquished her booty. Bodies crowded the decks. Pungent odors and sibilant words filled the air. Lissa picked a way among them, bound aft. When she thought some hailed her, she responded with a nod or a wave and passed on. It was all she could do. They had their medics and others tending to the hurt among them. She was ignorant of their requirements, and in any case wrung dry, wanting no more than to creep into her cubicle, draw the bunk sheet over her, and sleep.

Her course took her past the laboratory. Esker saw and shambled to the door. "Milady," he called in an undertone. She heard urgency and stopped. He beckoned her to enter. They were alone there, the others having gone to their own places. His back was bent and fatigue showed leaden in every gesture. Nonetheless the ugly face grinned.

"What do you want?" she asked.

He rubbed his hands together. "I wanted you to know first, milady." He leaned close. She was too tired to draw back. He spoke in a near whisper, although no Susaians were in this corridor and probably none but Orichalc knew any Anglay. "As we were finishing the evacuation, milady, I saw one of them carrying a data box, and what'd be in it but their observations? Different model from any of ours, but it had to be a data box. Things were crowded, confused. I shoved in and slipped it right out of that ridiculous straw-fingered hand. The bearer didn't notice; walking wounded. Nobody did. I've got it here, and I'm about to copy off the file. Then I'll leave the box for them to find, as though it got dropped accidentally. But when the stuff's translated, we'll know what they found out, at least this part of what they did. So our efforts paid off that much, didn't they, milady?"

You little tumor, she thought. I shouldn't accept this. But I suppose I must. Maybe I should even congratulate you.

He peered at her. "I did well, don't you think, milady?" he asked. "You'll put in a good word for me when we get home, won't you, milady?"

"I'll stay neutral, if I can. It's up to you." She turned and left.

Orichalc, bound forward with his personal kit, met her farther on. They halted. "How fare you, honored one?" he greeted. Under the flatness of the trans, did she hear concern? "I have not seen you since you went to aid in the rescue."

"I'm all right," she said. "Everybody is, or as much as could be expected, I guess. You?"

"*Sh-s-s,* I hold back. The Susaian officers know that a member of their race has been aboard this ship, but they know no more than that. Captain Valen agrees it is best they not meet me. On his advice, I seek the Number Two hold."

Slightly surprised, Lissa noticed herself bridle. "I should hope, after what we've done, they won't cause trouble."

"No, but why provoke emotions? I can bide my time. Soon we make rendezvous and transfer our passengers. After that, in view of our condition and the delta vee we have expended, Captain Valen says we shall go straight home. Surely other researchers will come from Asborg, and from many more worlds."

"I don't imagine those beings are so grateful to us they'll make their discoveries public."

"Would you in their place, honored one?"

Lissa laughed a bit. "No, probably not." Though in the long run, now that the great secret is out, everybody will know everything that can be known about it.

She stroked Orichalc's head. "Go rest, then," she said. "Pleasant dreams."

"I fear yours will not be," he replied.

Her hand froze where it was. After a space she said, "Well, of course you feel what I'm feeling."

"I feel that you are woeful. I wish I could help."

"And, and him?"

"He was full of pride and gladness, until there came a dread I believe was on your account. That was the last I saw of him, about a quarter hour ago."

"Don't worry about it."

"I do not worry much about you, honored one. You are undaunted. He— But go, since that is your wish. May the time be short until your happier day."

Lissa walked on.

In the crew section, the assistant physicists had already closed their doors and must be sound asleep. Deck, bulkheads, overhead reached gray and empty, save for the tall form that waited.

She jarred to a stop. They stood for a time. Air rustled around them. "Lissa," Valen said finally.

"I should think you'd be resting, or else in conference with Moonhorn and Ironbright," she stated.

"This is more important." He made as if to approach her, but curbed the motion. "Lissa, why are you here? Why not the cabin? When you didn't show, I asked *Dagmar,* and—"

"If you please," she said, "I am very tired and need some rest of my own."

Bewilderment ravaged the haggard features. "Lissa, what's

wrong? We saved those beings, we're safe ourselves, why do you look at me that way?"

Get this over with. "*You* saved them. It was your decision, your will."

"But— No, wait." He swallowed, straightened his shoulders, and said, "I see. You're angry because I put your life at risk. No, that's unfair. Because I gambled with everybody's. Including mine."

"No," she sighed, "you do not see. It's because of why you did."

He stared.

"Worse than staking us, you staked what we'd gained here for our people," she told him. "It was in fact a crazy thing to do, from any normal viewpoint. Maybe, morally, it was justified. Seven lives, a valuable ship, and an invaluable store of knowledge, against half a hundred other lives. We did win through, and we may have gotten some goodwill that our leaders can draw on in future negotiations. But . . . Valen, none of this was what you had in mind. Not really. Was it?"

"What do you mean?" she barely heard.

She shook her head, like one who remembers a sorrow. "You redeemed yourself. You met again with the Terror you'd run from, and this time you overcame it, first in your spirit, then in reality. Even if you'd died, you'd have won what mattered, the respect of your peers back, and of yourself.

"I'd come to know you. Orichalc's now confirmed my understanding, but it wasn't necessary. I knew. What mattered to you above all else—the only thing that mattered—was your own redemption."

"No," he croaked, and reached for her.

She denied the wish to lay her head on his breast. "Yes," she said. "Oh, never fear. You'll receive the honors you've earned, and I'll speak never a word against them. But I can't stay with any creature so selfish. Please leave me alone."

She dodged by him, into her cubicle, and shut the door. The light came on. She doused it and lay down in the kindly darkness.

XXX

Hebo sat on the verandah of a lodge in what was once Nepal. A mild breeze bore a fragrance of jasmine and flaunted the brilliant hues of rhododendrons against cloudless blue. Birdsong blew on it. Before him woodland climbed upward, and beyond it shone the mighty snowpeaks. The scene and this small house belonged in the days of his first youth; he'd backpacked hereabouts. He suspected the place had been sited and shaped as it was just for him. Easily done, after those memories had been read. His stay here, these past two or three weeks, must be as much a part of the healing process as the mental exercises programmed for him. He didn't mind.

His head had felt so strange at first, a whole new landscape, blindingly clear, but with sudden emptinesses to come upon as he felt his way around. Yet there'd been a coolness too, a sense of detachment, as if somehow he stood aside watching himself. He'd wondered if somebody waking from a fever delirium had felt like that, long ago, before even his own time. Then bit by bit he settled in, coming to realize not only with his awareness but with his whole identity that he was still the same old person, simply with a lot of fog and underbrush cleared away. Yes, there were gaps in his memories, but nothing that mattered too much; he could look up the records of those experiences whenever he cared to, and meanwhile everything he had kept stood sharp and vivid, his life story ready to hand.

Including enough memories of blunders to give a healthy ruefulness. He dared hope he'd be thinking and behaving better for the next few centuries.

Though when could he start? He surged from his chair and paced to and fro, growling. Yep, he thought, the same old fiddle-footed Hebo. He wanted a drink. Bad idea, pouring this early in the day, but what the hell else was there to do? Oh, yes, a hike through the woods, something like that. Sensible. He was getting mighty tired of being sensible.

A light footfall brought him around on his heel. Avi had come out onto the verandah. His impatience didn't altogether fall from him, but cheer blossomed. "Well, howdy!" he exclaimed. "Welcome back!"

"How're you doing?" she asked. She spoke with him not only in Anglay, but in the dialect he'd grown up with.

"Lonesome," he admitted. "Bored. Restless. Christ, but it's good to see you!"

He strode over to embrace her. She was worth embracing, for sure, slim, chocolate dark, with luminous eyes in delicate features. A sari-like dress was exactly right for her. Her garb always was, whatever it might be.

She responded willingly, but less ardently than before. "I wish you didn't have to flit away so much," he said when they came up for air.

She stepped back and murmured, "That's been more on your account than mine, dear. You've needed solitude."

"Yeah, to do the drills and straighten myself out and so on and so forth. I couldn't have managed without you, however."

After the clinic and the machines, human companionship, consoling, heartening. Great sex, also lively talk and shared music and rambles around the countryside and—

Avi smiled. "I've enjoyed it."

How much does she mean that? he wondered, not for the first time. Oh, somewhat, I suppose, otherwise why'd she bother? But with how much of her attention on it?

In his regained clarity he saw how skillfully she'd always evaded his questions about where she went and what she did when she wasn't here. Her flitter seemed to drift away and back as lightly and meaninglessly as thistledown. Nevertheless, she was absolutely not a creature of impulse. Now and then he'd touched, barely touched, on enormous underlying self-control, before she fended him off with a word or a caress.

And seeing her stance, her gaze upon him, he understood: "You've got something new for me today."

She nodded. Light shimmered slightly on the coiled midnight hair. "Yes. Haven't you seen it coming? The verdict. Everything shows you're whole, ready to go back and take up your own life."

In spite of the warmth in her tone, he had a sense of impersonal kindness. Briefly he imagined stopping a minute to put a fallen fledgling back in its nest. Oh, yes, they'd charged for their services, a draft on one of his bank accounts, but very reasonable. When he'd asked what was worth their buying on yonder world, Avi had said that humans were too apt to misuse whatever they perceived as free goods.

The train-of-thought recollection gave him a moment's chill. "Humans?" Isn't she as human as I am? Biologically, yes—I suppose—maybe. In her head and heart—well, maybe, too; but what else is in there?

He pushed that aside. The tidings were not unexpected. "Hey, wonderful!" With even more sincerity: "I'll miss you, though, Avi."

Her eyelashes fluttered. "Thank you, Torben." Then she looked straight at him and said, "You'll do best to take up your life again as soon as possible."

"No argument there," he must agree. "One thing I won't miss is all this sitting around on my ass."

She raised her brows. "Why, what would you rather use?"

He grinned and shrugged. She did have a sense of humor, or, at least, she knew how to put one on, like a dress. Like anything purely human?

She turned earnest. "Have you considered what you'll do?"

"N-no. Been turning some notions over, but I never was one

to think really far ahead. Except—" he blurted, "I'd like to come back here once in a while and see you again."

She shook her head. "No," she told him gravely. "That would be very inadvisable, Torben."

"Why?"

"For you."

Heartbreak? he wondered. Or confusion, or what? Would she even exist anymore as this woman I've sort of known? She's maybe been only one—well, incarnation of her whole self. I don't know. I doubt if I ever will.

Once, when they'd grazed seriousness, she'd said, "The future is intellect." Thereupon she'd glided off the matter. Harking back, he suspected the remark had not been accidental. They, or it, or whatever reigned on Earth, had probably judged—one of their carefully reasoned, millisecond judgments—it was best not to let the patient get above himself, not to give him hopes that were bound to be broken. Old-fashioned, purely organic life had reached its limits.

Or so they believed.

Maybe they did.

As if directly sensing his flicker of resentment and rebellion, Avi smiled anew, took his hand—how slender hers was!—and said, "You won't care about that when you've heard what I've got to tell you."

He let go of all larger questions—did they matter to him, anyway?—and stared. Yeah, he thought through a quickened pulsebeat, there's no sort of regular interstellar news channel, but word does get around, and I imagine Earth keeps alert, the way I'd keep alert for outside things while I'm mainly piloting a ship. "Say on. Please."

Her steady voice overwhelmed him: the black hole collision, observed at close range by Susaians and by humans from Asborg, preliminary data speeding forth over the scientific grapevine. "Hey, Judas priest, sensational!" burst from him. "Have you folks sent a mission out for a good look?"

Her voice cooled. "No, that's not necessary."

Why not? tumbled through him. Did the Earth-mind have the whole thing figured out beforehand? Or doesn't it give a damn anymore about anything but its quantum navel?

No, that's unfair, downright stupid. I'm like a rat in a maze wondering why the experimenter doesn't want to run it too and find the cheese.

The sheer archaism of his symbol was a shocking reminder.

He heard Avi: "But I daresay that in the next several years there'll be quite a bit of activity in the neighborhood. Somebody like you could find a way to make a profit off that." Her laugh trilled. "And have fun."

Again his misgivings died down. And see Lissa Windholm, he thought. Though what I could actually do—

It struck him like a fist. He stood amazed.

Avi cocked her head. "Seems like you've suddenly had an idea."

"Uh-huh," he mumbled. "I, I'd rather not say anything. It's too vague yet. Probably too far-fetched."

"I understand," answered the warmth he had come to know so well.

Do you completely? he couldn't help wondering. If I can get this notion, others can. If the Earth-mind is interested at all, it will have already. Has her link with it told her?

He pulled himself away from that, back to the allurement before him. "Yes," she said low. "An adventurer, a loner. You'll want to take off straightaway, I'm sure. But—Torben, could you wait to make ready till tomorrow? We ought to have a little farewell party first, the two of us."

"You betcha!" he answered half gladly.

XXXI

How often had she stood with her father on the watchtower at Ernhurst while they talked—casually, merrily, sadly, intensely, starkly, always lovingly—just the two of them? Lissa had not kept count, any more than she kept count of her heartbeats.

It hurt to see the hurt on his face. "This is—very sudden, dear," Davy Windholm said low.

"I only got the message yesterday," she answered. The invitation to join a new voyage, back to Jonna.

"And you're accepting? With no questions, hesitations, conditions?" He paused. "I'd been informed of the plan. They'd like to have the *Dagmar* along. I haven't mentioned it here because the answer was too obvious. So soon after the black hole business, who'd want to leave home? Nor would the House ever agree to tie up our ship so long."

"We have others," she said automatically, uselessly.

"All committed elsewhere, except the *Hulda*, and of course she's not only too small but it'd be a downright waste to send her off with a destination like that."

Perforce Lissa nodded. The exploratory scout could venture into extreme conditions—high radiation backgrounds, deep gravity wells, or less foreseeable hazards—better than *Dagmar* could, and make planetary landings to boot; but she was meant for preliminary missions, gathering basic data, and had berthing and life support for no more than four crewfolk.

"It didn't cross my mind," Davy went on in quiet amazement, "that these people would then approach you personally, or that you'd even consider going."

"The message to me was from the Gargantuan Karl," she said. "I've told you about him."

"Oh, yes, a good person. But not human. The expedition will be nonhuman, do you realize that? A consortium of Gargantuans and Xanaduans—with, I understand, some Sklerons, interested in the colonization possibilities. But the main objective, to study that . . . Forerunner thing."

"I know. Karl explained."

"What can you contribute, dear?"

"Nothing to that part, I suppose. However, other kinds of scientists will go too. Pure scientists. A whole world to study! We didn't make a decent scratch in the surface, our little group."

Davy attempted a smile. "A deep enough scratch for quite a few research papers and theses in the next several years."

"I know," Lissa now snapped. "Though the black hole sensation seems to have driven real, detail-work science out of nearly everybody's mind, here on Asborg. We should be thankful that a few beings haven't gone cosmology-crazy but want to learn about matters that can be dealt with."

"Nonhumans."

"Yes. Not given to stampeding after the newest fashion like our breed."

He regarded her for a while before he asked softly, "Are you bitter about your own triumph? In God's name, why?"

She couldn't stay irritated with him, nor bring herself to lie to him. "Oh, I'm restless again, and here's a chance to work it off doing something worthwhile."

"Already? After all that stress and danger, you don't want any more peace and quiet"—he gestured at the lovely late-summer landscape—"than the little bit you've had?"

"If I don't grab this opportunity fast, it'll be gone."

"I've told you before about the trip I was on, away back in my second youth, the one man in a crew of Arzethi. Perfectly decent, yes, fascinating beings, who tried hard for fellowship with me. I may never have made clear to you how lonely I got. And that was for a single year."

"Karl informs me they hope for two or three humans. Versatility."

He raised his brows. "Would any besides you come from Asborg?"

"I suppose not," she said indifferently.

"Then they'll be foreign to you in their own ways. Besides, I can't see so few, in a setting like that, not getting on each other's nerves. More than with the aliens. During five years!"

She had thought about that, and how to cope, but didn't want to talk about it. "Long enough, maybe, to start actually understanding the biosphere."

"You're no biologist." Did she catch a note of desperation?

She sought to ease him. "No, I'll play the same role as I did before. I've got a bagful of woodcraft skills, and I'll improve them as regards Jonna. Dad, don't be afraid for me. I'll stay careful. I like living, really I do."

"If it's wilderness you want to study, Freydis is right next door."

"I've been there, over and over. Have you forgotten?" she couldn't help throwing at him.

"It's still far from being well-known," he persisted forlornly.

She nodded, "Yes. Our sister planet. I could call home every day, take furlough home every couple of months." Scorn spoke. "Anybody could."

"And still do good science. But to more purpose. You know I expect the cession of New Halla to your friend Orichalc's people will soon be approved."

She tossed her head. "It had better be. We owe him enough. Everybody does."

"Don't you want to help them get established?"

"I'm not indispensable for that. Plenty of Asborgans know the region, the whole planet, better than I do." Her mood began to soften. "Maybe after I get back. Yes, I'll certainly look in on them then. But here's a—a challenge for me that I can't resist." At once she wished she'd found words less pretentious.

He stood silent. A breeze murmured across the land. Its sunny odors tugged at her from the depths of childhood. She braced herself against them.

"A chance to go away, be away, for those years, don't you mean?" he asked most quietly. "Altogether away."

Her eyes stung. "Oh, Dad—"

He nodded. "Like Captain Valen. The hero of the magnificent rescue. He can have any berth he wants. But he's leaving too. Taking an offer from a company on Akiko, I've heard. Humans there, yes, but—also far away. Another language, other lifeways for him to learn."

Her tenderness congealed. "I imagine he's sick of the publicity and the fawning and the journalists prying into his life. I certainly am. And maybe he hopes to prove himself."

Davy's gaze narrowed. "He didn't, there at the black holes?"

Lissa clamped her lips together.

"Something happened yonder," Davy said, gently again, "something that nobody's speaking about."

She squared her shoulders and met his eyes. "Some things are nobody else's business."

He sighed. "I know you too well to keep arguing with you, dear." His hand reached for hers. "But if ever you'd like a sympathetic shoulder and a tongue kept on a tight rein, here I'll be."

She took his grip and, for a moment, clung. "I know. Give me time, Dad. Only time."

Time for healing, she thought. No, that's another smarmy word. Smacks of self-pity. I just need to get out from under and keep busy for a while. A few years. What does that count for, when we've all got hundreds or thousands ahead of us?

With luck. Well, you have to assume you'll be lucky.

Yes, indeed, I'll be fine. Why, already I can start looking forward, vaguely, to my homecoming. And new surprises.

She didn't know that they would begin with a new rescue mission.

XXXII

Arriving on Asborg, Hebo was surprised at the depth of his disappointment on learning that Lissa Windholm had lately departed and wasn't expected home for several years. He considered going back to Jonna himself.

But no, he couldn't make any further profit yonder. His capital had dwindled substantially. If he wanted to accomplish anything, he'd have to set in train the lengthy, complicated processes of transferring what valuta he had banked on other worlds to this one.

As for women, Inga was a lively town.

He found a small apartment in it and settled down to collect the information he needed. The database on the colliding black holes was public, huge, and rapidly growing. Most of it was quite beyond his comprehension. Interpretations of the material gathered yonder were streaming out, highly technical articles on this or that aspect, occasional popularizations interspersed.

More would be coming in. Two or three Houses, notably Windholm, were preparing in partnership to send some robotic probes that would conduct further observations. Probably a few of different origin were "already" there, though the Susaian Dominators, for one, would play such cards mighty close to the vest. However, it'd take a large fleet of those little craft, and an indefinite time span, to follow the course of post-collision evolution reasonably well.

Any proper expedition, crewed and in a big ship, would cost a bundle. Even what he had in mind, if it was feasible at all, would take more than he could pay for at the moment.

He must go ahead cautiously. The first order of business was to gain a better idea of what the situation really was, what to look for, what to provide against. Or try to look, try to provide.

Simply getting the gist of what was available meant slow, hard work. His brain wasn't built for theoretical physics. He studied at certain hours of the day, after which it was a relief to deal with knowledge less cosmic. Nor was he built for sitting unbrokenly in one place and filling his head. He sallied forth, sought recreations, struck up casual friendships, and, when opportunity offered, sounded people out. There was no Neocatholic church anywhere on the planet, but once in awhile he attended Josephan services.

He had been thus occupied for about three months, and local fall was turning into winter, when his phone chimed, lighted the screen with a visage he didn't recognize. Wall transparencies showed dusk setting in and the city coming aglow. The hills where he'd spent the day tramping trails, wind rustling fallen leaves while wildlife fleeted and flew around him, were lost to sight. His lungs missed that freshness, but his muscles were comfortably tired.

The face was pale of complexion, black of eyes and curly of hair, chiseled as sharply as it gazed at him. "Good evening, Captain Hebo," said the voice. "Do you remember me? Romon Kaspersson Seafell. I was with the *Dagmar* expedition to Jonna."

"Uh, sure," Hebo lied. Although he'd kept more of his newer than his older memories, he'd had the program remove what seemed like mere clutter. Not that he'd identified each recollection individually, of course—a practical impossibility. The program had learned *him* and his wishes, then exercised its own judgment. "You'll remember yourself, however, my partner and I only paid one courtesy call on your camp."

Romon nodded. "Otherwise your contacts were by communicator, with our leaders, and through them with the authorities here, negotiating a payment for your discoveries. Oh, yes."

Didn't he approve? Hebo wasn't yet familiar enough with Asborgan culture to always know what somebody meant by something. "How did you learn?" he asked curtly.

Romon's mouth bent in a rather stiff smile. "No offense. I quite understand your position, and was happy to see that you did get a reasonable reward. I've wondered how things went for you since then."

"How did you learn I'm in town?"

"You've made no secret of your presence."

"Nor blared it out."

"Still, you're not nobody, Captain Hebo. You're the man who made that remarkable find. Your arrival was a news item in these parts."

"Pretty small." What little brief fame might have been his was eclipsed by the black hole sensation, perhaps especially so on Asborg. He'd foreseen that, and counted on it. This felt like an intrusion on the obscurity he preferred for the nonce. "Why didn't you get in touch before, if you wanted to?"

"To tell the truth, the item escaped me. As you say, not exactly first-projection news, and not followed up. I retrieved it a couple of days ago, when I'd been told you were here."

"And?"

Romon appeared to suppress exasperation. "Captain Hebo, I simply want to be friendly, and trade anecdotes. And we might possibly discover we can do business. May I invite you to dinner? Tomorrow evening, perhaps?"

Hebo had been intending to meet a lady then. Well, he didn't think she'd be too annoyed if he called and apologized for suddenly having to reshuffle his plans. "All right, why not?"

He smelled something on the wind, whatever it was.

XXXIII

The Baltica enjoyed a setting as elegant as itself, a clear dome atop one of the tallest towers in Inga. City lights shone, flashed, fountained to the edge of sight, under a moon ringed with a frost halo. Designer flowers bedded among the tables deployed multitudinous colors, animated the air, and trilled a melody that evoked springtime in the blood. Stepping in and seeing the customers, Hebo felt distinctly underdressed. Nonetheless, when he spoke Romon's name he was conducted with deference to a table in a reserved alcove. He'd come a trifle early, so he wouldn't be in strange surroundings, and ordered a beer to keep him company while he looked around. Quite a few of the women on hand were worth looking at.

Romon entered on the dot, immaculate in blue tunic, red half-cloak, and white trousers tucked into silver-buckled boots. On his left shoulder, a ring of tiny diamonds glinted around the emblem of his House. Contrast made the man with him doubly slovenly. Besides, the fellow was short, squat, ugly—a kind of arrogance, not getting that dark, hooknosed face remodeled. He stood unsmiling as Romon introduced him: "Captain Torben Hebo, I'd like you to meet Dr. Esker Harolsson Seafell."

Hebo rose. The other ignored his proffered hand, though a shake was customary on Asborg, and gave him a nod. "Esker Harolsson?" Hebo blurted. "The physicist who—observed those black holes? But I thought you were a Windholm."

He never had been much good at tact, he realized, and doubtless never would be.

"I changed my patrons," Esker snapped. Evidently he hadn't

wanted that publicized. They could have arranged it.

"House Seafell was honored to adopt him," Romon said, as if to gloss over the surliness.

"And I'm, uh, honored to meet you," Hebo said. The honor didn't feel overwhelming.

They sat down. Romon ordered a martini, Esker a whiskey over ice. Hebo decided to bull ahead. "Why've you come along, if I may ask? What you did, what you're working on, is way beyond me."

"I thought you might have questions you'd like authoritative answers to," Romon made reply. His manner intensified. "Inasmuch as you've been retrieving not just popular accounts of the matter, but everything, including new interpretations and theories as they appear."

"How do you know that?"

The drinks slid up from the table port. Romon sipped his before replying, "You didn't request an anonymous address." Esker took a pretty deep swallow of his.

"No, why should I?" Hebo countered. "And why should you keep watch for everybody who wants full reports?"

"Everybody who has no clear reason to do so," growled Esker.

Romon frowned at him, obviously not liking even this slight giveaway. "You were from offplanet, and not in any registry of scientists known to us. Don't you agree, that's interesting?"

"Why?"

Romon shrugged. "A natural curiosity, reinforced by having previous acquaintance."

"You said 'everybody.' "

Esker leaned forward, tumbler gripped tight in a hairy hand. "The potentialities of this phenomenon are unpredictable," he stated. "Revolutionary new technologies may well spring from it. Dangerous, in ignorant or irresponsible possession."

"Those Susaians didn't go there from a disinterested love of pure science," Romon added.

And parts of the story are still untold, Hebo thought, not for the first time. And these two aren't about to share them with me.

He forced a laugh. "I don't qualify," he said. "Anyhow, that particular cat is long since out of the bag."

"Too many cats are."

The old saw had escaped Hebo without forethought, as old saws were apt to do. It surprised him that Romon knew this one. The man must be a reader. What more was there to him that didn't show on the surface?

"Even the discovery at Jonna should not have been broadcast to any and every world," Romon continued. "We should at least have released the data gradually and discreetly. House Seafell urged it. But no, the other Houses knew better."

The bitterness in his tone made Hebo wonder aloud: "Who're you afraid would benefit, besides us? The Susaians?"

Romon's manner turned thoughtful. "I suppose you mean the Dominance. No, not that *per se*. I don't share the paranoia of too many people about it. We may not much approve of the regime, but we have no military or political conflict with it worth worrying over, and, as a matter of fact, it's having internal problems."

Hebo had likewise heard such news, leaking out across light-years, economic troubles and unrest which refused to stay repressed. Susaians as a race seemed to fare no better under totalitarianism than humans. Nevertheless, he didn't quite agree with Romon's assessment. That interstellar violence made no sense and hadn't happened didn't mean it never could.

He realized fleetingly that once upon a time he had had a different opinion. His revised mind didn't think in quite the same way as before.

Romon was saying, "I simply have in mind whatever technology may be gotten from the knowledge. And, no, we'd not be able to monopolize it for long. But a head start, a competitive advantage—"

Better return to our muttons, Hebo thought. Aloud: "Well, amongst all those big astropolitical questions, why such a concern over me?"

Romon lifted a palm. "Please. It's entirely friendly. I recognized your name when I was most recently checking the list of retrievals. Naturally, I was surprised, but also glad of a chance to meet you again."

Esker sneered. "Alas, the fair Lissa Davysdaughter wasn't here to greet you."

He's heard about us on Jonna, Hebo thought. His feelings on the subject sound pretty strong. I wish there were more grounds for it. "I'll admit I was disappointed," he gave back. "What man with his glands working right wouldn't be?"

That must have hit a nerve. Esker glared.

And did Romon wince ever so slightly? He made haste to interpose a smile and a chuckle. "Well, of course, a very natural reason to come. But the only one? The black hole material has been sent to a number of institutions elsewhere. Scientists communicate to and fro."

"Why is a *layman* like you downloading it?" demanded Esker. "What use to you?"

"Sir, I don't appreciate your tone of voice," Hebo said, truthfully enough. "Is this a reunion dinner or an interrogation?"

"I'm sorry," Romon responded fast. "We both are," which Hebo doubted. "We seem to have expressed ourselves poorly. Of course we don't expect anything . . . untoward. I repeat, I'm simply curious, and it occurred to me that Dr. Esker might be of some help to you. Or I might be."

He drew breath. "Yes, I checked further," he went on. "You're collecting information on Freydis as well, the planet and the proposed Susaian colony. That suggests to me your main reason for coming to Sunniva has to do with it. You're an entrepreneur. House Seafell is business-oriented, you know. If you care to discuss your ideas, we might perhaps find we can cooperate."

Hebo took cover behind his beer mug while he reassembled his thoughts. Be wary, he decided, but not too standoffish to learn whatever may be here to learn. "I see. Well, I'm not broadcasting it yet, when nothing may come of it. But if the colony does get started, there'll be a lot of work to do, a lot of inventions needed, and, if the project succeeds, a lot of money to make."

Romon laughed. "Ah-hah! That's what I thought."

"But why your preoccupation with the black holes?" his companion persisted. "You must be spending hours per week sifting through the information in search of bits and pieces you can halfway understand."

"Esker," Romon clipped, "if you don't keep a civil tongue, I'll regret inviting you along."

"I'm entitled to be curious too," said the physicist. "Or am I merely another machine of yours, to be switched off when you aren't using it?"

Hey, better lighten the atmosphere, or I'll have wasted an evening that looked promising yesterday, Hebo thought. He constructed amiability. "It's no riddle, Dr. Harolsson, and I do appreciate your taking the trouble to join us. If you've looked closely at my queries, and I'll bet you have, you know I'm not only asking about astrophysics, or even mainly, but about the whole little-known stellar neighborhood. The event's bound to have effects across parsecs. Radiation effects on biospheres are just the most obvious."

"Slight, and in the course of correspondingly many years," Esker retorted. "Those studies can wait."

"I gather they are in fact waiting. Sure, the new hole is the urgent case, and has a lot more to teach us. However, later on, exploration may turn up things farther off."

Romon raised his eyes and his drink. "Profitable things?" he murmured as mildly.

"What else, for me? I'm keeping an eye open, while I carry on my current fishing expedition."

"Excuse me, but doesn't that flood of . . . abstruse data and calculations . . . almost blind you?"

Hebo spread his hands. "At this stage, who can tell what's going to give a new opportunity? Besides, it's kind of a challenge."

"Why?" muttered Esker. "You'll never be a scientist."

"I see," Romon put in. "You want to keep expanding your mental horizons. And your physical ones." His voice dropped to a murmur:

> "Yet all experience is an arch wherethro'
> Gleams that untravell'd world whose margin fades
> For ever and for ever when I move.
> How dull it is to pause, to make an end,
> To rust unburnish'd, not to shine in use!
> As tho' to breathe were life!"

Esker scowled, puzzled by the archaic language and resentful.

Hebo blinked. "Hey, Tennyson's *Ulysses,"* he exclaimed.

"Oh, do you know it?" Romon asked, in surprise of his own.

"Yeah, sure, and a bunch of other mostly forgotten stuff. I may not be any literary type, but I do go a long way back, and there's been plenty of time with nothing better to do than read."

"Well, well. I hope we can get together over drinks now and then and cap quotations."

Esker broke in. "This is very fine, no doubt, but it makes me wonder still the more why you're trying to understand astrophysics and cosmology."

Hebo decided to smooth things over. "Just incidental, as I thought you realized." The hell it is. "A change of pace from the Freydis work. And just in short little forays."

"A hobby?" said Romon, likewise anxious to maintain politeness. "Good for you. To get practical, though, I repeat, possibly we can help each other as regards Freydis."

"Possibly." As he thought about it, Hebo felt more and more that the possibility might well be very real. Don't tip the hand, though, especially bearing in mind that Lissa Windholm once mentioned having a certain coldness toward House Seafell. "I'll have to see, or try to gauge, how things are developing. Maybe I'll decide the business is not for me at all, and go away before I go broke. If something positive should occur to me, sure, I'll let you know." He knocked back his beer. "Before we have another round, what say we screen the menu?"

"Sheer genius!" Romon exclaimed with a bonhomie that Hebo didn't think came natural to him. "Yes, indeed."

The rest of the time passed fairly pleasantly, since Esker didn't say much.

And then the next five years were amply eventful. And then Lissa returned.

XXXIV

At first the aircraft shone above the sea so much like a star that she felt something catch at her throat. Freydis was beautiful in the morning and evening skies of Asborg, but on Freydis itself there was never a glimpse of the sister planet, nor of anything in the heavens other than a vague sun-disc when clouds thinned to an overcast. Suddenly, sharply, a longing seized her for the cool green hills of home.

She thrust it away. Ridiculous. She'd had three months in them after her return from Jonna—when she wasn't elsewhere boating or skiing or among the pleasures of the cities—and then barely as many weeks at New Halla and here. And right now she had a life to save.

If she could.

Recognizing the approaching object for what it was, she turned and trotted off the headland toward the landing strip. At her back, the ocean murmured against cliffs. It glimmered yellowish-green close in, darkened to purple farther out. A storm yonder hulked black and lightning-streaked, but overhead and eastward stretched silver-gray blankness. Before her rose forest, a wall of great boles, vines, brakes, foliage in hues of russet and umber, brilliant blossoms, shadowful depths. It dwarfed the clearing where the Susaian compound stood. The multitudinous smells of it lay heavy in the heat and damp.

Long, limber bodies were bounding from the huts. Glabrous hides sheened in a variety of colors; the New Hallan colonists were from many different ancestral regions, alike only in their faith and hopes. Several still clutched tools or instruments in their delicate hands. Excitement often spread with explosive speed through beings so directly perceptive of emotions. Not that it wasn't justified. Lissa's own eagerness had driven her onto the promontory to stare southwestward, once the curt acknowledgment came that help was on its way.

She reached the strip. It lay bare, soil baked bricklike. A hangar of wood and thatch gaped empty. The camp's flyer had borne casualties away to medical care or eventual cremation, after leaving off the uninjured here. Impatient, she squinted up. "C'mon, move it," she muttered. "What're you dawdling for?" A drop of sweat got past her brows, into an eye. It stung. She spoke a picturesque oath.

Coppergold arrived and joined her. The botanist had thought to bring a translator. It rendered rustles, hisses, purrs into Anglay. "That is a cautious pilot, honored one."

Lissa replied in her language, which the Susaian understood though unable to pronounce it intelligibly. "Well, I suppose this area is new to him, and he doesn't want the airs to play some trick that catches him off guard. I've learned to fly warily myself." She begrudged the admission, and knew that Coppergold felt that she did.

However, fairness compelled. She mustn't lose her temper, her judgment, when she had Orichalc to save. The fact was that Freydis remained an abiding place of mysteries, and within some of them were deathtraps.

A whole planet, after all, she thought. (How often had she thought the same, here and elsewhere?) Not the global hell of jungle and swamp that most people imagined; no, as diverse as Asborg. But dear Asborg was well-nigh another Earth, renewed and again virginal. Humans soon made it theirs, and in its turn it claimed them for itself. Throughout the centuries that followed, few ever cared to set foot on Freydis, and none to make a home there. Occasional explorers: now and then a handful of scientists—until damned, destroying Venusberg Enterprises sprang up—scant wonder that most was still Mundus Incognitus, that she herself was more familiar with several planets parsecs away.

"Hs-s-s, he descends!" Coppergold exclaimed. She laid her blunt-snouted head on Lissa's shoulder, an oddly mothering gesture. Glancing about, the human looked into big eyes that were not really onyx, being so warm. "Take heart, honored one. Our waiting time has been less than it seemed; observe your chrono. Surely Orichalc lives and you will find him soon enough."

Could any human have been quite that sympathetic, in quite that way? "May it be, may it be," Lissa half prayed. "For your sakes too, and mainly."

Coppergold withdrew a few centimeters. "His loss would indeed strike a blow deep into us." The trans failed to convey a gravity at which Lissa could well guess. "He is more than a symbol, the hero who won our new home for us. He has become a leader, in ways that I fear we cannot fully explain to your kind. Yet we, like you, would grieve most over the passing of a friend."

Side by side, surrounded now by the rest, they gazed back aloft. The teardrop shape had ceased to hover and was bound slowly down. Landing gear made contact. Through the silence that followed, the nearby screech of a leatherwing and the distant roar of a deimosauroid sounded as insolently loud as the wild blossoms were gaudy.

Lissa advanced to meet the pilot. He slid a hatch aside and sprang to the ground. For a moment they stood motionless.

He was big, muscular, coverall open halfway down the front. The head was round, rugged-faced, blue-eyed, the brown hair less thick on it than on the bare chest. Amazement paralyzed her.

He grinned and offered a hand. "Greeting, milady Windholm," he said. "I've waited a spell for this."

Her tongue unlocked. "You're . . . Torben Hebo," she whispered.

"Last time I looked, I was."

"But, but we called Venusberg headquarters—asking for help—do you work for them? I had no idea."

"Not for them," he said. "I pretty much am Venusberg. I

haven't publicized it, but I am, as you'd've found out if you'd inquired. Me and my old partner Dzesi of Rikha. You remember her, don't you?"

She could not have foreseen the disappointment, almost dismay that shocked through her. Nor did she quite understand. The hand she had reached toward his dropped to her side. "I can't believe—If you're the head of that thing, you'd come yourself?"

"That's exactly how come I can take off on short notice, or do whatever else I jolly well please."

"But why? Somebody who knows the search area, has the skills, that, that's what we need."

He scowled. She saw him curb the temper she recalled. "Look," he growled, "Forholt Station is ours, a Venusberg base on this continent, right? I helped start it up, bossing the job in person. I've scrambled around in the environs. Also, just reminding you, I've kicked about in space for more hundreds of years and in more different places than anybody else you've ever met, lady."

She swallowed. "Well, then, this is—good of you, C-captain Hebo."

He unbent a little. "Too bad I couldn't bring Dzesi along. She's got a real nose for tracking. But she's at company HQ on the far side of the planet, or rambling somewhere else and out of touch. Nobody knows much about the section we've got to ransack, but I can cope there as well as any other human and better than most."

"It's . . . lucky for us you happened to be when you were."

Now he laughed. "Not by accident. When I heard you'd come home and were visiting on Freydis—news, in so tiny a population—of course I wanted to look you up. But word also was that you don't like what Venusberg is doing. So I squatted me down at the station, where they can use some straightening out of their operations anyway, and watched for a chance. This was it."

Somehow, that jolted her back to—if not hostility, then a certain coldness. "We can't stand here gabbing," she snapped. "A life is at stake. I have an outfit ready to go. Let me fetch it and we'll be on our way. We haven't too bloody much daylight left."

An inward fraction of her wished flickeringly that matters were different. He had passed through her thoughts oftener during these years than she wanted to admit. And, yes, his treatment on Earth did seem to have taken at least the edges off the arrogance and crudity.

But he was still headlong and self-centered. He must be, or he'd not have been working toward the ruin of a world, merely to get rich.

If she was going to wish for the unreal, it should be that Freydis's cloud cover didn't blind landsats that would soon have found Orichalc on Asborg, or that the forest roof didn't screen him from aerial search.

Hebo matched his stride to hers. Was he curious about this outpost? "I brought my own stuff, of course," he said.

"Is it suitable for such an excursion?"

"I've spent more than four standard years on this world," he answered, offended afresh. "What about you?"

She bridled in turn. "More than one fairly extensive and intensive expedition in the past. And I too have experience on several planets—including wilderness on Asborg. Some of it isn't totally unlike what we'll find today. We'll take what I've packed. In flight I'll inspect yours and rearrange it if need be."

He clenched his fists and bit his lip. That was tactless, Lissa realized. Almost as tactless as he's sometimes been toward me. But, oh, Orichalc—

Trying for peace, she blurted, "Have you any information about our wounded?"

"No," said Hebo. "They hadn't reached Forholt when I left."

She had expected as much. Her group's aircraft was capacious but slow, his the exact opposite. "I only know several Susaians and one human are hurt enough to require hospitalization, at least overnight," he added, perhaps also wanting a truce. "How badly?"

"Uldor Enarsson worst. Not to the point of mortal danger. They gave him first aid in camp, and then I went along when our flyer picked them up and did some more for him on the way back here. But I'm afraid he'll be out of action for weeks at best, and we may have to retire him from the project, return him to Asborg. Chaos take it!"

"A Windholm client, isn't he?"

"Yes, though actually he's been more on Freydis than off it for decades, independently surveying and researching."

"I know. He did first-chop work before he . . . joined you."

With an effort, she ignored that last. "My worry goes beyond a patron's obligation. He was, is, a comrade—an equal, as far as I'm concerned. And close to indispensable. Without his information and skills, unless we can find a replacement, our progress will slow to a crawl."

"Suitable for lizards, hey?" She glared. "Sorry, that was a bad joke, wasn't it?" He didn't sound overly apologetic. "But I do kind of resent the notion I've begun to hear about, that nobody but pure-hearted ecologists are fit to get the Susaians established. God damn it, that's the business I'm in!"

"To get as rich as possible as fast as possible, and never mind what happens afterward," burst from her.

"Do you expect me to work for nothing?"

They clamped silence upon themselves and stalked onward.

XXXV

As they entered the compound, she saw him surprised. He must have been too little interested, or too busy with his exploitive business, to learn more about this undertaking than the fact of its existence.

A stockade, erected to keep animals out and serve as a windbreak during storms, enclosed a dozen buildings. Some were living quarters, some for storage or utility, one a laboratory. All were cylindrical in shape, built of rocks and hard-dried mud, roofed with sod. Chimneys showed that several contained fireplaces. Doors and fittings were wood, supplemented by sauroid leather; windowframes held glass, unclear, obviously made by amateurs from sand.

"Judas priest!" Hebo exclaimed. "How much labor went into this?"

Lissa didn't recognize his phrase, doubtless archaic. Yes, he'd have wanted to keep many memories from his first youth. "Quite a lot," she replied. "Less will in future. We're learning as we work."

"When you could have assembled readymade shelters? We make them, you know."

"Yes. Just as you've made most of the buildings and utilities on New Halla. A main purpose of this expedition to the mainland is to find out what can be done with native resources—and I don't mean clear-cutting whole forests or poisoning the waters with tailings from mines."

"Huh? Do you suppose, once your precious Susaians start breeding and expanding in earnest, they won't need an industrial base?"

"Of course not," she snapped. "The wise ones, like Orichalc, want to find ways that won't gut the planet. Besides the direct damage Venusberg is doing, it's sapping the incentive for such an effort."

"You mean we provide them with what they need, low-cost and *now,* instead of standing back and leaving them in poverty for the sake of some future Never-Never Land—" He broke off. "Well, I'm not saying they shouldn't make inventions of their own. How does this adobe withstand the kind of rain you get?"

They'd gotten off on the wrong foot again, she thought. It hurt worse than she might have expected. But maybe he felt the same, and was trying to change the subject. "The Susaians experimented under Uldor's direction. They found that the local soil needs only water, a little added gravel, and some hours kept dry, to set like concrete," she answered almost eagerly. "You noticed the surface of the airstrip, didn't you?" With relief: "Here we are."

She led him into the hut that was hers. He peered around, but in the gloom saw little of her personal things before she had taken up her pack. They were few anyway: pictures of her kinfolk and the Windholm estates; a player and numerous cartridges of books, shows, music; a sketch pad and assorted pencils; a flute. The rest was equipment.

Emerging, they found the Susaian had likewise returned. "Not many," Hebo remarked.

"Most are in the field, investigating," Lissa told him. "These are busy with lab studies or chores."

"What were you yourself doing before the, uh, incident?"

"I've hardly begun here, I want to help. No lack of opportunities. I was taking a party of canoers along the Harmony River. Teaching them how. This work is still mostly exploratory, research and development, but it's beginning to assume an instructional function as well."

He smiled. How attractive he became, all at once. "Then you received the call about an emergency, and the flyer took you off and brought you to that scene. What about your tenderfeet?"

"I left them on an islet in midstream. They'll be all right for a few days, if air transport is pre-empted that long. I can even hope they'll learn something by themselves."

It was as if he couldn't keep from taunting: "The better to occupy the continents later, and breed lots of young to overrun them, huh?"

Coppergold and Stargleam approached, saving her from making an angry retort. "Are you certain you do not wish any of us to accompany you, honored one?" the botanist asked.

"Thank you, no," Lissa replied. "My new companion claims expertise. No harm should threaten me, and we can move faster if we're alone."

"We are most grateful, benevolent one," said Stargleam to Hebo.

The man grinned. "Customer relations." Lissa wasn't sure the trans could render that. Best if not. The Susaians did look a bit puzzled.

"Come," she said, and walked away fast. They must be sensing the tension between her and him. It would worry them.

Silent, the humans proceeded back to the flyer, stowed her pack, and settled down side by side at the front. "Do you have the coordinates?" she inquired.

"The autopilot has them. Up in the foothills of the Sawtooth, right? We aren't all of us tunnel-vision moneygrubbers in Venusberg, whatever you suppose." His finger stabbed the control board. Power whirred.

And again I've blundered, she thought. Not that he's altogether undeserving of it. "Apologies. No offense meant. I'm anxious, you see, tired, overwrought."

"Then shouldn't you have rested before we go, or sent somebody else?" His tone had smoothed. "That would have to be a Susaian, I imagine, but why not?"

She shook her head. "I dare not delay. Orichalc can come to grief at any instant. He was on New Halla till lately and has had time to learn virtually nothing about wilderness survival. Besides, under the circumstances, I think I may be the only person of either species on this planet who could find him."

If that can be done at all, she thought. The trail is already cold.

They gained altitude and bore east. The ocean, the curving shoreline slipped from view. Below them reached another sea, ruddy-brown, the crowns of trees in their millions, from horizon to horizon and beyond. Wind made great slow billows over it. Here and there gleamed a lake or the meandering thread of a river. A marsh passed beneath vision, nearly hidden by antlike forms, browsing animals that in reality were huge. Often a flock of winged creatures, thousands strong, scudded above the forest. Far ahead, cloud banks towered beneath an opalescent sky. Air conditioning made the cabin blessedly cool.

"Well—" In almost Susaian wise, Lissa felt how Hebo tried to veil skepticism. "This, uh, Orichalc, I gather he's important?"

"Why, yes. I thought you'd remember. It was a sensation, six years ago. How he led us to those black holes about to collide, at risk of his life, such a scientific prize that my House was glad to award him the island he asked for."

"Oh, *that* one? Of course. I'd forgotten the name, that's all. Asborg may be just a quick flit away, but we on Freydis, we're preoccupied—isolated—" He drew breath for an explanation he'd have to make sooner or later. "And, to tell the truth, Dzesi and I lie as low as we can. You must've heard Venusberg is a joint stock corporation. That's a front. Forty-nine percent of the shares are held by her Trek back on Rikha, where the nominal president is, and we two have the rest. That's how come you didn't know I was even on Freydis. You'd have had to search databases of forgotten news items to discover it."

"Why the secrecy? Doesn't seem like you."

"To keep journalists and other pests off our tails and out from under our feet."

Insufficient reason, she thought. He's holding back something. But what, and why?

The Venusberg operations may not be advertised, but they aren't hidden. I wish I could say outright that what I learned about them when I came home was what brought me here, dismayed, indignant, hoping I can make such a position for myself among the Susaians that I can get something done to curb the destruction.

No. Not now. I can't afford a quarrel. Yet.

She swallowed. "Well, I'm grateful you came out of hiding to help."

He gave her a glance. His tone mildened anew. "Orichalc means a lot to you, plain to see. After what you went through together in space."

"And our correspondence and meetings since then. Any life matters, of course, but his more than most. They revere him on New Halla. His words, his leadership may make all the difference in what happens during the next few centuries. He came to the mainland to learn for himself, in hands-on detail, what's being accomplished there and now. The whole idea, which the Old Truth itself promotes, is not to destroy the natural environment but to fit into it."

"As if you could do that without causing an upheaval's worth of changes." Hebo sighed. "Hey, I don't want a fight, But could I ask you to study some history? Pioneers, voortrekkers, yeah, they do your minimalist, economical sort of thing. They haven't the means to do more. But after them come the farmers, the miners, the cities, the factories—and that's the end of anything you could call nature."

"We've kept Asborg green." Mostly.

"Domesticated," he snorted. "Manicured. What virgin growth and wildlife you've got are in carefully managed reserves. Anyway, the case is completely different on Freydis, and you know it."

At the aircraft's speed, they were already beyond the coastal plain. Ground rose in swells and ridges, still densely overgrown but with lighter-hued foliage and frequent shrubby openings. Rainclouds shrouded the Sawtooths themselves and spilled westward beneath the high permanent overcast.

After a silence too full of the thrum and whine of their passage, Hebo said, "I've got to admit the problem today isn't clear to me. All I was told, in the hurry everybody was in, was that a camp had been attacked by predators, several persons were hurt, including the human leader, and one was missing. Your Susaian friend, it turns out. Doesn't he have his radio bracelet on?"

"Radio collar," Lynn corrected. "No, but that wasn't due to carelessness. The trouble was unforeseen—unforeseeable. The Susaians were familiar only with New Halla, an island, and getting some acquaintance with part of the continental seaboard. Uldor had worked in the highlands, and deemed the time ripe to start exploring and experimenting there. In many respects, he said, they might prove to be the best site for the first mainland colony."

Hebo nodded. She hurried on: "Orichalc went along to observe. The Susaian leaders need to know how these efforts are conducted. Uldor's party was conveyed to a suitable spot and left to itself. The first couple of days went to settling in. Then everybody relaxed last night, before commencing their studies. They held a party to celebrate. Perfectly sober, Old Truth believers don't use recreational drugs of any kind, and Uldor might have a single well-watered shot of whiskey if he's feeling expansive. They saw no need to post a watch when they went to sleep, but did. In short, they took every precaution.

"A little before daybreak, a pack of silent-running large carnivores entered the camp. As dark as the night was and as fast as they moved, the lookout doesn't seem to have been aware of anything till they were almost on her, and then probably only through her emotional sense. We don't know; she barely had time to cry out before being torn apart. The creatures ran wild, blood-frenzied. Uldor and a couple of others had kept loaded firearms handy, and shot several, two fatally, but fangs slashed them nevertheless. After a horrible battle in the dark, the beasts retreated and our people called the base. We evacuated them. You know the rest."

"No, I don't," Hebo said. "What sort of beasts? You say dead ones were there to look at."

"Lycosauroids. I asked Forholt for data, and they identified them from my transmission, and were astounded. None had ever been seen this far north. Why should Uldor provide against them? Getting struck by lightning seemed more probable."

"Hm." Hebo rubbed his chin. "Did some weird set of chances take a single pack hundreds of klicks from its hunting grounds? Or is this an early sign of an ecological fluctuation? The ceratodon herds do seem to be declining in the southern range, and that's the principal lyco prey. . . ."

His almost scientific language bemused Lissa. It was she who must say: "Such problems can wait. No, I take that back. It can well be a very practical question. Another deadly stunt pulled by a world never really meant for us."

But just homelike enough to draw us into its snares, she thought. If Susaian and Freydisan and Terran life didn't happen to be biochemically similar, able to provide nourishment of sorts for each other, none of us would have dreamed of any such ventures here as ours.

"Or for anybody," Hebo said sardonically. "Not that I object, understand. I'm in business because of it. But I have wondered what's eating the settlers, to take all this risk and hardship."

"An ideal."

"Yeah, an ideology." He sounded contemptuous.

She shook her head. "Nothing so simple. Susaians aren't completely alien to us. Look back at human history. You'll find any number of parallels to this. You know"—whether or not you understand—"how the Old Truth people have needed a place of their own. Discriminated against on the Susaian worlds, even persecuted, for centuries—though their standards of honesty, industry, all-around decency put most of our race to shame—"

He laughed. "Quite the little idealist yourself, aren't you?"

She wouldn't let the gibe sting. She wouldn't. "I'm sorry. I didn't mean to preach. When I got home, my father told me how he'd had to explain things over and over to Asborgans who knew practically nothing and cared less about the subject till suddenly they heard they were getting nonhuman next-door neighbors. I guess that affected me."

He turned his eyes back to the ruggedness rising ahead. "Okay. What's become of this Orichalc?"

"The Susaians remove their transceivers when safely on the base or in camp," she told him. "You can well imagine a collar around the neck is uncomfortable in this climate, not like a bracelet, their wrists are too thin and flexible for that. Most are unarmed, and when the beasts attacked, naturally they fled every which way. Trees in the immediate vicinity aren't climbable, mingled thornbark and flexy. When the attack was repulsed and first light came, those who could made their way back. Searchers quickly found the injured, and three more dead, and brought them in. Except for Orichalc. He was gone. Some comrades beat the bush—within a narrow radius, as difficult as that was—and when we arrived in our flyer, we scanned from above before returning. Not a trace.

"I wanted to stay and commence hunting on the ground, but that would have been crazy to do by myself. Also, Uldor and a couple of the Susaians urgently needed further attention, which I was best able to give. So I called Forholt, and . . . you were good enough to come."

"Could the reason that Orichalc didn't show up be that he's dead?" the man asked bluntly.

She swallowed. "That's what we're going to find out."

"Can we?"

"We can give it a damn good try." Lissa arranged her words with care before she uttered them: "I do need a partner, someone who knows that kind of region. I've gained a certain familiarity with both lowlands and highlands from my past visits, though not these particular hills. Uldor had some, which is why he led that expedition, but Uldor's disabled. So I called for such a helper, and you came."

"If you're a stranger to the area, what can you hope to do?"

"I have my ideas. You'll see."

He was silent a while before he said, "Look, I've never been in just these parts myself. The lycos would have caught me off balance too. I can't guarantee nothing else will."

Blast, she thought, he infuriates me, and then turns right around and charms. I wish he'd make up his mind. "Nor I. Another reason not to hare off alone. Uh, I was going to check your gear."

"I thought you meant to heed the voice of experience."

I've flicked him again. To chaos with it. "This mission is special. You've never had anybody lost, have you? Not with their bracelets."

"Did you ever, on your expeditions elsewhere?"

Is he implying incompetence? "Natives, a couple of times. And it baffles me how your outfit imagines it can learn much about wildlife without old-fashioned tracking and stalking."

She unharnessed and wriggled into the rear of the flyer. Cramped, she carried out her inspection slowly, unconscious at first of thinking aloud: "—clothes serviceable, but one change is ample, we won't be gone long. . . . Rifle, by all means. I'll leave my pistol but keep my machete. If those creatures are still loping around, I'd as soon we didn't become part of the ecology. . . . Rations, yes, we can't take time to live off the country. . . . Cookware, no, unnecessary weight, we'll eat cold food. . . . Tent? M-m, more weight and bulk, but goes up faster than making a shelter. We'll give it a try. . . ."

She returned to her seat. The aircraft slanted downward. "Kind of high-handed, aren't you?" Hebo said. As if he never was. "Be warned, in case I have doubts about your judgment, we'll follow mine."

"Oh." Beneath the frostiness, she felt shaken. There had to be a boss. It was a bad oversight of hers, not to have made clear at the outset who that would be. Haste and anxiety were a poor excuse. "I reserve my right to disagree. But we can't squabble now. I trust you'll listen to reason."

"The same for you!"

XXXVI

The landscape on which they descended reached enormous, heights and depths forested except where steeps were eroded to the bare rock. Rivers foamed down gorges. Mists eddied in hollows and along the intricately folded flanks of hills that in many lands would have been called mountains. Clouds drifted low and murky above. From the west, where lightning danced, Lissa heard thunder come rolling. Wind hissed. The aircraft quivered within it.

On a horizontal shoulder halfway up a hillside, woods ringed a glade where a spring bubbled, Uldor's campsite. Perforce Lissa admired Hebo's skill as he landed. Nothing grew underneath except a rough, low ground cover and some shrubs, but air ramped wildly in the narrow space, while around it the big trees bristled with thorns and the lesser ones lashed about like whips. When Lissa climbed out, the wind struck at her, almost cold. The smells on it recalled musk, vinegar, cloves, and things for which she lacked names. Through them wove storm's ozone.

Hebo followed and stared about. He ignored strewn supplies and equipment left behind at the hasty evacuation. What caught his attention was the camp itself, thatch tipis and a rough stone fireplace grill. "Not even tents?" he blurted.

"I told you, a large part of our project is to find out what can be done with local resources," she flung back. "This is an experimental design. Perfectly adequate. Now go unload our packs and batten down the vehicle. We'll set off as soon as I've found the trail."

"Have you brought a chemosensor, or what?"

"I wish I had, but we've got nothing adapted for this kind of work, and I doubt they do at Forholt either. I did bring my eyes and my wits."

He grimaced but yielded. She walked to and fro, peering downward. Presently she went on hands and knees to examine leaves, twigs, soil. Altogether engaged, she forgot time and him.

Emerging at last, she saw him considering a stone in his hand, and joined him. "Well, have you found anything?" he asked. His intonation said that he didn't believe so and that the lengthy wait had annoyed him.

She nodded. "It took a while because those amateur searchers ruined a lot of spoor, but I've figured out what must have happened and which way he set off. Let's saddle up and go."

"Really? I'm afraid you'll have to convince me. This is dangerous terrain, not for heading into blind."

"What? You expect me to teach you right now what it took me years to learn?"

"No, if it is in fact an art, not a hunch. But you'll show me you know what you're doing, or we'll flit straight back."

"We will? Listen, you—" Lissa gulped acridness. *Just when he's begun to seem fairly decent, up comes the arrogance again.* "Very well. Kindly pay close attention. That's what tracking is mainly about."

She led him to a chosen spot, hunkered down, and pointed. "Traces often last a considerable spell. Years, under certain conditions." *Or geological eras if they happen to fossilize.* "But they generally weather fast, at a rate that also depends on the type of ground, the depth of the impression, et cetera, et cetera. So I took care to retrieve area weather records from the radar satellites for the past several days, before we left base. Observe. The wind has strewn leaves and dust and other debris, but uncovered a trail—four feet, three-toed, about one hundred and seventy-five centimeters apart front to rear, stride indicating short legs, occasional traces of a tail. I can't identify many Freydisan animals this easily, not yet, but no mistaking a Susaian.

"Now, these other pockmarks over it were made by rain—a shower, not a downpour—and the last time any fell was four days ago, about one hundred and twenty hours. Therefore the Susaian track is older, and of no use to us. Except that at this point and a later moment, as I can tell by the sharpness of the impressions, another four-legged creature crossed it, bounding. The pattern of the prints indicates the gait. A big beast, clearly a lyco. The claw marks are faint, but if you lie prone and squint your eye just over the surface, you can identify them, and they're pointed downhill. So that's the direction the pack fled in. Which is obvious from the mangled brush and dried flecks of blood farther on, but I've illustrated the principle. Finding where Orichalc went was a process of elimination."

"I get the idea." Did she hear respect? "You needn't go on. I'll follow your lead."

Gladly, she bounced to her feet and made for the packs. "With due caution," he added.

"Sure. You said something about the terrain."

"M-hm. I've conducted my own look-see. I've had to learn some Freydisan geology and such. The rocks lying around are friable. The reddish dirt is another clue. Iron in the region, and a particular microbe's been at work. It gets its energy by oxidizing iron. The result is crumbly formations, quickly leached. Be extra careful on steep grades. And even on a level surface, you might fall into a sinkhole hidden by deadfall or whatever."

"I see. Uldor never mentioned that bug. Is it confined to a few areas, so he hadn't encountered it? Yes, I definitely need you with me." We need one another.

They donned their packs. "It's pretty clear about Orichalc," Lissa said. "He fled into the woods, uphill as it chanced. One lyco pursued, but only a short ways, because the growth hindered it more than a Susaian, and the killing was better back in the glade. The noise behind Orichalc and, yes, the ravenousness that he sensed, those made him move as fast as possible for his race, which is quite fast, and keep going for some distance. Philosophers can panic too. Finally he—after calming down and resting, I assume—must have tried to return. Where else was there to go? But in dense woods, an inexperienced person can get completely lost within less than a kilometer, and wander farther and farther astray. It's especially easy on Freydis, where you have no definite shadows or heavenly bodies or anything to steer by. I only hope he soon realized the sensible thing was to settle down and wait to be found. And hope he survives the wait."

They entered the forest. For some meters the going wasn't bad. Lissa wove among hooklike thorns; arms before her face, she parted withes, passed through, released them slowly enough for Hebo to intercept before they slapped him. Then the trail, hitherto clear to a practiced eye, went into the thicket that had baffled the lycosauroid. No, not a coppice, more like a wall, too wide to go around and have any likelihood of finding the track again on the other side. It was a duckwalk or all fours, machete, long pauses to search for the next broken twig, bruised sapling, disarrayed tuft marking where fear had gone. Gloom and rank odors closed in. Sweat runneled over skin, hung in clothes and reeked, grew sticky under the gathering chill. Cries, croaks, whistles jeered from unseen mouths.

Hebo cursed. Lissa marveled at his vocabulary. She'd have to remember some of those phrases. Glancing back, she saw how he struggled. "I was afraid of that," she sighed. "Your tent pack's catching on everything. Get rid of it. It could cost us hours we can't afford."

"After lugging it this far? Bringing it was your idea," he grumbled.

"I don't claim omniscience," she snapped. "And you didn't object."

Lips twisted upward in the wetly gleaming face. "Well, my sleeping bag's waterproof. I hope yours is." He lessened his burden.

When they won free of the brake, progress wasn't much faster. Though this was only slightly more altitude, trees grew farther apart and underbrush became sparse. That, though, meant stretches of bare dirt or exposed rock where it could take minutes to make sure of the traces. Wind moaned louder, leaves soughed, clouds raced low and swart overhead.

"You'd think the lizard would backtrack himself," Hebo growled once.

Lissa told herself not to resent the word he used. She'd been guilty of it too, now and then in the past. "It's all I can do to find out how he went," she reminded him. "Do you expect that a stranger to wilderness could?"

"N-no. You're right. Stupid question. I'm tired, brain going numb. How do you keep fresh?"

She must laugh. "And fragrant? After enough running around in woods, you learn ways to save your strength. No, *you* don't; your body does."

"I wouldn't've thought experience on one planet's useful on another."

"Oh, there are countless differences, of course, but the principles are pretty broad and the techniques pretty adaptable. When I mentioned that to Orichalc, it gave him the idea of persuading me to join the explorers for some years."

"He didn't do you any favor."

She resisted a sharp answer.

The traces angled off. Orichalc had evidently noticed that he had gone above the camp, and sought to turn downhill. Unfortunately, on this irregular ground that was not a simple either-or proposition. A check against the flyer's radio beacon showed that the general direction of the lurching path was almost at right angles to what might have helped. After a while, the descent sharpened. Here creep and erosion had thinned soil, so that trees stood three or four meters apart and gnarly knorrig was commoner than thornbark. In between gray trident bushes, dirt littered with windblown detritus, boulders, and bedrock.

"He must have known by now this was the wrong way." Hebo's voice came hoarse.

"Certainly," Lissa agreed. "I suspect he was fire-thirsty, in random search of a streamlet or a puddle or anything." They had drained their canteens along the way, and refilled them at a pool she had found and the Susaian had not.

The man glanced aloft into roiling, hooting gloom. "No dearth of water by nightfall."

"Which isn't long off. Damn, oh, damn."

"We have lights. I can keep going if you can."

She did not so much reach decision as feel it thrust upon her. "No. In rain and the Freydisan dark, they'd be useless. We'd better hole up, get some rest, proceed after dawn."

Once more, as often during the past hours, they shouted their throats sore. No response. No response. Lissa's vision strained straight ahead through gathering dusk. Beyond the nearest trees, woodland merged into a single blackness. She could still perceive how rapidly the slope rose yonder, and recalled from her aerial view that on its other side the ridge gave on a canyon which Orichalc would surely not enter.

He can't be far. We arrived late, and had to find the signs and read them, but I swear they show him slowing down, closer and closer to exhaustion. Maybe we've less than a klick to go. But in exactly what direction? The cursed wind blows our cries back onto us. Oh, dear kind Orichalc, thirsting, hungering, shivering, alone, alone.

"Too bad we had to leave the tent behind," Hebo said. "No matter how sturdy our bags, if I know hill weather, we'd be glad of a roof."

At least he doesn't blame me, he admits it was necessary. "We can arrange that," Lissa told him, "provided we hurry. Will you hop to my orders?"

He sketched a salute. In the haggard, grimy, stubbly countenance, how boyish his grin flashed.

With her machete she chopped down a slim flexy and lopped off its boughs. Propping an end in a forked knorrig, she leaned the larger branches against the pole and wove the lesser ones between to make a framework. He had gathered withes, leaves, deadfall, whatever small stuff he could find. Together, she directing, they plaited and heaped it over the lattice. "Got to pitch the roof carefully," she explained, "but this will keep us snug."

"Yes, and I notice how the ground slopes," he replied. "We won't get runoff. Good job."

Weary or no, he possessed a quick intelligence. "It's an ancient device, primeval," she said. Unable to resist showing off a bit: "Ordinarily I'd pile a circle of stones outside the entrance and bank a fire there, to reflect heat inside, but we haven't time, it'd probably drown anyway, and our bags will serve. Hoy, pass that vine over the thatch, or it'll blow loose during the night."

The first drops flew heavy, cold, and stinging. "After you," he said with a bow. She crawled into the narrow space. Best avoid possible misunderstandings and undress in the dark. By feel she arranged her things, got out of her stinking clothes, slid into the bedding. Never mind a bath, toothbrush, all ordinary amenities. "Your turn," she called.

He took her hint and also left his light in his pack. Often, inevitably, groping and twisting about, he bumped her. She grew acutely aware of it and commanded herself to be an adult. That didn't quite work. Which was ridiculous, she thought exasperatedly. There had after all been a couple of other humans on the Jonna expedition, and it had become good between her and Jomo Mkato from Brusa, clearly understood on both sides as just physical and friendly, and then after she returned to Asborg she'd renewed two old acquaintances. Had she now a feeling of desperation, the body wanting whatever comfort it could grab?

Well, it wasn't going to get any for a while, not of that kind.

XXXVII

Rain rushed, wind brawled, branches creaked. Where did Orichalc huddle? He'd never been taught how to make a shelter, a fire drill, snares for small game, or, or anything.

Lissa heard a slight metallic pop. She felt more than she saw that Hebo lay raised on an elbow. "I've broken out rations," he said. "You may not be hungry, but I'm starved."

"Hoo! How could I have forgotten? Let me at it."

"Have a spoon— Sorry. I was searching for your hand."

Despite herself, she must suppress a giggle. "That isn't where it grows. Here. Thank you."

Avidly, they shared hardtack and meat paste. "This does beat lying in the open, no matter how well wrapped up," he admitted. "Don't worry. We'll find your friend tomorrow."

Alive, let's hope, said neither of them.

"How'd you acquire all this woodcraft?" he asked. "Sure, I remember how slickly you got around on Jonna, and you mentioned taking outdoor vacations on Asborg, but I had the notion you were mainly a spacefarer."

"One spacefares to someplace," she replied. "I like it best when they're places where a human can breathe."

"How'd you get started on it, anyway? I should think the daughter of a head of a House would find plenty to do at home."

Though her muscles ached, she wasn't sleepy yet. Talking kept thought of Orichalc at bay. "Interest in one kind of nature led to interest in others. Frankly, I'm surprised you haven't learned more about native life, in four years."

"I learned as much as I needed to, and as much more as I

got a chance to." Did she hear a defensive note? "I've been kind of busy, you know."

"I wonder why," she heard herself say.

"Huh? To make money. What else?"

"But in this particular way— No, I don't want another argument. Not tonight. It's only, well, as I said, I can't help wondering."

"What do you mean?" He sounded genuinely puzzled.

She had no choice but to be straightforward. "I've seen the screenings, read the accounts. Those facilities, mining, pumping, refining, synthesizing, lumbering, wrecking the natural environs. Monstrous already, and growing. And now you've established Forholt as a seed of the same thing on this continent too. Why?"

"Somebody would've. Or will your Susaians agree to limit their births and huddle on one island forever? They don't act like they will. Nor should they. Law of life, isn't it? A species expands to fill all the living space it can."

"Nonsense. Natural species keep within bounds." At once she wished she hadn't said that. Population explosions and crashes happened to wildlife also, and ultimately extinction. Before Hebo could seize on her mistake, she continued: "The colonists aren't that many to begin with. Yes, they're looking toward the future. But they hope they can grow in a sane fashion. That's what we're working on, developing nondestructive technology for them."

"Good luck. Meanwhile, though, they need housing, tools, vehicles, robots, factories, chemical plants, every damn thing. Cheaper for them to buy stuff made on the planet than import. Which, if you want moralizing noises, means they spend less of their slim resources than otherwise, and can get on with whatever else they aim to do. Or would you rather they started from scratch in a Stone Age?"

She resolved not to resent the sarcasm, or at least not show resentment. "Of course not. Please believe me, I'm not fanatical. Some modern technology is essential. But on this scale? With more to come, and worse—no. That's what desolated Earth. Restoration there took centuries, and was never complete. It'd most likely be impossible for Freydis."

She caught her breath. The night roared around her. "But I said I'm not looking for a fight. Later, if we must. Here— Well, Captain Hebo, I realize you have your living to make. But why are you doing it with this dirty work?"

"I'll pretend you didn't say 'dirty,' " he answered from low in his throat. "All right, I came to Sunniva from Sol because I thought I'd find people I'd met on Jonna, friendly people on Asborg, who'd maybe give me some ideas, some information about what to try next. And I learned about this need to fill, this opportunity, next door on Freydis."

Again he was holding something back, she felt. Maybe that he'd expected to find her? No, he'd openly admitted as much, yet it certainly wasn't the major reason he stayed. Greed for quick wealth, then? He'd flaunted that. But she'd come to know him yonder, just a little, and it didn't ring true to her that the motive could be so simple.

However, his words offered an opening. "An investment for your capital, as well as your labor?"

"More labor than capital," he said wryly.

"Yes. From the moment I learned it's you who started Venusberg, I've wondered. Those facilities are huge. Even with robotics and nano, they can't have grown from a mustard seed. Not to speak of the land they occupy and exploit. I checked that back on Asborg. Seafell claimed it long ago. They'd never done anything with it before, but I know damn well they wouldn't make you a free gift of the lease merely to help the noble Susaians.

"You never claimed to me that you're a rich man. On the contrary. And the time on Earth must have been costly. Where did you get your capital to invest?"

He was silent for a span amidst the storm-noise. She feared she'd overstepped. But when he responded, it was quietly. "From them, among others. Some from my savings, some from Rikha, and some from Seafell."

"Yes, obviously you've made a deal with them." As for its details, the Houses maintained what secrets they saw fit. If every member knew, there'd have been a shipwreck's worth of leaks, but one or two financiers could keep lips closed and databases secured. "That big, though? You told me you and your partner control Venusberg."

"We do. Their part amounts to a loan, or a mortgage if you like. It's being repaid out of profits, and afterward they'll get a share of those. The contract won't let me say more. Maybe I shouldn't have said this much, but—" Through the gloom she made out that his head was turned her way, his eyes upon her.

"Still, the lender must expect a big payoff, or he, or they or whoever, wouldn't have lent. That by itself is enough to explain why you operate as you do," she said, abruptly bitter.

"I told you, Dzesi and I are free agents."

"Absolutely free?"

"Uh, naturally a couple of their people have positions with us. Advisory."

"And you'd better follow the advice, or they'll call in the loan and close you down."

"God damn it," he exploded, "try being reasonable for a change!" A fist struck the ground. "You're the one who first wanted the Susaian colony, aren't you? How long do you think it can last, hugging Mother Nature? Come the day, they'd mucking well better have a global industrial base!"

Lissa's fingers tightened on the edge of her sleeping bag. "I've been through that argument before."

Memory rose in her, as if she sat again by her father, listening to him explain to some protesters who had invoked their right to be heard at a council of their House:

"Yes, we should perhaps have studied the situation more thoroughly before we made our agreement," he had said in his grave manner. "But though we knew the basic facts, the exact values of the parameters weren't established until our announcement of the decision prompted an intensive research program by the Institute of Planetary Science.

"May I lay out the results? I'll be telling you what several of you, at least, already know, but I wish to make clear that the council understands.

"Freydis is perpetually on the brink of catastrophe. Sunniva was cooler gigayears ago, when the first life developed there, and evolution kept pace with the slow warming, but today the planet is at the inner edge of the habitability zone. Nothing maintains liquid-water temperatures except the worldwide forests. Vegetation from outside can't replace them; nothing else known to us takes up carbon with the same efficiency. At that, the forests barely maintain the composition. If Freydis loses any significant fraction of them, with nothing done to compensate, its biosphere is doomed."

Runaway greenhouse. Increased atmospheric carbon dioxide trapping more solar energy. Rising temperatures evaporating more water, whose vapor is itself a powerful greenhouse gas. Drought, fire, dieback, desert spreading and spreading, while the heat mounts. As the life that renewed them vanishes, oxygen and nitrogen become locked in minerals. The oceans boil. Water molecules go on high, where ultraviolet splits them asunder; the hydrogen escapes into space, the oxygen is soon imprisoned in the rocks. When at last an equilibrium is reached, it prevails over a searing hell, it is the peace of the graveyard or the slag heap.

"And you'd let the Susaians breed till they've crowded out the trees?" somebody cried. "Don't you care?"

"We have pledged our honor," Davy answered. "Remember what a tremendous service the Susaian Orichalc did, not only for Windholm or Asborg or humankind, but every sentient race. If the Dominators had kept a monopoly of what we've since learned, the future might not be very pleasant."

"But we can keep the colony on that island. It's big and fertile. Pretty generous payment, I'd say." The speaker's companions muttered agreement.

Davy shook his head. "That was discussed behind the scenes. Some of the Old Truth leaders felt it would be fair. Unfortunately, it would be unenforceable. One fundamental of their belief is individual liberty. We can sympathize, can't we? Generations to come would revolt against forced limitations on family size. Best to face reality and help them cope with it.

"Besides, by now more Houses than only Windholm and Seafell support the idea. A Susaian population expanding over the planet means a growing market—for goods, services, everything—which pays out of its own productivity. Freydis will at last become profitable."

"At the price of its life!"

"The scientists don't extrapolate serious ecological trouble for another five centuries."

"I plan to be alive then. Most of us do."

"Mass extinction won't happen. Haven't you seen the proposals?"

"Yes, and we here don't like any of them."

Nor did Lissa. She hadn't had the heart to say so, then and there, nor much about it afterward, for she knew that her father wasn't happy about it himself.

She heard the mighty rushing of wind through the trees and across the heights. From somewhere resounded a call, a wild creature. It was like a trumpet in the night. It sang of marvels, mysteries, and nobody knew what insights to gain, or what profits of understanding and inspiration could be forgone forever.

"Yes," she told Hebo, "I've seen the grandiose, expensive schemes. Increase the planet's albedo, for instance, by orbiting a cloud of reflective particles around it. Or cut down the sunlight with a giant reflector at the L2 point. Or— Never mind. No doubt it can be done, if money's to be made. But hardly any of Freydis' life can survive a change like that. There'll be nothing but cities, machines, and drab gene-engineered plantations. A corpse with worms and fungi feasting on it."

The bags side by side, she felt him stiffen. "How dramatic," he said. With a sneer?

"We can do better. That's what we've begun on, a handful of Susaians and humans, finding the ways. Already—"

"This's turned into a head-butting contest," he growled. "I'm dead worn out, and we've got work to do in the morning. Your work. Goodnight."

He rolled over, his back to her. The rainfall loudened. She lay staving off anger, fear, despair, until she blundered into an uneasy sleep.

XXXVIII

She had set her brain to wake at the earliest clear light. In these latitudes at this time of year, nights were short. She sprang to consciousness, gasped, and sat up. Hebo's eyes were already open. They widened—in appreciation, she felt fleetingly—but he put an arm across them before she could cross hers over her breasts. "Do you want to dress first or shall I?" he mumbled. Laughter broke from her of its own accord and shook her to full alertness.

The rain had ended a couple of hours ago, easing her worst dread. When she emerged, she found mist a-smoke over the ground and among the trees. The cold didn't belong on the Freydis of popular imagination. A whole world, though, a whole congregation of miracles like none other in the universe— How was Orichalc? She sped to the last signs she had found yesterday.

"I'll fix breakfast," offered Hebo at her back. She nodded absently, her mind concentrated on brush, dead leaves, mud. It was not easy to trace the spoor farther; the rain had obliterated much. In vague wise she noticed him gather deadwood, use a lighter to start a fire, make a grill of green sticks on which to heat food in its containers. Well, naturally he'd have elementary skills.

He brought her a serving, together with his own. She glanced up from her crouch. He didn't look as though he had slept well, either, but if he could smile, so could she. "Here." She lifted a branchful of crimson berries she had cut off a chance-encountered bush. "Redballs for sweetener."

"Have you eaten any?" he exclaimed.

"Not yet. I meant to share— What's wrong?"

"Whew! That's not a proper redball, it's a highland species, poisonous to us. Those little yellow dots on the leaves mark it. You'd have been one sick girl."

"Thanks." You *are* necessary, damn you. And you are trying to be friendly again, damn you. And I think you're succeeding, damn you. Lissa took the opened container, set it down, spooned food from it with her right hand while her left hand turned debris over.

"Can you really still pick up sign?" he wondered.

"Yes. Tracks in the dirt don't all slump away under rain. Many collect water before silt starts to fill them, and are temporarily more visible than before. Leaves blow onto others and protect them. Bent twigs and such don't disappear overnight. The problem does get extra complicated. I find plenty of breaks in the trail. Just the same, I'm getting an approximate direction. Once this flinking fog lifts I'll have better clues. Orichalc wouldn't move purely at random, you see. No animal does. Whether or not he had much consciousness left, the body itself would tend to follow the least strenuous course. If we look ahead and study the contours—A-a-ah!" A breeze made rags of the gray. Dripping trees, begemmed shrubs, wetly gleaming boulders hove into sight.

Having gulped their ration, swallowed some milk, and separated to do what else was needful, the searchers moved onward. Lissa led the way, slowly, often pausing to cast about or for eyes and fingers to probe, yet with a confidence that waxed and tingled in her. Up the slope they climbed, topped the ridge, and gazed across vastness.

The air had cleared, though it remained bleak, and heaven was featureless, colorless, save where the unseen sun brightened it a little, low above eastern bulwarks. Ground slanted downward, begrown with bushes and dwarf trees well apart, otherwise ruddy-bare to a narrow ledge. Underneath this a talus slope plunged into unseen depths. The far side of the gorge reared a kilometer beyond. Its course zigzagged north and south, a barrier between distant plain and distant mountains.

"Look!" Lissa shouted. "The trail, straight and plain!" Runoff had gouged the slight hollowings unmistakeably deeper. Wavery as the footprints of a man staggering at the end of his endurance, tail dragging behind, they pointed to her goal.

Hebo caught her arm. "Easy," he warned. "Remember what kind of soil and rock we've got hereabouts. You could lose your footing at best, touch off a small landslide at worst."

"Orichalc didn't." Still, she placed her boots warily, one, two, one, two, on the way down.

The reddish body lay coiled in a clump of scrub. Lissa fell to her knees, crushing branches, to cast arms about it. "Orichalc, Orichalc, *s-s-siya-a,* shipmate, here I am, how are you, comrade, comrade?"

Cheek against skin, she felt not the wonted warmth but a faint incessant shuddering. Otherwise the Susaian barely stirred. Glazed eyes turned toward her and drooped again. The least of sibilations reached her ears.

She scrambled erect. "Hypothermia," she heard her voice say; it rang within her skull. "Extreme. Fatal, I think, unless we act fast."

"He didn't wear any clothes?" Hebo asked, as if automatically.

"None of them foresaw the need, when they'd spend every night in camp." Her own tongue likewise moved of itself. "You know, you ought to know, Susaians seldom do. They're warm-blooded, with thermostats better than ours. But the wind chill factor last night overloaded his. You or I would be dead. He's dying."

"What to do?"

"We haven't got a thermal unit. Quick! Unroll your sleeping bag, open it fully, spread it out." Lissa released her backpack, dropped it, squatted to pluck at the fastenings of her sack.

He followed suit while he asked, "What've you got in mind?"

"Warming him, of course. Putting him between the padded fabrics and ourselves." She glanced about, saw a spot that wasn't truly level but was not so canted that they would roll off, and brought her bag there. Returning, she said, "It'll take both of us to carry him. Susaians are massier than you'd think."

Hebo had the strength to be gentle as he hauled the limp form up across his shoulders. Lissa took the head end. Grunting with effort, they bore Orichalc over and laid him down on her bedding, stretched out. Hebo fetched his and put it above. "Now what?" he inquired.

"Clothes off," Lissa directed. He gaped. "Strip, I said! To chaos with modesty." She ripped at her garments.

He removed his more slowly, eyes at first locked on her. Then, doubtless realizing how he stared, he swiveled his head away. A moment later he turned his back while he completed the task. She was already between the bags. As he faced her again, he tried to cover himself with one hand. Though big, it wasn't quite enough.

Lissa couldn't help herself. Laughter pealed. "Oh, fout, don't worry!" she called. "I'd feel slighted if you did not react. C'mon, join the party."

He grinned and obeyed. They snuggled close on either side of Orichalc. That put their arms in contact across the Susaian while glance met glance over his head. The chill made them shiver too. Then as heat flowed from them, replenishing itself within, and the victim's blood began to respond, they felt a growing voluptuous comfort.

"Yeah, I recall hearing of this trick," he said. "Never had to use it before, and I doubt I'll ever do it again with so shapely a trailmate."

Respond amicably, but don't be too encouraging, Lissa warned herself. "Thank you, kind sir. We'll be here a fairish while. May as well relax and enjoy it, now that we know it's working."

"It does feel good, saving a life. Uh, that sounds smug, doesn't it? Wasn't meant to be."

"You mean it doesn't fit your rough-and-tough image. Well, I admit to a touch of smugness in me, and consider it well-earned. Relax, I said."

"How to pass the time? Not with more wrangling, I hope."

"Me too. We must both have a lot of stories from our pasts that we haven't swapped."

"Good idea. Want to start?"

"What?" she teased. "A man doesn't snatch at a chance to talk about himself?"

"I know my biography." A shadow passed over his face. He could not yet be quite sure how much of it was gone from him. He lightened again, but she decided to steer clear of talk about Earth. "Yours is new."

"No, do go first, please."

He regarded her for a moment. "You want something to get your mind off fretting about your friend, don't you?" he asked softly. "All right, I'll try."

So he has that much sensitivity, she thought. Maybe I shouldn't be surprised. Still, it's good to know. She let her hand brush across his. "Thank you."

"Um-m-m, something really different from right now. . . . This happened maybe fifty years ago, to a fellow I knew. You not being a girl fresh out of convent school," whatever that meant, "it shouldn't offend you too much."

The anecdote was bawdy and funny. Two hapless lovers, stranded on an asteroid with supplies and equipment but otherwise only their two spacesuits, and nothing else to do until the relief ship would arrive and rescue them, weeks hence, applying their engineering ingenuity to the problem—Lissa whooped laughter. Only later did she wonder who the man was to whom the incident had really happened.

As if in response, Orichalc writhed a bit, raised his head, let it sink again but whispered a few words. Lissa's trans was in her pack. However, by now the Susaian understood Anglay. "Everything is well," she said gladly. "Rest. Get warm. We'll soon take you home."

"To New Halla?" Hebo asked.

"To our base on the coast," Lissa replied. "From there, we

can call for further transportation if need be, but I don't think we'll have to. A couple of days' relaxation ought to put Orichalc in fine fettle."

"What'll he do with it? Isn't the upland project spoiled?"

"Not permanently. First he can join another group, maybe my river cruise—"

The muzzle brushed her cheek. "S-s-s," she heard, and words that must mean something like, "I would enjoy that, your company, darling comrade." She patted the big bald head.

"Meanwhile somebody can talk with Uldor at Forholt," she continued. "If he's up to it, and I bet he soon will be, we can arrange audiovisual transmissions, so a new expedition can have the benefit of his advice till he's recovered himself. I can lead it, once we've taken care of my canoers, if nobody better is available."

He studied her for a spell before he murmured, "My God, you're a hopeful one still. But just what is it you're so hopeful for?"

"I've tried to tell you."

"In snatches. We keep being interrupted." He smiled ruefully. "Or interrupting ourselves. I only got from you what I'd heard about in a fuzzy, general way. It'd always seemed too far-fetched to me to bet the store on. Maybe, while we wait here, you could rightfully explain."

Now she was happy, yes, eager to discuss immediate reality. "It hasn't been a secret, but it hasn't been publicized either, so I suppose I can't blame you for not knowing more. Partly that's because the people working on it don't want to make overblown promises. They, we need more scientific evidence, more data on the Freydisan biosphere and its ecologies, before we can draw up a comprehensive scheme."

Go ahead, take the risk. "Also, if we raise premature expectations, they'd be bound to cause public disappointment and disbelief. This is a long-range, gradual thing. And there are those, even on New Halla, who'd take advantage of that disappointment to undermine support and build opposition. No offense, Torben. Honestly, none. We know full well the colony needs a base of conventional industries to start from, to build on. What we want to prevent is them becoming much larger and more widespread than they are. That leads toward over-commitment, outright dependency, and the end result—I've spoken already of the end result. Certain interests want exactly that to happen. They stand to profit hugely. Not just in return on their investments, but in the power that control of such a system will give them." In a rush: "I believe as independent a spirit as you would stand against that."

He nodded, showing no resentment. "In principle, sure." He grinned a bit. "I don't care for fat cats. Keep 'em lean and hard, I say." Soberly: "I'm here to make money, but within decent limits. Trouble is to figure out what they are."

Yes, she thought, he is looking toward something else. And dropping no hint about it.

"What is your alternative, anyway?" he went on. "How much chance has it got of working?"

"The basic concept is almost ridiculously simple and obvious," she told him with mounting enthusiasm. "It went far toward rehabilitating Earth, till Earth civilization became so—so ethereal that industry and commerce are irrelevant. It's used in different ways and degrees on several other planets, including Asborg. It isn't striking there, because the settlers began with a remarkably Earthlike world and with state-of-the-art technology, nano, robotic, self-recycling, that doesn't need to draw heavily on the environment. Besides, huge territories are still held as preserves by the Houses."

"You mean gene-modification. Sure. Can you do it on the scale you'll need for a global civilization?"

"That's what we're working toward. It'll take a tremendous lot of research, sequencing and reading the genetic codes of millions of species, detailing their biochemistry, working out their evolutionary histories, understanding how they interact, everything, on a world that is *not* very Earthlike. In the end, though—

microbes that extract and refine minerals, buildings that grow out of the soil, food, fiber, chemicals, not from farms or factories but from the forests that keep Freydis alive."

"What'll that do to your beloved wilderness? Sounds to me sort of like the nightmare you were laying out yesterday."

"No, not truly, not at all if things work out the way we hope. Of course there'll be some conventional artifacts and processes, but minimal. Besides, 'wilderness' is a relative concept. It doesn't mean chaos. The life you see around you is in balance, though it does change with changing conditions. What we dream of is a civilization not opposed to nature, but integrated with it, both in and of it. Something altogether new. No telling how it will develop, what shapes it will take, what the rest of the galaxy might learn from it."

"Visionary."

"We mean to move toward it step by strictly practical step. If we're given the chance."

" 'Bold,' I should've said." Hebo smiled into her eyes. "Except that's too weak a word. A scheme bound to appeal to one like you, Lissa." His gaze dropped. "Could I think about it for a while?"

"I was wishing you would," she answered softly.

The silence that fell beneath a rising wind grew more and more companionable.

Finally Orichalc stirred, making as if to move from between them. Lissa had been feeling renewed warmth in the smooth, muscular body. "I think we can let go of you," she told him. "But you stay under covers for now, hear me?"

She slipped forth, bounded to her feet, and hastily dressed. Hebo followed suit. They were careful about keeping back to back till they were done.

Thereupon she said, "Our patient's out of danger, I suppose. But you must have noticed how cut and bruised he is—thorns, rocks—and probably still weakened, in poor shape to travel cross country. Can we do an airlift?"

He frowned. "You'd better stay with him while I fetch the flyer. Whether a safe landing is possible hereabouts, I don't know. If not, I can try hovering and lowering a stirrup cable, though that might be tricky in this weather. Let me look around for a more promising spot close by."

The wind had strengthened as the air warmed. It boomed, slewed about, shook boughs, sent dust devils awhirl. He's right, Lissa thought.

His tall form zigzagged away from her, stopping to examine outcrops and dig bootheel into gravel, till he reached the ledge above the canyon. She saw him glance at his bracelet, and well-nigh read his mind. Guided by the radio beacon, he could make most of his return distance on that bare strip instead of struggling through the brush. A new smile tugged at her lips.

The rock broke beneath his feet. He flailed his arms, then pitched downward out of sight.

XXXIX

Lissa screamed and bounded forward. Orichalc sibilated an alarm behind her. Whoa! she told herself amidst the hammers in her pulse. No use two of us going over. If the stone betrayed him, how easily it could fool me.

Slowed to a gliding walk, she sought Hebo's footprints and took that exact route until it approached the verge. There she hunkered down, peered at the rock and rubble ahead, piecemeal made sure of where it had crumbled and where it might crumble and where it seemed reasonably safe. Cracks meant water seepage, which occasionally froze and expanded; but you must also shun bands and blotches of soft iron oxide. . . .

Prone, she thrust her head over the edge and squinted. Talus littered a slant into remote mistful depths. Hebo sprawled on its darkness, come to precarious rest after sliding some four meters. His face, turned skyward, was smeared with blood, and he did not stir; but the brilliant red stream out of his right thigh showed a heart still beating.

A sharp edge cut a major vessel, she knew. He's exsanguinating. If he doesn't get help fast, he's dead. Eternally. We couldn't bring him to revival before the cerebrum cells that make him human decayed beyond restoration.

Pebbles gritted under clawed feet. She felt Orichalc plucking the trans out of her pack. "You should have stayed," she answered automatically.

"One can summon up one's ultimate reserves when one must," the Susaian replied. "I believe I can assist you to recover our comrade."

"Our" comrade, she noticed. The thought flickered past and was gone. She weighed her chances. Did Orichalc overestimate his own strength? Maybe so, but if she took care, then she needn't perish, though Hebo certainly would. Trapped on an unclimbable hillside, she could nevertheless call Forholt by radio satellite, and a rescue party would arrive. Unless, of course, her efforts triggered a slide. Then she'd lie chopped to flitches, smashed to pulp, buried beyond finding.

No time for worries. Glancing about, she saw the bush Orichalc plainly was counting on. It grew within centimeters of the edge, but inspection showed thick roots that must go deep, and above them a bonsai twisting that decades or centuries of wind must have wrought. Probably it could withstand a few hundred kilos' worth of stress.

A dash back to fetch cords or straps would take too long. Cutting a stick, she put it between her teeth. She pulled off her shirt, slashed it in two, knotted the halves together at the bottoms and one sleeve around Orichalc's neck. The other sleeve she took in her hand, with a bight to secure her grip. Orichalc curled his tail around the lower stem of the bush. Lissa sat down and went over the side on her rear end.

Shards rattled, slid, slashed at pants and boots. The Susaian strained backward, easing her descent, paying out his length bit by bit until at last he was stretched taut. The scree must be cruelly painful against skin, but she heard no murmur.

At the end of her line she lay side by side with Hebo. She dared not kneel, but by cautious use of palm and elbow she could support herself well enough to work on him. Her sheath knife slid forth again. Best single tool the mind of man has yet hit on, she thought, not for the first time. She ripped the trouser leg, exposed the wound, cut a cloth strip, made a tourniquet with the stick and tightened it. The lethal flow ceased.

Sweat beaded his face under the blood, he felt clammy and his breathing was shallow, yes, he was in shock. Got to get him upstairs quick. Slip her improvised hawser under his back, below the arms, and secure it. "All right, Orichalc, haul away!"

Could he? If not, she'd yell for help and try to keep Hebo alive where they were. Whether she could or not was a crapshoot. It was just about as uncertain whether his weight, as he was drawn higher, would start a rockslip fatal to her.

Somehow it didn't. Somehow, from somewhere, Orichalc got the power to haul him aloft, undo the line and cast it down, raise her in turn. She went backside under, keeping her bare torso above the flinders that would have lacerated it. The tough material of her trousers didn't give way, but she'd be seating herself gingerly for the next couple of days.

Pulled to the ledge, she lay briefly, heaving air in and out of her lungs, before she clambered to her feet. Orichalc was almost as limp as Hebo. "I can drag him the rest of the way by myself," she mumbled. "Can you make it? You've got to."

"I . . . can . . . since you . . . wish—" her friend whispered. "And then?"

"Why, then—" Laughter shrilled. "We apply naked bodies to him, you and I."

Once between the covers, both humans unclad and Orichalc on his other side, Lissa sent her message. A voice from Forholt Station sounded faint but crisp out of the bracelet: "We'll dispatch our ambulance immediately. It should reach you in about an hour. Can you manage that long?"

"I'd better, hadn't I?" she retorted.

She could not simply lie waiting by the man. From time to time she must tend him, massage, loosen the tourniquet and tighten it anew. The blood that ran out made a gluey mess, but some went into the injured limb to keep the flesh alive. Of course, if gangrene set in, a surgeon could amputate, and at a clinic on Asborg they could regenerate what was lost. However, she didn't want him subjected to that.

Strong and healthy, he responded well. Before the medics appeared, his eyes fluttered open to hers.

Lissa must needs admire the adroitness of the rescuers. The

ambulance hovered high and lowered a platform which had thrusters to stabilize it against the wind. A paramedic started work on Hebo while they lifted him. "You did fine, milady," he said. "This shot's the only added thing he needs to put him out of danger. Thanks. We're pretty fond of the old man."

Aboard the vehicle it was possible to wash, receive treatment for injuries, and don fresh clothes. Lissa hadn't minded the masculine looks she received—to the extent that she noticed them—but how good to settle down warmly swaddled and fall asleep by Orichalc.

Neither woke till they landed at Forholt. The director greeted them courteously and offered overnight accomodations, that they be well rested before they were flown back to their base. They accepted, and emerged from bed only for dinner. Nonetheless, at the meal Lissa enjoyed telling the staff what had happened. Nobody mentioned the dispute.

As they returned to their quarters, Orichalc asked, "Can we visit honored Torben Hebo in the morning?"

"I'm sure we can," she said. "I mean to."

"With some privacy."

"Hm?" She caught the implication. A thrill shot through her. "Well, we'll see what the conditions are."

XL

They slept luxuriously late and enjoyed an extravagant breakfast before they walked over to sickbay. Morning had brought a mild, silvery rain, filled with odors of growth and cheery animal cries. It veiled the ugliness of prospecting operations. The buildings immediately around were for housing, recreation, and the like, almost deserted while the day's work was under way.

As Lissa and Orichalc rounded one of these, they saw a man coming in the other direction. She jarred to a halt. Sensing tension, the Susaian dropped to a half crouch, taut beneath the healpatches scattered over his wounds.

The man neared them and stopped too. Raindrops glistened in dark curls. The sharp features drew into a smile. "Good day, milady," he greeted. "I was hoping we'd meet again."

"Good day, Romon Kaspersson Seafell," she replied formally.

He sketched a salute. "And to you, honorable Orichalc," he said.

"Likewise," the Susaian answered through the trans, "although we are not acquainted, sir."

"I've heard of you, however, seen your image, admired your deeds. Who on Asborg and now Freydis hasn't?"

Lissa wondered whether Romon really felt the cordiality he expressed. Probably not much. "I didn't know you were here," she said.

"I'm fairly often on the planet, milady," he told her. "House Seafell has a substantial investment in Venusberg Enterprises, and naturally wants to keep up with what's going on, beyond what scheduled reports we get."

She nodded. "And you're the observer."

"One of them. Perhaps the main one. I do have a suitable technical background as well as experience on other planets. Besides, Captain Hebo and I have been associated from the beginning. I first introduced him to the financiers who've backed his venture. In fact, I'd say I had more than a little to do with persuading them to it."

"That was good of you."

Romon made a new smile. " '—a good deed in a naughty world.' " It must be one of his quotations, for she barely got the meaning of the antique words. "Actually, I confess to self-interest, as well as the interest of my House. We expect to gain from this. And, yes, the undertaking's fascinating, often exciting."

"I daresay the news about our rescue flashed from here, around the globe to headquarters."

"Of course. I'm glad I was on hand." Momentarily, his voice shook. "And, and you'll never know how glad that you came through safe. The greatest poets couldn't have told—" The bland mask came back down. "I flew over as soon as possible."

"Thank you . . . for your kind thought."

"You have come from seeing our friend?" inquired Orichalc.

"Correct," Romon said. "He's doing excellently." He stood for an instant in the soft rain before he added, "I wanted to see—both—all three of you, and offer my best wishes." The tone went dry. "Besides, I hadn't had time to visit Forholt before, it being so new. I'll take the opportunity to look around; the Seafell sponsors ought to be interested in a first-hand account." Again the mask cracked. "If only we could talk more." Hastily: "But there's a great deal for me to do back at headquarters. I'll stop by in a few hours and call on Captain Hebo again, briefly, just to reassure myself, then I must return. I hope we can meet with more leisure sometime before too long, milady and . . . sir. May your stay here be pleasant and your trip home happy."

"Likewise, sir," they responded. He strode onward.

Lissa kept herself from staring after him. "Is he really that rushed?" she wondered. "This isn't quite like him, unless he's changed in the last several years."

"I sensed conflicting emotions," Orichalc said. "They are warm toward you, I think, although with an ambivalence. I believe he would have liked to linger, but feels stressed. Or is 'eager' more appropriate? Perhaps he is indeed anxious to get on with his business in the opposite hemisphere."

"Not necessarily skulduggery," Lissa conceded.

"You are clearly not cordial toward him."

"Nor hostile, really. He's always been polite enough, even made amiable overtures I pretended not to notice. Because I've simply never been able to like him. Due mainly to conflicting views of the universe, I suppose. I wouldn't have expected he'd be this brusque." Lissa shrugged and grinned. "So I should be relieved he didn't suggest we share lunch! C'mon, let's go."

They found the infirmary nearly vacant. The injured Susaians had been returned to New Halla after getting preliminary care, and Uldor Enarsson was being given preliminary physical therapy prior to making the same trip. The medics would soon decide whether he could finish his recovery there or had better be taken from the spaceport on the island to Asborg for it. The prognosis was favorable in either case.

An attendant conducted Lissa and Orichalc to Hebo's room. It was small but adequate. A window stood open to the wet wild air, which sent fragrance eddying from a vase of fireblossoms on the bedside table. Pale from blood loss, he nonetheless sat propped up, alert, screening a book. A biopromoter encircled his thigh, humming mutedly as it hastened cellular renewal.

He stopped the screening when they entered. She identified the text. *Rachel Irvingsdaughter's Saga*, from pioneer times on Asborg, why, that was a favorite of hers. His hail rang forth. "Milady! Comrade! Welcome!"

She offered her hand. The clasp lingered. "How are you?" she asked.

"Fine, considering. I should be on my feet and out of here in two or three days at most. Meanwhile, the place is programmed for halfway decent food."

She nodded at the vase. "Nice of them to give you the flowers, too."

"Oh, Romon Kaspersson brought those. From clear across the globe."

"That hardly sounds like him."

"Yeah, he's mentioned knowing you." Hebo laughed. "Don't stand there so astounded. He was only the courier. They're from a lady in my office."

Lissa discovered she wasn't quite happy to hear that, even though it explained what might otherwise have been an unsuspected side of Romon's character. And Torben's? "She must . . . think highly of you."

"Well, we're pretty good friends. Romon himself didn't have much else to convey. He'll look in again later today, then take off."

"Yes, he told us. We met on the walk."

"Hey, for God's sake, why're we gabbing about that? Sit down, please do. I've been waiting and waiting for you."

And I didn't bring flowers, Lissa thought. Not that I had a chance to get any. She took a chair beside him. Orichalc coiled on the floor, head raised.

An unwonted awkwardness came upon Hebo. His voice stumbled a bit. "It seems I owe you two my life."

"As I owe mine to both of you," Orichalc replied. "Yours would not have been imperilled had you not come after me."

Lissa made a flinging gesture. "Spung the sentiments! We all three clowned our way through a string of bollixes that should never have happened in the first place. Because we were ignorant, right?"

"I wouldn't call you that, ever," Hebo said. "And this makes twice you've saved me, milady Windholm. I haven't forgotten the time on Jonna. I never will."

Orichalc gazed at him before briefly bowing his head and

whistling three low notes of melody. Lissa recognized the sound and the gesture; they had been given her in the past, a sign of sympathy and respect. It struck her like a wave that the Susaian felt directly what she could merely guess at, how much it signified that this man thus opened his heart.

"I'm Lissa, Torben," she blurted. "After everything we've been through together."

He was silent for a few heartbeats, until, very softly: "Thanks. Thank you."

Orichalc's look upon him seemed to intensify, almost to glow.

"Maybe we can see more of each other, oftener?" Hebo proposed. "Peaceful-like, I mean."

Lissa half wished the Susaian weren't here. It complicated fibbing. "I'm afraid we'll both be awfully busy."

"Not that much. If we don't let ourselves be."

"Take time off?" He nodded. She decided on blunt honesty. "I'd like that if the situation were different. I could try to arrange it without disrupting my work. But— I'm sorry, Torben, I truly am, but I doubt I could ever quite get out of my mind that it's work to oppose what you're aiming at, and my side is the underdog."

"That's not right!" he protested. "You agreed Freydis needs some regular industries."

"Yes. A minimum, and the goal should be to phase them out as far as possible once the colony learns new, better ways. Which it has to start doing soon, or Venusberg will have taken the planet over."

"A somewhat exaggerated dread, my dear," Orichalc said.

Lissa scowled. "You both know what I'm getting at."

"But do you know what Captain—Torben is talking about?"

She stared.

Hebo turned his own look on the Susaian. "How much do you sense?" he demanded.

"I cannot read your mind, sir."

"What can you read, then?" Hebo asked roughly.

"Good will. Hesitation. An inner loneliness."

"Him, lonely?" exclaimed Lissa.

"Perhaps I should say nothing further. I have no wish to give offense."

Lissa wasn't used to being abashed. "Well, I—I don't want to intrude—on your privacy, either—Torben. Maybe I'd better say goodbye." She started to rise.

He reached a hand toward her. "No. Wait. Please, damn it."

She sat back and could not escape smiling.

He pondered for half a minute, then slapped his sound leg and laughed aloud. "All right!" he nearly roared. "You win. And I'm glad."

Lissa's pulse jumped. "Do you want to tell us something? We want to hear."

His voice dropped, his face tautened. "If you'll both first swear secrecy. I mean secrecy. Not a breath or a hint before I give you leave, which I don't expect will be for several years." He looked at the Susaian. "Your mates will know you're keeping something from them, Orichalc, but I'm betting they won't pry."

"That perception will of itself motivate them not to," replied the other. "This is a basic ethic."

Hebo's gaze returned to Lissa. "And—I think we've learned quite a bit about each other, we three," he said.

"Enough for trust," Lissa answered low. "More than enough. Yes, you have my promise, Torben. My oath, by the honor of my House."

She hoped with sudden passion that she wouldn't regret giving it. Well, if so, maybe she could talk him out of whatever he intended.

"I have nothing to offer but my bare word," said Orichalc. His people didn't need spoken pledges.

"Plenty for me," Hebo sighed. "I must admit it's been lonely. Oh, I've got friends here, fun, the kind of ties that shared work makes. But always I'm hiding the thing that really matters, from everybody but Dzesi." And she isn't human, Lissa thought. "It's a kind of permanent lie. Now—"

He leaned back, pausing again, before he went on, his tone gone decisive: "You'd have learned anyway, in due course. Everybody would have. Supposing anything comes of my notion. Today I can share it with you."

"Who knows but what we may be able to help a little?" said Orichalc.

He kens honest intentions, Lissa realized. Warmth flowed through her.

Hebo drew breath and plunged into his explanation in the headlong way she had come to know.

"I've thought about the Forerunners quite a lot, off and on, because of what happened on Jonna. When I heard about the black hole collision, and how you were there for it, maybe that's what made the notion click together. A grazing crash, of a sort probably unique in the history of the galaxy, almighty rare in the whole universe. Did the Forerunners predict it, way back when they or their machines were scouting this neighborhood? Wouldn't they have wanted observation from close by?"

"Do you believe they could have calculated the event?" asked Orichalc, incredulous. "The latest traces we have of them are some three million years old."

"Not terribly long ago, when you remember that an orbit around the galactic center takes close to 200 million years at our distance from it. Besides, their oldest things we've found seem to go back at least five million years. Which gives 'em maybe two million to collect astronomical data and run the calculations with computing power I imagine makes our best look puny. Yes, I know about chaos theory, but my own amateur figuring convinces me that times and distances weren't so great that exact prediction was impossible. After all, those were two pretty damn massive bodies. Not easily perturbed."

"We detected no probes or anything else foreign when we were there," Lissa said.

Hebo grinned. "You were kind of busy."

"But neither have later expeditions."

"Would you expect them to? We're talking a volume of something like a cubic light-year. Hell, we today can build probes that're bug size and radiate practically nothing."

"But things coming the whole way from wherever the Forerunners now are—"

"Oh, they'd've established a local base before they left these parts. At a nearby star, seems obvious to me."

"That could mean any of thousands," Orichalc objected.

"As a matter of fact, several of the nearer ones have been looked at since I was there," Lissa added. "Negative, at least as far as Forerunner spoor is concerned."

"I know," Hebo retorted. "Think I haven't been following every scrap of such news that comes in? What those crews wanted to see was whether there're planets with biospheres to be affected when the radiation gets there. Which means they went to likely stars—and, sure, found three that scientists will want to keep an eye on. But those are small stars, more or less like Sol or Sunniva. It would be hard, maybe out of the question, to forecast their exact trajectories that far in advance.

"A fairly massive one, however, that's something else. And the observations—starting with those your *Dagmar* took as a matter of routine—show a type B5 giant only about fifteen light-years off."

Amazement gaped at him.

"My guess," he said. "That kind generally has planets, or at least asteroidal junk for von Neumann machines to reproduce off of. Why haven't I already gone for a look? Well, those are mighty fierce environments. My little *Tramp* does okay around smaller, cooler suns, but at that, she'd better steer clear even of big planets, subjovian and up. Whoever goes yonder will need top-of-the-line powerplant, radiation screening, and whatnot else. A complete retrofit for me, or better, a whole new ship. Expensive."

He nodded. "Yes, I'm keeping this to myself because I mean

to get there first. If I find what I'm hoping for, all that information—an entire, working Forerunner base—will make my fortune. Not that I'd want to monopolize the place, or could if I did want to. But just the fact that it exists, plus whatever knowledge I can pick up on the first trip—remember, Lissa, how I said once on Jonna, the only real interstellar currency is information? In spite of being interrupted, Dzesi and I did fairly well on discoverers' awards and so on. This one would let us retire, to live however we jolly well please till the universe burns out.

"I came to Sunniva from Earth—oh, sure, thinking you'd be on Asborg, but also because I'd gotten wind of an opportunity to make the money I'd need. Which turned out to be true, and is why I'm here, doing what I am, Lissa. Till I've made my stake. A few more years, I estimate. Meanwhile, you've admitted that Venusberg's work is useful. Maybe we could've gone at it a tad more heedfully, but the investors wouldn't've sat still for that, and the damage to the planet isn't so terrible or unrepairable, is it? When I'm ready to sell out, I'll ask you to help me make the terms and arrangements."

She could only think to mumble, "Seafell won't like this one bit."

Hebo grinned. "Seafell will be stuck with a, what d'you call it, a *fait accompli.* Not that they'll be cheated. Everything will be within the contract, and they'll have gotten a fair return."

"They might not think it is—" But this is the dreariest detail stuff, she thought. He's talking of adventure and glory. Maybe of everybody's future.

"Has no one else thought as you have?" Orichalc wondered.

Hebo shrugged. "Evidently not, or we'd've heard. Unless whoever it is has more reasons than getting rich. In which case, I suspect we'd do a public service by finding out. The gear I want on my ship includes weapons."

"I see. I see," Lissa said in slight shock and rising exhilaration. "I don't know yet if I quite agree with your plan, but— Oh, Torben!"

She sprang to her feet, leaned over, and kissed him. He responded. Positive feedback set in until they remembered Orichalc. He had kept tactfully still; nonetheless, they broke off, he somewhat rueful, she coloring.

"Oh, yes," she breathed, "we will be seeing each other again, Torben."

It happened sooner after she left Forholt than she had expected, and was less joyous.

XLI

The thought struck her a day after she had returned to New Halla, too late for her to warn him. And maybe an unnecessary, even stupid notion, she told herself over and over. Certainly there was no point now in passing it on to him. She'd risk looking like a fool in his eyes. Or would she? He must have had far more experience of trickery in his long and checkered centuries than her comparatively innocent life had met with. He'd appreciate wariness. Wouldn't he?

And did it matter so much what he felt?

Anyhow, as things had worked out, for the time being she and only she could do something about the situation.

She considered calling her father, or actually going to him, for his help. But no need yet. In fact, it might narrow her options. He was a dear; he was also a traditionalist of sorts, whose concept of honor sometimes got unreasonably stiff. Without much better evidence than she could offer, he might feel that her idea was a gratuitous insult to House Seafell, and therefore unworthy of Windholm.

A private investigator? She had never dealt with any. Besides, what she wanted done was simple enough. All it required was discretion, and perhaps a few connections here and there. Her sister Evana and brother-in-law Olavi Jonsson qualified on both counts. They happened to be back on Asborg, taking a few years to personally cultivate their investments. She gave them a call—encrypted, just in case. Yes, they could easily oblige her; and when she didn't say why, they didn't ask. She'd doubtless let them know eventually. Meanwhile, and always, the children of Davy and Maren trusted each other.

Lissa resumed her work on Freydis. Not quite three months later, she came into bush camp at eventide and found a message on her communicator. Thereupon it took three planetary rotations to plead private emergency, arrange for her replacement, flit to the colony, and commandeer a flyer. It wasn't a speedster; the six or seven hours it spent going halfway around the globe became interminable.

Nonsense, ridiculous, she muttered in her mind. There can't be this kind of urgency. Can there?

Night lay over Venusberg when she arrived. She was faintly glad of that. The vast scars that mining and manufacturing had gouged in highland forest were amply infuriating on video. Or simply depressing, and she in reaction against sadness? After all, Torben was right, this was inevitable in the early stages of settlement. It shouldn't have been, but mortals being what they were, it was. And the wound, the ulcer, was still tiny on the body of a whole world.

It must not be let grow much bigger.

Though operations sprawled, habitation huddled mostly dark. More machines than people labored here. The airfield glared out of a surrounding murk. She set down and sprang forth, leaving her vehicle to the servors. A solitary live figure waited at the edge. Hebo. He hurried, well-nigh ran, to meet her and seize both her hands.

"Jesus, how good to see you!" Then, with the wry, lopsided grin she remembered from past moments: "I wish you came to gaze into my eyes, not on an errand, but welcome anyhow." A servor brought her bag. He took it in his left hand, his right on her elbow. "You've got a room at the hostel, of course, and I'll escort you—right away? Or would you like a drink, a snack, a gab, or whatever first?"

She beat off temptation. "I'm wide awake, thanks; not hungry, but, yes, a drink would go well. Unless you're politely pretending not to be dead tired."

"No, I'm keyed up like a grand piano." Another of his archaisms that she didn't recognize. "Whatever we do, let's get inside out of this steam-bath air. I know an all-night pub. Noisy, but it has booths."

They started walking. "Only good for small talk," she told him.

"Yeah, your call said you have top-confidential information. You really feel like diving into it straight off?"

"If you do. That'll probably mean a sleepless night, but I'm impatient. However, the site has to be absolutely secure."

His stride checked for an instant. "I think my digs are. I double-checked them myself, after your call."

"That'll be fine." Keep this strictly business. Even a casual romp could prove too distracting. Especially since she suspected it wouldn't stay casual. "Then you can ferry me to my lodging, and I'll sleep till noon."

Did she hear the slightest chuckle, feel the slightest tightening of his hold on her arm? Did she care?

His groundcar whirred them to a house apart from the rest. The interior reminded her of his shelter on Jonna, basic cleanness and order, casual clutter strewn about it, oddments, tools, a half-completed model of a sailing ship, probably one that had plied the seas of ancient Earth. An animation on the wall showed mountains in the background, trees she didn't recognize waving sinuously under a softly booming wind in the foreground, souvenir of some world where something had happened that mattered to him. Another screen was blank. Did it ordinarily show a woman? Glancing around, Lissa saw no traces of feminine visitors. That didn't mean he hadn't had any.

He ushered her to a seat and, at her request, poured a whiskey and splash for her, a neat shot for himself. Briefly, sharply, she remembered an evening in Gerward Valen's apartment. It faded away as he sat down before her and raised his goblet.

"Cheers," he said. "Also *salud, prosit, skaal, kan bei,* et cetera. Again, welcome, Lissa."

She clinked rims with him and wondered how ancient that

gesture was. "I'm afraid I don't bring the best of news," she forced herself to say.

He shrugged his massive shoulders. "Didn't expect you would, from the tone of your voice. Proceed."

She gathered breath. "Romon Kaspersson and Esker Harolsson have left for Susaia."

"Hm?" However lightly he spoke, she sensed the sudden tension. "What's that signify?"

"You know Romon, but probably not as well as you may believe."

"Probably not. And Esker's, um, the physicist who was with you on the black hole expedition. I've met him a time or two." She heard a certain distaste. "Go on."

She drank a longer draught than she had intended and leaned forward. "I admit I'm prejudiced, but the fact is I've never felt easy with either of that pair. After I'd said goodbye to you at Forholt, I fell to thinking about those flowers Romon brought. Yes, legitimately, no doubt—you'd have learned otherwise once you got back here"—and never mind about that girl in the office—"but an opportunity? Why did he make a second visit several hours later? Why come at all in person, when telepresence would've been perfectly adequate, in fact more suitable for a coolish relationship?"

Hebo's eyes widened while the pupils contracted. "Judas priest," he whispered. "He knew you'd be here too, and after what we'd been through together, it was natural, maybe likely, we'd open up to each other—"

She nodded. "Yes. A microbug in the bouquet. When he returned to you, he could scrape it off with a fingernail. What had he to lose?"

"He went home sooner than he'd been scheduled to," said Hebo grimly.

"Which proves nothing. I had only a hunch. But—what harm?—I had a watch put on him. Not intensive, simply an eye out for anything unusual.

"And now— Obviously he's been in hyperwave contact with Susaians. Because a Confederacy ship has come to take him there. Him and Esker. To the mother planet. Which means the Dominance.

"It can't be hidden, no, but it's been kept as inconspicuous as possible. The ship took a remote cometary orbit, and they were brought to it on one of the few interplanetary boats the Seafells have. Which implies that higher-ups in that House have approved the whole undertaking. They did give out, very quietly, that the trip is for purposes of discussing a joint venture. The implication was that it's fairly minor. Nothing for anybody else to worry about."

"Except us," Hebo growled.

"Maybe all of us. Who can tell what capabilities the Domination may gain, and what that may mean in the course of centuries? Remember how they tried to keep the black hole collision itself secret. Most Susaians are nice people, yes, lovable, but the Dominators aren't."

"Same as with humans. This wouldn't be the first time in history businessmen looking for a quick profit cut a deal with a government that in the long run intended to hang them." Hebo rose and prowled the room. "Yeah, I can see it plain. They send an armed ship or two to the giant star for a look-see. If my idea about it turns out to be right, they'll claim 'discovery,' then 'security,' and mount guard over the system, same as they meant to do with the black holes, while they milk whatever technology they can from the site. If others protest and invoke the Covenant, why, keep the arguments and diplomacy dragging on and on for decades. After that, if they've gotten what they hope for, it'll be too late."

His fist crashed against the wall. "If I could arrive first, and announce the discovery! I can't!"

Lissa got up also and went over to him. "Easy, Torben, easy." She laid a hand on his. "I've been thinking about this, you know. It'll take Romon time to persuade the Dominators, and then time for them to organize an expedition. Meanwhile, we have a chance."

Chance indeed, she thought. The stake might include their lives. It thrilled in her.

XLII

Once more she spoke alone with her father atop the watch-tower of Ernhurst.

They could have been as private in his study, and warmer. The northern half of Asborg had slanted into winter. But when she told him that this mattered greatly to her, he made a slight gesture, she nodded, and they clad themselves for outdoors and went up. She wondered fleetingly how much their race lived by such unspoken symbolisms. And what of other races?

The air rested quiet and keen beneath an enormous blue. Breath smoked. Paler blue shadows crossed snow lately fallen and still pure. The forest afar stood in its coppery-umber phase. The village and its works showed themselves as knife-sharp. The line of sea to the south sheened too bright to look at for long. A flight of swartwings passed high overhead. Their cries drifted down, a faint steely ringing.

He regarded her for a silent span before he smiled. It didn't mask the trouble in him. "Well, what's your newest recklessness?"

"None," she declared. "Not my style. Really." While she would never outright lie to him, she could make her own interpretations of the truth, couldn't she? "I'm still alive."

"Frankly," he said low, "I've paid my thanks to God for that."

"You know I don't charge blindly ahead. I like living."

"Especially living on the edge."

"Once in a while, maybe. Though that's more fun to remember than experience." Don't get sidetracked. Persuade. "Daddy, some risks have got to be taken. Else we'll never gain anything." And we can lose what we do have to those who will take them.

"Knowledge, or treasure, or achievement—" Davy sighed. "You are what you are, darling."

"I think the House has benefited a little."

"More than a little. Which I almost hate to admit."

Lissa gave him back his smile, hers less rueful. "You mean you're conceding me a point in advance?"

"I suppose so. Go on."

"You do trust me," she murmured.

"Yes."

She locked his gaze onto his. "I'm about to ask you for the most faith ever."

He waited.

"I have a journey to make that I can't tell you or anyone about, not yet," she said. "I can only give you my word of honor that it's not crazy, it may have a tremendous payoff, and, win or lose, I ought to come safely home. But it's urgent."

"What do you want from me?"

"The use of the *Hulda.*"

She saw him stiffen, heard him catch his breath. "What? Where are you going?"

"Nowhere like those black holes, I swear. However, yes, there are unknowns, there will be surprises, it calls for a ship that can cope."

"Recruiting a crew—"

She shook her head. "That's taken care of. I'm sorry, Dad. I wish—" in a tidal rush she felt how deeply she wished it, and for a moment her eyes stung—"I wish I could say more. I just can't. I—we—have to leave in a hurry. No time to collect the three or four who could fit in with me. Not here on Asborg," as slowly as such things always moved. The more so when the objective would raise a sensation she could ill afford.

Again Davy studied her before he said, slowly, "I might make a guess or two."

It angered Lissa to feel the blood hot in her face. "We know what we'll be doing, and we're able to," she snapped. "Don't you believe I've learned a few things in my life?"

"You have," he whispered. "Enough?"

Her heart and her tone melted. "I'll communicate along the way. *Our* encryption. The trip shouldn't take very long, actually. Afterward, oh, yes, you'll have the story, you and Mother and the whole family and the world!"

"*Hulda* isn't mine, you know," he said, "any more than *Dagmar* or— She belongs to Windholm."

"Of course. But you have authority to order a special, short, inexpensive mission, without giving notice, when a ship is currently idle."

If he knew what she intended, quite possibly his sense of honor would require that he consult his associates in the planetary governance, which would bring on the questions and debates and long-winded arguments that would eat up what time remained. She couldn't chance it.

"I'll have to answer to the council," he reminded her.

"That'll be then," she said, "and you'll give them a blaze of a good answer."

"Meanwhile," and she heard the pain, "I'll have to pray for that. Pray for you, Lissa."

"Oh, Dad!" she cried. Hardly thinking, she came into his embrace and laid her head against his shoulder. Yet soon she was crooning, "You will. You'll trust me. You always have."

At what cost to him? The question pierced. But she'd make it up to him, she'd make him proud and glad, truly, truly.

XLIII

Freydis shone against the dark as a tiny crescent. Sunniva light fell space-harsh over the little craft in high parking orbit. She waxed as Lissa's maneuvered to rendezvous. For a moment the woman imagined the sight from an outside viewpoint—*Tramp* a sharp-nosed cylindroid, battered and tarnished, *Hulda* a cone not quite so long but twice as broad at the stern, sleekly bluish, massive with the powerplant and equipment that left small room inside for living creatures.

Stillness hummed. The ships conducted their robotic dialogue directly by radio. Lissa almost heard her heart knock.

Smoothly, *Hulda* matched velocities and lay alongside. The slight, shifty weight of accelerations fell to zero. She undid her safety harness and floated free. Conjoined airlocks opened. A whiff of odorous Freydisan atmosphere mingled with hers. Hebo came through, grabbed a handhold to check his flight, and swung toward her. "Hi," he said. His manner was not as exuberant as she had expected. Diffident? Hardly like him. But how well did she actually know him?

Dzesi followed. As usual, the Rikhan was clad mostly in her spotted orange fur and a belt holding two pouches and her great, wickedly curved sheath knife. She smiled, though, a curious thing to see on that half-feline face, and greeted, "Honor to meet you again, milady of Windholm. Yes-s, I remember Jonna and what you did."

"Welcome aboard," said Lissa, surprised by a sudden hesitation in herself. She covered it with briskness. "Are you ready to start?"

"We hope so," Hebo answered. "Things are pretty well battened down at Venusberg, and I don't believe anybody thinks anything special about our taking a short 'vacation.' " Messages arranging for this meeting had been encrypted, but that was fairly common in business and private communication alike. "Shall we fetch our stuff and stow it?"

"The sooner the better." Lissa quivered with the wish to be on her way. Doing survey and science in the forests was well enough, but now she realized that before much longer she'd have grown bored. Today she was on the track of big game.

Maybe.

Man and anthropard went back, returning with their personal gear and other needs, neatly arranged, skillfully handled in microgee. Lissa showed them where and how to stow it. She noted a couple of firearms and a hand-held missile launcher. All right, she'd come heeled too, if not so heavily. This vessel wasn't armed, as he'd have preferred, but she didn't expect any hostility; they should arrive and depart well before the Susaians. Their personal weapons were mainly a psychological prop, she hoped.

She gave a quick tour. Life support was adequate but austere—recyclers, synthesizers, basic facilities for sanitation, cleanliness, and medical care, four cubicles for sleeping, an area where a table and benches could be extruded—that was about it. Nor was there much cargo space. Most of *Hulda* lay abaft the bulkheads, barred from any crewfolk, meant to keep them alive and the ship active in environs that were often lethal.

The group sought the command compartment and harnessed themselves. The viewscreen before their eyes held a wilderness of stars. "Proceed to initial destination," Lissa ordered.

"To initial destination," repeated *Hulda,* displaying the coordinates. Lissa accepted. With faint noise and gentle motion, the spacecraft closed their airlocks and disengaged. Power purred as acceleration began, dropped to a whisper, and thence to silence. The travelers boosted outward at one standard gravity.

Weight steady beneath them, they released their bodies and

rose from their seats. For a while they stood mute.

"Well," Lissa said at length, because somebody ought to say something, "we're on our way."

"This—" Hebo cleared his throat. "I've been trying to find words— This is so good of you."

Odd how that put her more at ease, seeing the big man stand half abashed before her. She smiled. "I have my motives, you know."

"But it's—it is kind of a long shot. Suppose we don't find anything, or anyhow nothing useful?"

"That's the chance we take. You were prepared to invest a number of years and all your earnings."

Did she have the power to restore his self-confidence, or did it—more likely—revive on its own? Nevertheless he stayed earnest. "Yeah, but it's my gamble. Mine and Dzesi's. If we'd lost the toss, we'd have sniffed around through the neighborhood till we had to give up and begin again from scratch, something different. Wouldn't be the first time. You, though, you've stuck your neck out with a lot more to lose."

"Not really. If we draw a blank, I'll explain things to my people, and they'll understand."

"If you return," said Dzesi from where she sat on her haunches.

"Uh-huh," agreed Hebo. "The physical risks, whatever they turn out to be. Why should you take them, Lissa?"

"The case looked important." She glanced at the Rikhan. "Why you, Dzesi?"

The anthropard made a gesture that perhaps corresponded to a shrug. "It is a hunt. And I was wearying of endless cloud, swampy air, trees crowding in on me."

Yes, Lissa remembered, she is a drylander, and her folk are nomads of the steppe. But she's not human; she can never make her feelings entirely clear to me. Throughout these years, she doesn't seem to have missed the company of her kind.

And yet—"Whatever the outcome," Dzesi finished, "my Ulas

Trek will remember such a quest. They will tell of it by the campfire. Unless, of course, we leave our bones yonder." She appeared to take the possibility almost casually.

"That's us," Hebo said. "You, Lissa, I've been wondering about you. Are you acting on account of politics, to head off the Dominators and Seafells, or for the glory of your House, or for the hell of it, or what?"

All those reasons, she thought, and maybe others, tangled together in me till I'm not sure which is which. This is no time or place for baring our souls. She summoned coolness and replied, "I have my price. We've already agreed on it."

He bit his lip.

"Whatever happens," she pursued, "whatever we do or do not find, you'll turn management of Venusberg over to"—she stumbled the least bit—"persons I'll name."

I still have to decide, she knew. Certainly Orichalc and various fellow colonists must be included, but I suspect they're too naive and trusting. Some tough-minded, reliable Asborgans. We shouldn't offend other Houses by excluding them, either. Dad can advise me. In fact, I dare hope I can turn the whole thing over to him.

And then what, for me?

Did Dzesi trill a laugh? "It is well," the Rikhan said. "I have in truth grown restless, I desire newness."

"I didn't promise to throw everything at Freydis overboard," Hebo objected.

"You'll have a fair payment," Lissa said with a flick of irritation. "Every investor will. The details can be worked out. But unless you agree to the principle, swear to it, this ship is turning straight around."

"Hey, I did, I do!" he cried. After a moment, softly: "Besides, it's worth plenty to go adventuring with you."

He has more than one sort of adventure in mind, Lissa understood. Hold off on that. She made her voice impersonal. "We have about forty-four hours to hyperjump point. None too much, considering how little time or opportunity there's been for planning and preparation."

"Planning, against the unknown?" gibed Dzesi.

"Contingency plans," Lissa snapped. "Emergency doctrine. Let's review what we do know, and take stock of what we have, and get some food and rest while we can."

Hebo grinned wryly. "I'm afraid you're right."

XLIV

Jump.

Abruptly the sky was strange, constellations Lissa had not seen since *Dagmar* was at the black holes. She glanced in what she knew was their direction, but found nothing. The light from their impact would not arrive here for several years yet, the particle radiation trailing after it in the course of decades. If any glow of their discs was naked-eye visible across four and a half parsecs, the sun she had reached drowned it out of vision.

With more than six times the mass of Sunniva or Sol, the giant shone a thousand times as fiercely. At the fifty astronomical units she had judged was a prudent distance for arrival, it gave two-fifths the blaze that fell on Asborg or Earth, luridly blue-white. Even heavily stopped down by the viewscreen, that was too much to look into, and in a well illuminated compartment it cast shadows.

Briefly, she must suppress terror. Free fall gave the body a senseless sense of tumbling down toward the fire. And they were, of course. *Hulda* had gone into hyperspace with an intrinsic velocity of some fifteen hundred kilometers per second. Potential differences could have changed it only slightly. She emerged with the vector pointed straight at the target star.

But that was all calculated beforehand. B types were rare enough that instruments had long since studied this one from afar. The basic parameters were known. Lissa had ordered *Hulda* to plot a course which put her north of the equatorial plane, her vector aimed inward. If she continued on the trajectory, she'd take more than a month to reach the distance at which she'd be too deeply in the gravitational well for hyperjump to work. Obviously, that wasn't going to happen.

Dzesi hissed, Hebo whistled, sounds of awe, faint within the silence. "The sooner we commence observations, the better," Lissa said.

The man regarded her for a second. "Sure," he agreed slowly. "It's just kind of an overwhelming sight."

"Don't let it be."

He shook his head and clicked his tongue. "Well, women always were the practical-minded sex."

Dzesi said nothing. Lissa wondered what she thought about the males of her own race.

They unharnessed, floated from their seats, and got to work. Mostly that was a matter of telling the ship what to do and trying to evaluate the results, but it quickly and utterly gripped them.

The instruments and computer programs aboard were meant for research, responsive to minimal data inputs. They scanned the equatorial plane, where they were likeliest to find anything extraordinary, to and fro across billions of kilometers. Glints appeared. Velocity gave parallaxes. "Yes," Lissa whispered, "there are planets."

Few giant suns seemed to have them, which was one reason that still fewer had yet been visited. Any such worlds must be barren. A star like this had only about eighty million years to exist on the main sequence, before it swelled and then exploded as a supernova. The scientific prize wasn't judged worth the cost and hazard, when the galaxy swarmed with so much mystery and promise.

Hebo nodded. "I kind of figured we'd find an exceptional case here," he said, himself gone prosaic again. "Planets provide stable platforms for observing, bases for expeditions to the site, and unlimited raw materials. Though if the sun was lonesome, I thought the Forerunners might have orbited something of their own anyhow. It didn't form very long ago, cosmically speaking, which would've helped predict exactly where it'd be at crash time."

"Have the Forerunners now returned?" wondered Lissa.

"That's what we aim to find out, no? I doubt it, myself. Not their style. Makes more sense to leave some robots, probably dormant till the right time came nigh, that'd then build the necessary stuff and establish contact with the masters, wherever *they* are."

After waiting at least three million years? Lissa shivered. This conversation was trivial, saying nothing they hadn't said over and over to each other, but it comforted.

"Any signs of activity?" she asked.

"Nothing clearly identifiable," the ship replied. "The signal-to-noise ratio should improve at lesser distances."

Dzesi bristled. "Why are we waiting?" she demanded.

"For lunch," Lissa said. More chatter, more fending off—less of fear than of a rising eagerness that could too readily override caution.

Then, jump.

The star flamed as brilliant as Sunniva over Asborg. The disc showed just a tenth as wide, but when the screen blanked it out, a corona sprang vast into view, rimmed at the hub with red tongues of prominence which could have incinerated a planet, its hue less pearly than fiercely white, the outer edges a breathtakingly lovely filigree.

Hulda reported a stellar windstorm. Any living creature caught in it, spacesuited or not, would take a lethal radiation dose within minutes. The wayfarers were safe. Their ship was made to survive terrible environs. Forcefields deflected particles well before they came near, so smoothly that the photons they spat when thus accelerated were a low-energy bombardment that the hull shielding easily absorbed.

However, no cause for complacency. The sun's thermal emission peaked at a far harder wavelength than did a G-type's. X-rays and even gamma rays abounded. They struck straight through, as did the neutrons they knocked out of atoms along the way, and the secondary particle showers they could touch off were worse. Simply the heat, the infrared, would make a furnace of the ship if she got too close.

At thirty AU, though, it was bearable. And—

"Definite indications from the second planet." *Hulda*'s impersonal voice thrilled the three like a trumpet call. "Emission patterns characteristic of artificial conversions; some neutrino background suggesting nuclear processes, although not identifiable with any in my database."

"We'd hardly expect that, would we?" muttered Hebo.

Displays and readouts gave details. Too vague, too sparse. Lissa instructed the ship to plan a pattern of movements and observations.

They ventured closer. Jumping from point to point across interplanetary distances added perspectives, making a kind of interferometry possible. Hour by hour by hour, truth emerged.

At the end of one leap, the hull tolled. *Hulda* bounced off on a wild new trajectory, whirling crazily. The travelers were flung back and forth against their safety harnesses. Outrageous gyrations left them fighting nausea.

Yet they found they were alive, unhurt, their ship intact.

Hulda won back to control of herself. She told them what had happened.

Apparently asteroidal debris was strewn throughout the system. That was no surprise. The typical giant star had nothing more to companion it; radiation and gravitational gradients inhibited further condensation from a primordial molecular cloud. This one was exceptional in having a few attendant globes, none much larger than Asborg. Everything else that orbited it was minor, and not quickly detectable from a distance. By sheer unlikeliness, *Hulda* had returned to normal space in front of a solid metallic mass some ten kilometers across.

The collision would have proven disastrous for any vessel less resistant. Forcefields stronger than most took the shock. Perforce they transmitted some of it to the ship. But they distributed it, and that hull was built of materials well-nigh as tough as the laws of nature permit, to a design intended to withstand impacts. *Hulda* simply recoiled and, briefly, tumbled. The scarred, pitted mass dwindled away into remoteness.

Hebo and Lissa stared into one another's eyes. "My God," he stammered, "you, you could've been killed."

"You too," she dimly heard out of a mouth gone dry.

"Nobody was," Dzesi snarled. "Carry on."

They did.

It was impossible to approach the planet that lured them. Mars-sized, eccentrically orbiting at about one AU, an airless, waterless waste of rock glowing red-hot by day and always spitting induced radioactivity, it revealed little more than that at half a dozen points on its surface there were centers of electronics, nucleonics, hyperonics, and who could tell what else?

"We couldn't make anything like this," Lissa murmured. "They knew more about high-energy conditions back then than we do today."

"We will learn," Dzesi declared, "whether they want us to or no."

Lissa tautened. "If they don't, we won't."

"Are you certain?"

Hebo's hand chopped air. "Friends," he said, "at this stage those aren't questions, they're gabble."

Yes, he can think, Lissa thought.

Hebo rubbed his chin. "But, y'know, this does seem a little odd. Sure, stations on yonder ball would have all the power, free, they'd ever need. But one hell of a set of background counts too. Sure, the instruments can filter out the noise as well as quantum mechanics allows. But would that satisfy? Especially when other sites are available as well. I say we should look wider, as long as we're here." He paused. "Might even find things we can look at close up."

His companions agreed. While *Hulda* retreated outward, Lissa sent a hyperwave message home. Whatever happened, their discoveries must not be lost. She sent it encrypted, though, addressed to her father with a request for secrecy. Not wise to publicize the expedition at once. Too many unknowns, rivalries, tensions.

Why couldn't humans, and other mortals, simply get on with the business of understanding the miraculous universe that was theirs and becoming one with it?

Maybe because they were mortals?

She shrugged. More urgent and interesting questions lay at hand.

Hulda leaped and peered.

Yes!

Activity, not identical with that at the inner world, but as clearly technological, on another planet, nearly a hundred AU from the great sun.

Hebo nodded. "Makes sense. Long-base interferometry. And you can take advantage of the low temperatures to do stuff you couldn't easily do close in. They complement each other."

Dzesi leaped in microgee, caromed off two bulkheads, came to a midair stop in a crouch as if readying to attack a foe. "We can land there!" she cried.

"Maybe, maybe," Lissa said, though the idea thrilled in her too. "Let's take a rest—we certainly need one—and then talk about it."

She never did quite get to sleep. Maybe her shipmates didn't either. Well, Dzesi. . . .

The decision was to go, carefully, calling home again in the course of it. To shed their velocity, they would hyperjump to a point from which they could back down on their goal, decelerating at one-half gravity: more slowly than they left Sunniva, but giving more time and space for forewarning of danger. This enterprise was chancy at best.

The crossing from emergence to destination would take about seventy hours, almost three standard days and nights. That would also let them prepare themselves.

XLV

At their second meal after that, when Dzesi had finished the food suitable for her biochemistry, she rose and said, "I go to *kshanta.*" She slipped aft, currently down, to the dorm section. Lissa and Hebo heard the soundproof panel of her cubicle slide shut.

The man got up too. "Let's sit more comfortably," he suggested. Lissa nodded. They used the rungs along the bulkhead to climb the passageway to the control compartment. Behind them the table and benches retracted, converting the saloon to a small, cramped exercise area.

Settling into her chair, with no need for safety harness, Lissa looked out the viewscreen. Interior light was dimmed, making more stars than usual visible, gems of frost strewn through a crystal darkness. How often had she beheld this? Yet it never failed to stir awe deep within her.

Hebo took the seat on her right. All four were close together. For a moment she heard only the whisper of ventilation. Full health on a long trip required weatherlike variations in air. At the present stage of the cycle it bore a slight, electric tinge of ozone.

"What's, um, *kshanta?*"

"I don't know," Hebo answered.

She glanced at him. The rugged profile turned and the blue gaze met hers. "You don't?" she exclaimed. "After how many years with her?"

"Not steadily. Off-and-on partnerings. Total, maybe twenty years. And, no, I don't."

"Hasn't she done it before when you were there?"

"Now and then. It involves being alone for several hours. She's never said more, and I haven't pried. Could be something private or religious or— I don't know."

"I imagine human xenologists have noticed it among her kind and tried to investigate."

His smile twisted wryly. "Somehow, the casualty rates of xenologists on Rikhan planets went pretty high. They got discouraged after a while."

She nodded. "That's a fierce and touchy race."

"Let's just say that many people in it are. I wouldn't call anything except their biology true of every culture and every individual in any race."

Yes, he thinks. And he can sympathize. "Agreed," Lissa said. "Seafell—But no, that's merely another Asborgan House, nothing alien about it. And the members aren't all alike by any means."

"The basic biology really is basic, though. Also to ways of thinking, feeling, picturing reality. Has any human ever figured out how the sexual machinery of Susaians affects their psychology?"

Dear Orichalc—"We can be good friends."

"But not like two humans, or, I suppose, two of them. The, uh, the aspects of nonhumans we can sort of understand and interact with in ways that sort of make sense, they're those that happen to be enough like aspects of us. And vice versa, of course." He spoke not intently, but earnestly, as if opening himself to her, something she hadn't quite heard him do before. "For instance, I've gathered that Dzesi, Rikhans generally, can't comprehend our idea of the Incarnation of God."

Your idea, Lissa thought. It puzzles me too, a bit. I'd like to know more—because it is yours?—Veer off!

"So maybe Dzesi realizes I'd never understand her *kshanta,* however hard she tried to explain, and doesn't bother," Hebo finished.

"As I imagine you haven't preached at her."

"Or at anybody else. Who am I to say what relationship they have to God? Besides, I'd be lousy at it."

Another archaism? Well, I catch the drift. He's tolerant. By nature? Or did he have to learn to be if he was to survive as long as he has? I'd like to find out.

"She and I do have working knowledge of each other." Hebo laughed. "Could be, she's simply made an excuse to give us some privacy."

"What?" Lissa murmured, and felt the blood in her cheeks and was angry with herself.

"She can be very tactful," Hebo said. "Armed and dangerous folks had better be, most of the time."

"But—you and I—"

"Our first chance to talk freely, just us two, isn't it? And days ahead of us."

Wariness: "Had you something particular in mind?"

"Yes," he admitted cheerfully. "However, that's up to you."

"What do you mean?" As if she didn't know full well.

"Don't worry. I won't repeat my mistake on Jonna. That's one memory I made sure I'd keep."

She didn't reply at once. The air rustled, cooling off, smelling more and more like a rainstorm drawing nigh. He waited.

I could be evasive, she thought, but I don't want to. Nor do I want to charge blindly ahead. Once was enough.

She met his eyes again and softened her tone. "You're really a rather lonely person, aren't you?"

He lifted a palm. "No, no, I can always have company when I feel like it." He grinned. "I'll bet you often do when you don't feel like it."

She let the little jape go by. "All those centuries, wandering—"

He shrugged. "Would've gotten scum-dull staying put."

"But some people must have become dear to you, and then you drifted apart or—" She winced. "It's already happened in my much shorter lifespan."

He went almost somber. "Or they die. We may hang on for a long while, but one way or another, at last the Old Man is coming for everybody."

"Don't you find belief in a life after death comforting?"

"Mainly, to be honest, I think how nice it'd be if the faith is true. Whatever the facts of that are, we'll never get back what we've got now. Let's make the most of it."

"Is roving around the only way? Didn't you ever try making a home?"

"Three times."

"And?" she murmured.

His voice flattened. "Twice, it simply didn't last. The third, she died. An accident that was ridiculous, unless there is something beyond this universe that sets injustices right."

"I'm sorry. I didn't mean to intrude."

"No offense." He smiled. "Instead, I'm glad you're interested."

"Why wouldn't I be?"

He brightened further. "That's a great question, coming from you."

"We've already . . . been through . . . quite a lot . . . together."

"And we're still busy at it. Think you might like to keep it going afterward?"

Why am I suddenly so lightheaded? "I don't know—"

"Why not try it out? No cost, no obligation."

She regained balance. "Oh, there's always a cost."

He nodded. "Yeah. I'm willing to pay. Got a notion I'd make a mighty big profit."

Does he mean that? wondered bewilderment. If he does, how much?—He didn't *have* to come to Asborg from Earth, even for his purpose—

Hebo leaned closer and with an odd gentleness laid an arm around her shoulders. "The accomodations aboard aren't exactly luxurious, and we haven't a lot of time, but—"

"No," she interrupted, stiffening beneath the touch. "We

can't afford to, to get involved." Not yet, she thought while her pulse accelerated. Maybe not ever. Gerward—

But he was a phantom, pale and fading.

Hebo grinned. "Have no fears. I'm only talking good, honest lust."

Is he? Am I?

We're both grown, both tough, we can both think coolly in a crisis no matter what our emotions. Can't we?

Anyhow, there's no crisis today. If I were cautious and forethoughtful, I wouldn't be here.

"Only?" Lissa breathed.

"No," he said, quickly serious. "But you're right, we'd better postpone anything more. Meanwhile, though—"

Their lips were centimeters apart. Fire kindled. "Well—"

The bunk was narrow, its cubicle cramped and bare. They hardly noticed.

XLVI

At a hundred AU the giant sun cast a tenth the radiance that Sunniva did on Asborg, ample for human eyes; but it was discless, a point of blue-white blaze too brilliant to look anywhere near, drowning most other stars even in empty space.

Mars-sized, the planet shone wanly in that light, a motley of darkling rock, white ices, dull brownish reds and yellows where ultraviolet quanta had forced low-temperature chemistry. Those temperatures were low indeed, ranging around one hundred kelvin. A wisp of atmosphere, a few millibars of pressure at the surface, nitrogen with some methane and argon, scarcely hazed the limb. The axial tilt was small, the rotation period a bit under forty-nine hours.

Such were the facts gathered by the ship as she approached. The sight close by sent shivers along the nerves. Here was a whole world, with all its unforeseeable strangenesses. And here was Forerunner work at work. The instruments had caught enough enigmatic emissions to prove that. What more escaped them?

Otherwise there had been no message, no sign. "I can't imagine them not having detectors, and equipment to react with," Hebo muttered. "They couldn't have predicted that no trouble would ever come in from outside. If nothing else, a comet strike."

"Those may be only blind machines," Dzesi suggested.

Lissa shook her head. "They'd have to include robots with at least as much capability as our ship," she said. "Probably much more." The thought was cold: that this could be so much more as to lie beyond the imagination of merely organic creatures. She mustered the resolution to add in everyday fashion: "Well, we've received no threats thus far. Let's try for a look."

Hulda slipped into a forty-five degree orbit, two thousand kilometers out. That was too close for hyperjump or hyperwave; in the near neighborhood of a substantial rotating mass, which drags slightly on the inertial frame, the function steepens from the smooth potential-well dropoff of astronomical distances. However, a hard boost would quickly bring her to an escape point. Meanwhile, here was a good altitude for observation, with a period neither inconveniently long nor short. And there had been no sign of hostility, opposition, anything other than those stray pulses she intercepted.

Acceleration ended. The three hung weightless in harness and silence.

After a long half minute, Hebo hunched his shoulders and growled, "All right, search." The viewscreen display shifted from stars to planet, swept across desolation, steadied and magnified.

They were lucky, happening just then to be where a site was in daylit view. Seen slantwise, three slim helices reared gleaming against a broad ice-field, a horizon rimmed with murky cliffs, and a cloudless blue-black sky. Spread around and among them were several delicate, intricate three-dimensional webs. Lesser shapes moved over bare rock which had been rendered mirror-flat. Sunglare made vision difficult. When the optics filtered that out, a subtle, shifting veil seemed to remain; the scene was almost dreamlike.

"I think," Lissa whispered, "what we see is framework and, and attendants, and—yes, that thing yonder looks half finished, with activity on it—construction, preparing for the wave front. . . . I think most must be not matter but forces, maybe subatomic, maybe the energy of the vacuum itself—" She was no physicist, but this epiphany wakened learning that had lain half forgotten.

"When did it start?" Hebo asked. "Yeah, three million years ago or more. I should guess that'd be a von Neumann type operation. A kind of seed left, with a clock that germinated it at the right time, to begin making the machines that'd make the machines—but maybe 'grow' is a better word than 'make.' Or 'generate' or—"

"Probably it began before the black holes met," Lissa ventured, faintly amazed to hear how calm her tone had become. "Building probes to be present at the event and afterward. I suspect they're there yet. Expeditions of ours wouldn't spot them except by super-unlikely accident. Meanwhile, newer machines have been making ready to conduct long-range studies in these nonviolent surroundings."

Again they were repeating ideas they had uttered before, back and forth, apes reassuring each other with chatter, a need that was not in Dzesi—but not entirely so. Reality stimulated a certain hardheadedness that abstract speculation never could.

It spoke through Hebo: "Whatever knowlege can be had here, whatever power, has goddamn got to be kept out of the wrong hands."

Lissa shuddered a bit. "Whose are the right hands? And how long will they stay clean?"

"I dunno. But I remember reading a historian on Earth, writing way before I was born. 'The only thing necessary for the triumph of evil is that good men do nothing.' We can hope we're more or less amongst the good." Hebo's hand sought hers and closed on it. His voice went warm. "You are, for sure."

The eeriness below neared the edge of sight as *Hulda* swung on toward the night ahead.

"We'd better send these data straight home," said Lissa. While we still can, said her mind.

"Uh-huh. You're smart, too. And beautiful, I might add."

She drew a breath to order the ship back to hyperwaving distance.

Desi yowled. *Hulda* sang an alert. "What the hell!" roared Hebo.

A gleam lifted from darkside into sunlight. It arrowed at them. In seconds it had waxed to a complex of coils and strands, half the size of their vessel, shimmering like the constructs down on the planet. At the center pulsed an iridescent sphere: a heart, a brain? With no trace of jets, of any propulsive force, maneuvering as deftly as a barracuda in the sea, and with no sign of deceleration stress, it glided to a relative halt and poised three hundred meters away.

Dzesi crouched a-bristle, right hand gripping the arm of her chair, left hand on her knife. Both humans kept still, staring, shocked into that coolness and clarity, that weird detachment, which sudden extremity can throw upon their kind. The compartment, the control board, the huge day-crescent of the planet were blade-sharp in their eyes; they heard each murmur of the air; they smelled its fragrance of summery meadows and the observers in their heads noted how inappropriate that was—but meaningless, meaningless; they waited for whatever would befall.

Set for broad-band reception—though how did the thing know which band?—the radio said forth in a calm human contralto and unaccented Anglay: "Outsiders are forbidden access. You shall depart immediately. There is no wish to harm you. However, in token of what can be brought to bear against intruders, your hyperwave communicator is now disabled. Bring the warning home, and broadcast it to all your societies. Make known that further attempts will suffer penalties more severe, up to and including destruction. But make known, also, that otherwise no one has anything to fear from this quarter. The prohibition is in large part for their own sake. Think about this."

After a moment the voice changed to flutings and rumbles that shaded off into the humanly subsonic. Lissa recognized the principal Gargantuan language. She had acquired few words of it, but grasped that the message was the same.

"How about that hypercom?" Hebo demanded.

"Ruined," *Hulda* replied. "Circuit elements burnt out, quantum superpositions decohered, programs wiped. My systems registered nothing while it occurred."

No, Lissa thought, the Forerunners would have means more subtle than an energy blast. But I'll bet they—their robots, or whatever these are—can call up as much energy as they want, any time they want.

The voice became Rikhan. Dzesi snarled.

"Yep, everybody," Hebo said.

"We haven't much choice but to obey, do we?" Lissa asked needlessly.

"Reckon not. Still, I expect we've got a grace period, at least till it's run through its repertoire. Plain to see, it doesn't know just who or what we are. And since it wants us to take the news back, if we're still here when it's done talking, logically it ought to say, 'Scram, I *mean* it,' maybe with some extra token that doesn't really hurt us either, like turning our food stock to charcoal. Then of course we'll say, 'Sorry, honorable sir,' and skedaddle. Meanwhile, though, we're up against heap big medicine, but not God Almighty. How about we collect any more information we can?"

Recklessness? No, Lissa thought, boldness. Taking a risk, yes, but you can't cross a street without taking a risk. He's my kind of man. "Keep scanning," she ordered the ship.

Susaian turned into clicks, while an Arzethian image appeared on the visiscreen and went through the body language that was most of its converse.

Hulda and the alien were not precisely co-orbital. They drifted slowly apart. The alien kept sending. The sun slipped behind the planet, which became a circle of blackness, very faintly edged with light, and stars sprang into heaven.

"Another site," *Hulda* reported, displaying and amplifying—not quite the same as the first, though it was hard to distinguish between such foreignnesses.

Having run through every known spacefaring race, and three or four that Lissa couldn't identify, the radio returned to human. Han, this time. How many important languages would the sentry try before it—lost patience—and struck again? Already it had dwindled to a small, exquisite piece of jewelry.

Something high caught sunlight and flashed.

"Hoy!" Hebo exclaimed. "Give us that!"

The optics locked on and magnified. The thing hurtled inward. Plasma jets made ambient atoms fluoresce, ghostly sparkles. Velocity already closely matched, the vessel needed little adjustment to lay her nearby, in adjacent orbit. She must have emerged from hyperspace about as far down the gravitational well as possible.

"Jesus Christ, what a piece of navigation!" blurted Hebo.

Lissa knew that lean body, those flat turrets from which projectors reached out like snakes. A Susaian—no, a Confederacy warship.

Hulda's receiver continued dispassionately. But the Forerunner machine must have observed too. Was it transmitting the same command, backed by the same disablement?

A streak leaped from the newcomer. The viewscreen muffled a fireball to a flare. Then incandescent gases dissipated into space, and the sentry was gone.

XLVII

A tactical nuke," Hebo mumbled into the abrupt void. "No, we're not confronting God. It's worse than that."

The warship still looked small at her remove, toylike athwart the stars. Another missile could cross the distance between in a second or less. Lissa seized his hand.

"Receive any communication," Dzesi coolly ordered *Hulda*.

The visiscreen flashed to life with the blunt head and snaky neck of a Susaian. Lissa caught a gasp. She knew that countenance, that rufous, cloudily spotted skin. "Naval unit *Authority* of the Great Confederacy, Dominator Ironbright commanding, calling Asborgan vessel," rendered a trans. "You are under arrest. Make no attempt to escape or otherwise resist. If you do, we shall fire upon you. Acknowledge."

"Do you wish to transmit?" asked *Hulda*.

"Yes, and challenge this outrage," Dzesi rasped.

Hebo made a shushing motion. "Better let Lissa speak for us," he said. "You seem to've met yon bugger before."

She nodded, again abruptly cool, totally alert. "He was second in command of their expedition to the black hole."

"And you saved his slippery ass. Some gratitude."

The pickup focused on her. Recognition became mutual. "Greeting, Milady Windholm," said Ironbright. The nonhuman voice sounded as imperturbable as what came out of the trans. "We thought very possibly you would be here. We trust you will understand that necessities of state force us to take stern measures. Cooperate, and you will live."

A part of Lissa noted a change in the underlying timbre and, yes, barely perceptible to a human who knew what to look for, the posture and manner. During the years since their last encounter, Ironbright's life cycle had changed gender. She was no less grim now for that—if anything, was more so. That could well be part of the reason for giving her this mission, that and past experience and—

We're caught, knew the detached observer and calculator. No weapons except for what we brought along ourselves. We can't reach hyperjump distance if they don't let us. Oh, we can outaccelerate that craft by more than enough to make pulp of us. However, we can't a target-seeking missile.

She had a far-away sense of feeling cold, but her body did not tremble or sweat or even uselessly tense very much. "Why are you doing this?" she heard herself ask.

"It ought to be fairly obvious." Was Ironbright capable of dry humor?

"That was insanely reckless, blasting the Forerunner guardian. I hope we aren't included in the retaliation."

"It has not happened thus far. Observation leads us to think that there are no others." Ironbright leaned forward, as if to stretch across the kilometers till she hissed in the woman's ear. "Still, delay among countless unknowns does certainly court disaster. For your own survival, you will do well to obey orders promptly and fully."

"How can we unless we know what this is all about?" This nightmare upset of everything.

"Suffice it for now that the Great Confederacy has established sovereignty, which you have violated. You are therefore prisoners subject to what penalties any agent of the Confederacy sees fit to apply." A pause, as though to give weight to what followed. "Do not claim innocence. At the black hole event, an agent of Asborg committed massive theft of data obtained at large cost and sacrifice, belonging to the Confederacy. Since then, Asborgans have freely made use of the information and disseminated it indiscriminately. Consider this the first of the sanctions to be imposed."

Yes, Esker Harolsson did "borrow" and copy that file, recalled the calculator in Lissa's head. How did the lizards find out? We never publicized the fact. It somewhat shamed House Windholm. We simply released the data, because suppressing it would have been worse. . . . Well, the deduction was rather simple, after all. But what more about the incident has their intelligence service collected over the years? I wonder if Esker kept his own mouth shut. It'd be like him to at least drop what he imagined were sly hints—and at last be such a fool as to go to the lizards!

"No more delay," snapped the trans. "Have your scanner sweep the compartment where you are. Identify each member of your crew. At once."

Lissa cast a glance at Hebo. Though rage whitened his face, he shrugged. Dzesi hissed but sat still. "Do that," Lissa told her ship, and named her companions.

A human would have nodded. The skin rippled down Ironbright's neck. "This is as expected," she said. And who led you to expect it? wondered Lissa. I can guess. "If you are concealing anyone, that will come to light and be punished. Meanwhile, it hardly matters. You have been cruising around in this system for some time. In due course you will give the details. Again, it does not matter at the moment. You surely sent a few hyperwave progress reports as you scouted. But now the guardian has disabled your transmitter."

"And yours," Hebo put in. "How else would you know?"

"Silence. These are your orders. Listen well, carry them out faithfully, and redeem your lives. The alternative is immediate death.

"We want all the information we can possibly get before reporting back. *Authority* is not designed for planetfall, nor does nest-honor let us risk her and our mission further in the possible hazards of closer exploration. You will make landing at one of those Forerunner installations, examine it as best you can, and keep us continually informed. We will take synchronous orbit, to observe and receive from above."

Up in hyperjump escape range from this small planet, Lissa knew, though not too high for instruments with resolutions of less than a meter to follow what happened. Nor too high for hurling a missile. Transit time—Torben probably knew something about such weapons. He could figure out how long theirs would take to strike. A few minutes, at most. . . .

"Do you understand?" Ironbright demanded. "Repeat."

"We're to land, look around, stay in touch, and try to stay alive," Lissa said mechanically. Then: "But just where? How? What'll we *do* down there?"

"As for deciding on location, in our present state of ignorance that is a question of practicality," replied the Susaian. "You may pool whatever information you have with ours, bearing in mind that your lives depend on accuracy. Since none of us know what the machines will do next, discussion will commence at once, decision be reached in minimal time, and maneuvers commence directly thereafter. I will turn you over to Navigation Officer Leafblue." Again a brief span of silence. "If all seems to be going satisfactorily, you may thereafter converse with a human among us. He can further clarify the situation for you."

XLVIII

Hulda curved slowly and cautiously toward a construction site in a low northern latitude not far east of the sunrise line. Lost to naked-eye visibility, the Susaian ship maneuvered to her station while always keeping the Asborgan in line of sight.

The three sat in the control compartment under a slight weight of deceleration. The silence between them seemed to thrum. Finally Hebo cried, "Oh, Christ, Lissa, I'm so sorry!"

The woman looked at him and raised her brows. "For what?" she asked.

"Getting you into this mess."

"Don't blither. You know damn well I got myself into it. And *I'm* not sorry. See what I've gained."

They leaned as closely together as harness allowed. Arms encircled, lips clung. To hell with the fact that they weren't alone. This could be their last time.

They let go when Dzesi said, "We are not foredone yet."

Hebo regained a measure of balance. "No, by God," he agreed. His fist smote the arm of his chair.

"Although if we are," the anthropard murmured, "can the Ulas Trek somehow, someday know how we died, and that we died well?"

It oddly touched Lissa. What other wistfulnesses lay behind that tigerish face?

"Incoming communication," *Hulda* announced.

Lissa's pulse fluttered. "Accept," she directed.

Romon Kaspersson Seafell's image appeared on the screen. Hebo stiffened, Dzesi bared teeth. Lissa met the gaze. It was surprising that the man was not triumphant, but white-lipped, unkempt, and a tic at the right corner of his mouth. "Yes," she acknowledged icily, "Ironbright said you might call."

"What do your keepers allow you to tell?" Hebo jeered. "And is it the truth?"

Lissa shook her head at him. "No sense in quarreling," she whispered. He scowled but nodded.

Although the pickup scanned all of them, Romon's eyes were wholly for her. His voice stumbled. "I'm free to answer—most questions. . . . Lissa, Lissa, I never expected this!"

She caught the undertone of a trans rendering their Anglay into a Susaian tongue. "What did you expect, then?" she demanded.

"I— My House— You know what loyalty to one's House means."

"And status in it," Hebo couldn't help snorting, "power, personal profit."

It stung, maybe, but it also stiffened. "Yes," Romon gave back, "I spied on you. Why not? I'd always suspected you had some ulterior motive, above and beyond the profit you claimed you craved. When the chance came to learn more, the situation suggested that there was in fact something to learn, something you'd kept hidden from your backers, your partners."

"My own business."

"Must you humans always make those smug noises?" Dzesi muttered.

Romon spoke again to Lissa. "I should think you, at least, would understand. House Seafell needs an advantage. The big ones like Windholm have dominated our politics, our world, too long." Hastily: "No offense to you, though, none, I swear."

"Enough self-justification on both sides," she snapped. "What did you do?"

He drew breath. "I took my information to the Seafell magnates. What else? It looked far-fetched to them. And yet, who knew? Our House couldn't send an expedition. And if we did have the means, how could we keep possession of whatever we found? Nor did we want to bring in some rival House. Besides, yes, Torben, you were right about how that would have meant endless delay and debate and publicity, giving the game away to anyone ready to take prompt, decisive action."

"Meaning the lizards," said Lissa with scorn.

He showed more pain than anger. "That sort of insult is unworthy of you."

"All right, the Dominators of the Great Confederacy. But I'm no friend of theirs," as I am of those Susaians they have persecuted. "Nobody ought to be."

"Why? What threat have they ever been to us? What might be gained by cooperating with them instead of denouncing them and intriguing against them? Why not try to win their amity and trust?"

"As the chickens wondered about the foxes," said Hebo aside. His archaism went by.

"It seemed reasonable," Romon insisted. "Didn't it? After all, as Ironbright explained, they have a legitimate grievance. This could make it good."

"Well, nobody's judgment is perfect," Lissa admitted, mainly to encourage him to go on. Ours, for instance, dashing off the way we did, she thought. But at least we can still live with ourselves. He sounds like being on the verge of breakdown.

"Esker Harolsson strongly recommended the idea when I consulted him," Romon said. "In fact, he was afire with it; he insisted he should go too." The tone wavered. "He— In spite of everything, he's been horribly lonely."

And here was possible new fame to win, Lissa thought. And glory attracts some women to even the most repulsive men. . . . No, I'm being unfair, maybe downright cruel. I could never stand him personally, but he is brilliant in his field, he'd have much to give us if we let him.

Romon continued in a rush, words he must have rehearsed: "Our message was carefully nonspecific. We just told that we had certain interesting clues to the Forerunners, which the Susaians might like to discuss with us confidentially. We anticipated months of negotiation back and forth. Instead, they responded within two weeks. They offered to send a ship for our representatives.

"Of course I volunteered. This was my doing, in a way, and—I am a man." He was looking straight at Lissa. She saw the hunger and realized, faintly amazed: Why, he's in love with me. How long has he been, and not dared speak because that would most likely bring his flickery hopes to naught?

Romon's voice steadied. "Esker came along. No one else. We supposed this would be only the first meeting, only a mutual feeling out. But—almost immediately, the Dominator committee proposed an equal partnership with House Seafell, provided that our news proved worth following up. We had to decide virtually on the spot; they said hyperwave consultation with Asborg posed too big a risk of the secret escaping. Esker and I thought this might well be so, and took it on ourselves to reveal what we knew. Again, it was stunning how fast they moved. In a few days they had outfitted *Authority* and dispatched her."

"I wouldn't have been surprised," Hebo said. "That government's been wallowing deeper and deeper into trouble. The Old Truther emigration is a minor symptom. All their traffic and communication restrictions, all the light-years around them, can't quite hide economic breakdowns, provincial unrest, armed coups—" After a moment he remarked quietly, "Well, human or nonhuman, totalitarian regimes aren't any more stable than democracies, often less. The Dominators must be near the point where they'll try damn near anything."

This rough-hewn man has lived through a great deal of history, Lissa thought, and he's studied a great deal more in his spare time. I'd like to learn how deep his thinking runs.

"We came to this sun," Romon stated flatly. "We cruised about as you did. Finally we made for this planet."

"And you were ordered off, and your hyperwave decommissioned, same as with us," Lissa said. "Why didn't you head straight home?"

"Why didn't you?"

"We were about to. But whatever becomes of us, they know in my father's council that we arrived and explored a little."

"As they know about us in the Dominance. However, Ironbright is determined to do everything possible before giving up. If we are destroyed, others will follow."

"A warrior soul," Dzesi said. "My compliments to her."

"Pretty inconvenient for us, though," Hebo added sardonically.

Romon's resoluteness cracked. "Lissa, if I'd known! If I could have warned you!"

"What actually happened?" she asked sharply.

Still shaken, he regathered himself. "We withdrew, but didn't leave the system. We cruised at a distance, observing whatever we were able to. Nothing pursued us, nothing called to us, we detected nothing alien in space except the one guardian, keeping near-planet orbit. Esker, especially, got some more data. He has ideas. Ironbright's reasoning was that if the machines were—mortally serious—about us, they'd probably let us know by less than lethal means. That's when we'd depart. Otherwise our duty was to linger and look till we weren't learning anything further."

"Like us, sort of," Hebo put in, "except she's willing to gamble an expensive ship and a whole crew." He shrugged. "Well, the Dominators never did set much of a price on individual lives."

Romon gulped. "And then," he continued harshly, "we detected you, and followed your progress."

Hebo nodded. "Naval-quality instruments. Naval doctrine. It didn't occur to us. Damn!" he sighed. "Too late now."

"If, if I'd known you were aboard, Lissa," Romon stammered, "I'd have—" He broke off in futility. What could he have done?

"So friend Ironbright guessed that we'd get the same reception she did," Hebo said. "Your ship kept watch from a few light-minutes away and pre-matched velocities to ours before she jumped."

"To blast the guardian was daring indeed," Dzesi said.

"Ironbright—she'd concluded the Forerunners are, or were, probably very peaceful," Romon tried to answer. "They wouldn't have foreseen a, a devotion like that."

"Besides, she's got us to bear the risk," Hebo said. "At gunpoint."

"A plan doubtless made as fast as everything else the lizards have done," Lissa said. That word didn't really taste bad. "Yes, Torben, I agree, desperate people are dangerous."

"Small consolation to us if the Dominance collapses in ten or twenty years," Hebo replied. "Unless we're alive to enjoy the circus."

"Lissa," Romon pleaded, "believe me, believe me, I—"

"We are close to final approach," *Hulda* interrupted.

"Till later, then, Romon," Lissa said. "Maybe." She shut off the com and the sight of his anguish.

11

Few spacecraft of *Hulda*'s size or greater could land on a planet without docking facilities. Descending on an unprepared surface, the plasma jet would melt it. Ironbright must have recognized her type and known what she, meant to meet unpredictable hazards, was capable of. Lissa wished grimly that the Susaian weren't such an able spacefarer. But the Dominance had known it when making the assignment. Ordinarily, at least in human services, a captain who lost a ship, whether culpable or not, never got another command.

Having positioned herself and verified every vector, *Hulda* cut drive and fell. Dropping some two hundred klicks under this gravity, she would have struck ground at one kps. Her hull could readily have taken that impact, but her crew were less hardy. She extended the forcefields that had helped keep them alive when she collided with the asteroid. Other vessels, liners, freighters, warcraft, carried no such generators. For them the contingencies were too unlikely to justify taking up the mass and volume. As for landings, some models had boats. *Hulda*'s machine spread its invisible shields to distribute weight over square kilometers and decreased their strength at a measured rate. Touchdown was feather-soft.

The silence that followed seemed to ring.

The riders stared at the view. Extended landing jacks rested on a basaltic plain, scarred, drifted with reddish dust, but reasonably flat, about five kilometers north of the complex. Seen from their present height, it lay on the near horizon. Shadows reached long and irregular from a sun, shrunken but still too savage to look near, not far up into a sky almost space-black but with stars hidden by glare. A few dust devils whirled on a wind more ghostly than themselves. Hills reached raw across the western distance, streaked with ice that glittered and gleamed and was not simply frozen water.

It was the Forerunner works that captured Lissa's gaze and would not let go. Seeing them there, close at hand, herself in ready reach of whatever they might send forth, was altogether different from a view in space. An upward helicoid, a spidery polygonal dome, shapes less easily nameable, and smaller shapes that moved upon them, busy with mysteries, a shimmer over all like mirage or heat-waves, but it was cold, cold out there—

Hebo's prosaic voice hauled her back. "Weird place. Seems peaceful enough, though."

"Thus far," hissed Dzesi.

"We'll sit tight for a while and see if anything happens, okay?"

"Then what shall we do?"

Lissa's heart rallied. "Go and start investigating," she said. "Do we have a choice?"

"I do not need a choice, now," answered the Rikhan, and quivered with the eagerness of a hunter.

Hebo unharnessed, stood up, and stretched, muscle by muscle. "Well, let's brew some coffee—hell, a shot of brandy in it—and try to relax, try to think," he suggested.

Lissa had to smile, forlorn though it probably was. "If those aren't mutually exclusive." She and Dzesi rose too. Having steadiness underfoot, but weighing only about twenty-five kilos, felt oddly refreshing. "First chance we've had, really." Might it not be the last.

She suppressed that thought and helped with the small mundane tasks, making equally small talk with Hebo. That, and the companionable silences in between, while look met look, also brought back hope, even a bit of cheer. Underneath, she sensed reaction to what they had just been through, but it lapped down near the bottom of consciousness, a black tide rising very slowly.

Dzesi didn't act as if she had been affected at all.

The coffee tasted astoundingly good when they sat down again, like a promise that she would at last come home to the dear everyday. Her mind was thrummingly taut.

"Nothing has attacked us yet," Dzesi said. "Are the things unaware of us?"

"They could be," answered Hebo. His tone had gone slow and reflective. "Specialized for their one job of observation. Sure, that's a complicated set of operations, starting with constructing the apparatus, including robots, computers, and programs. Plenty of unforeseeables to deal with, decisions to make, things to modify or invent as need arises. But nothing that calls for what we'd call sentience. Nothing like us was ever . . . expected. I think the guardian was supposed to handle anything that came out of left field."

Once more Lissa must infer what an expression of his meant. "And it may well have been a, an afterthought," she said. "From Earth."

Dzesi pricked up her ears. "What say you?"

"Can you think of any plausible way a purely Forerunner—artifact—could acquire the principal languages of the modern space-going races, and knowledge of their capabilities, right down to the details of circuits?"

"How can we say what *they* have or have not mastered? It's as bad a mistake to overreckon as to underreckon another. It can well be deadly."

Hebo lifted a hand. "No, wait, Lissa's right. Or, anyhow, she's working along the same lines as me." He sipped deeply from his cup. "Let's lay our notions out, share 'em, tinker with 'em."

"You first," Lissa murmured in a rush of warmth. Practicality: "You've lately been on Earth."

Hebo grimaced. "And the more I look back on it, the stranger a place it seems," he said, as if with a slight inward shiver. "Oh, they put on a pretty good show for outsiders, but I've gotten pretty sure that a show is what it is. They're—cooperative, unanimous—in a way impossible on any of our worlds. . . . Linked, in some fashion, through and to a giant, central artificial intelligence." He paused. "Don't get me wrong. I believe they still have individual minds, personalities, as human as you and me." A smile barely flitted across his mouth. She wondered who and what he was remembering. Maybe best not to ask. Starkness returned. "But they're also in a sort of mental collective."

The idea was not entirely new or daunting. "Yes, weren't things tending that way for a long time?" Lissa asked. "Though we on the new planets grew too occupied with our own new lives, societies, troubles, adventures, to keep track; and of course nonhumans never did."

"I've seen how a few people here and there guessed this was developing. However, what they suggested was fairly well ignored, for the reasons you gave. There were no strong clues to the truth. It was easy to cover up."

"Easy for—for what they were becoming." Lissa summoned fresh courage. "That doesn't mean they're hostile to us, or, or evil. Why should they be? They may wish to spare us bewilderment and envy, or unnecessary fear. After all, the guardian didn't hurt us. I think it was only there to keep—amateurs—from bumbling around and interfering with the work."

"Now, looks like we've got to."

"We shall tread lightly," Dzesi said. She touched the hilt of her knife, as though to add: If we are left in peace.

"Of course," Hebo agreed. "As lightly as we can. *I* don't want to spoil the fun here."

Lissa smiled, trying for the same appearance of assurance, "Which they've been looking forward to for several million years."

"In a way. Actually, I doubt it matters much to them—to the Forerunners, at least."

Dzesi's whiskers registered astonishment. "What, this unique event?"

"Let's have a go at reasoning backward," Hebo proposed. "Why would Earth be involved in it, without any physical presence except, we're guessing, the guardian—why, if they didn't know about it from the Forerunners themselves? Otherwise, supposing they are interested in the spectacle, they could do their own observing, mostly on the spot, like us."

"Do you know they are not?"

"No, but I'm imagining that the Forerunners, foreseeing, set things up for probes to be built here as well as instrument stations, and operate out of here. As somebody remarked earlier, our people wouldn't likely detect them, in all that volume of space and violence, especially with their whole attention focused on the natural phenomena. This being so, Earth wouldn't need any."

"If Earth is in contact with the Forerunners," said Lissa. The sense of being on a chase thrilled along her nerves.

"That figures, doesn't it? One super-civilization is bound to become aware of another, wouldn't you suppose? Maybe by signs or means we don't yet know anything about. I suspect that thing in Sol orbit, what visitors call the Enigma and never have gotten any real explanation of, I suspect it's apparatus for the purpose. Not just straightforward communication. Interpretation of concepts. Earth probably has things to tell that the Forerunners find worth hearing, as well as vice versa."

"But where, then, are they?" growled Dzesi.

"At the core of the galaxy?" wondered Lissa.

Hebo nodded. "Yeah, that's my best guess. Otherwise, scouting around, our explorers ought to've found more spoor of them than a few relics of once-upon-a-time expeditions. We can't survive in there, and our probes can't go deep—so far."

"A high-energy environment." Excitement swelled in Lissa. "That explains how they can also have a base on the inner planet here. To them, child's play. It already was, those millions of years ago."

"Could they, could any life, have evolved yonder?" argued Dzesi. Evolved, survived, grown powerful in that hell of radiation, unstable orbits, stellar crashes and castings out, and at the middle a monstrous black hole devouring suns.

"Maybe, maybe not," Lissa replied. "We know so little. Perhaps they moved there once they'd learned how, because it's rich in energy and—and who knows what else? Perhaps they've become intelligent machines, or something less imaginable."

"And they've never bothered to come back to the boonies." Once more Hebo made commonplaces into armor. "They've learned as much about the stars and planets as they care to. That gizmo on Jonna may still be working, sort of, by sheer geological accident, but how can it be transmitting? As for sophonts, well, for the last two-three centuries, or however long it's been, Earth's reported the news, more or less."

"Which does suggest they're not totally alien," Lissa offered. "Not totally."

"Doesn't all intelligence have at least one thing in common? Namely, intelligence. Not that ours is in that league, but—"

Dzesi interrupted fiercely. "We shall not humble ourselves!"

"N-no. I'm not working on an inferiority complex, nor should anybody. But, still—"

"Does advanced technology bring greatness of spirit?"

"I dunno. You've got a point, however. Yeah, an excellent point, old chum. Stick around awhile and we may find out."

If we can stay alive, thought Lissa. Her verve chilled as she remembered the warcraft hovering watchful above the southern horizon. The tide of weariness flowed higher.

"To get back to a point I was making," Hebo said, "I suspect the Forerunners aren't especially interested in our little black holes anymore."

Dzesi seldom repeated herself. "What, this unique event?"

"I suppose, way back when they were visiting hereabouts and saw what was going to happen, they knew less than they've discovered since. So they made arrangements here for observing it. Now they may as well let the equipment run. However, I kind of doubt they'll collect any data that surprise them, these days."

Lissa stared again out at the incredible structures on the horizon. "Another abandoned relic?" she whispered.

"Oh, not quite," Hebo judged. "And Earth's people are interested. Enough to build the guardian—maybe with some gadgetry aboard that the Forerunners taught them about—and station it." He sighed. "Of course, they may just want to preserve it as an archeological specimen."

"Or keep us from learning things they don't think we should know," Lissa added.

Dzesi bared teeth. "We will decide that," she vowed.

"Let's hope so," Hebo said flatly.

Lissa gazed upward, as if through the blank overhead into space. "Haven't these ideas occurred to the Susaians?"

"Or to friend Esker, by now. I expect so. It probably won't change their course."

"Must we indeed do their seeking for them?" snarled Dzesi.

"For everybody," Lissa said. Perhaps, she thought through the waves of exhaustion. But should we? Who can tell?

"Let's hope for that too," Hebo said. He rose. "Well, we'd better get some sleep, no? Then a bite to eat, and then go ahead." His own voice was muted by his own conquering tiredness. Yet a clang remained in it, an answer to a challenge. Only his gaze on Lissa was anxious.

L

The sun in its slow course was not yet at noon when they ventured out. There was no need to leave a watch aboard. *Hulda* could do that herself, and respond to their radio voices, while three together stood a better chance than one or two. They went afoot in power-jointed spacesuits. Jetpacks would have been too bulky for them to carry much in the way of instruments, recorders, and other apparatus, and unlikely to give any critical advantage in an emergency. Even in this gravity, they were rather heavily loaded.

The burden included weapons, sidearms for all, a light electric rifle for Lissa, a high-caliber one for Hebo, and the portable missile launcher with its rack of explosive darts for Dzesi. Their one hope was that none would be needed or, if worst came to worst, some would be of use.

Hebo spoke for them to *Authority*: "We're on our way."

"That is well for you," replied Ironbright. "Remember that you will be judged by your results." The transmission lag was barely perceptible.

Hebo's face hardened behind the viewplate. "Don't you forget that they know on Asborg we're here. You'll be judged too."

"Do not waste time quibbling."

"Then don't you waste it by trying to manage our mission."

"Not unless that appears necessary," Ironbright agreed. "We have you under constant observation with good resolution. We scan considerably farther than you can see. If we detect something anomalous, you will be informed."

"Thanks," snorted Hebo, and switched off spaceward transmission while leaving reception open.

The three walked on. They could not hear the tenuous wind, merely see dust drifting before it across rock, sand, strewn boulders, now and then a frost-blanket in the shade. As the sun climbed and shone down where shadow had been, gases began to steam from these, white wisps quickly scattered and lost. Insulated boots muffled footfalls, but Lissa sensed them faintly through her bones.

After a silent while, Hebo said, "If we get out of this alive—no, God damn it, when we do—how do you figure you'll spend your discoverers' awards and royalties and whatever else they pay us? Ought to make us filthy rich."

"I will return home and fare again with my Ulas Trek, a chieftain," Dzesi answered. Lissa thought she heard an undertone of longing.

"I'll rest and revel on Asborg till I've had enough, whenever that may be," she herself said as cheerfully as she was able. "Oh, and we must make proper arrangements about Venusberg and so on, but that should be simple."

"What then?" Hebo pursued.

"How can I say? There'll be something interesting for certain. What of you?"

"I dunno either. I need a long vacation too, and can't imagine a better place for it than Asborg. Later, yeah, who knows?" He paused before going on, unwontedly awkwardly: "Would you, uh, like to continue this partnership?"

The question, not unexpected, nevertheless kindled a flare of happiness. "Yes," she replied. "Indefinitely. Maybe for always. We'll see." Brazenly indifferent to Dzesi's presence: "Once we're back in the ship and out of these suits, I'll show you. Save your strength, big boy!"

His glove gripped hers, his laugh rang. "I'll never have anything better to spend it on."

Joy and lust blew away like the ice vapors. Awe mounted. They were nearing the Forerunner work.

First they passed through the shimmering. It was like going

two or three meters in a bright haze; then they were beyond, inside, and vision cleared.

Delicate intricacies loomed high over them. The flat-fused ground below and between sheened darkly in the harsh light. Lesser things, some so small as to be scarcely more than sparks, were spread well apart in a kind of spiraling pattern. Machines went to and fro on their tasks; a broad radio band whirred, clicked, whistled with their communications. Most of these robots ranged in length from a few centimeters to perhaps one meter, bodies slender and rounded, scurrying on legs or wheels or whatever it might be underneath their beetle-like shells—until they extruded antennae, arms, tentacles that flowed themselves into unidentifiable tool-shapes. Twice the explorers spied Gargantuan-sized hulks moving with stately slowness. What they carried out was impossible to understand, except that it had to do with operation, maintenance, and further construction. On several helical towers and polygonal skeletons, machines climbing about aloft spun gleaming webs, almost like spiders. Another evidently shot forth a thin, invisible energy beam, for metal glowed and softened as it moved along, its manipulators dextrously shaping a structure, artistry alive. Another emerged from a closed dome, although no door opened for it, bearing a load of rods to still others, which carried them to the top of a half-finished spire. Others—

Step by tensed, cautious step, the newcomers advanced. The instruments on their backs extended and swiveled sensors, peered and listened through the whole spectrum, did not intrude with radar or sonar but surveyed and triangulated, micrometrically precise, a cataract of data pouring into their recorders. When a robot headed their way, they moved aside and it went on past. They spoke little among themselves, very softly.

Nothing happened to them. They searched through the complex on a zigzag route that brought them near most of it, seemingly altogether ignored.

Once Dzesi rasped, "Does it not, any part of it, have any awareness of us? Is it nothing but blind machinery?"

"I can't believe that," Lissa answered. "Something like this must require all kinds of sensitivities, yes, and computer power. If it isn't conscious the way we are, it must at least have capabilities for evaluating information and making decisions, like a spaceship's but surely greater."

The thought ran chill: Probably not a pseudo-personality like *Hulda*'s. We program for that because we feel more comfortable with it. What is this thing's mode of mentation?

Hebo nodded inside his helmet. "Yeah. To handle the unexpected. Bound to crop up now and then, if only a freak storm or groundquake. In fact, I'm getting a hunch that this whole system wasn't laid out from the beginning. How could the Forerunners know exactly what the planet would be like millions of years in the future? My current guess is, the original 'seed' wasn't a preprogrammed von Neumann device. It had as big a database as they could provide, and general instructions. When it 'woke' it designed things according to what best fitted local environments. As it gained 'experience,' it modified those specs. You might say the different complexes didn't 'grow,' they evolved."

The party searched onward. They seldom stopped to rest, and then just for a few minutes, with a gulp of water from their drinking tubes and a bite of food from their chowlocks. They were strung too tightly. Yet nothing ever responded or threatened or did anything but work its mysteries.

A few installations looked weirdly half-identifiable. Well, Lissa thought, maybe the Forerunners weren't really very far ahead of us today, three million years ago. Our scientific and technological growth curve isn't rising as steeply as it used to, but it's still upward. Give us a few more decades, and we may be able to equal everything of theirs we've come upon.

But what are they like now?

Meaningless question.

All right, what would we find if we or our probes could survive at the galactic heart? What have the Earth people learned?

What, maybe, have they taught?

The sun trudged westward. Shadows lengthened. Dust scudded thinly on an evening wind between the great shapes.

"Okay," said Hebo. "We've pretty well quartered the whole place, got enough stuff already to keep the scientists out of mischief for the next twenty years, and I, at least, hear some cold beers calling me, and dinner, and about ten hours' worth of sleep."

"You're not unique, my dear," Lissa sighed. Suddenly the weight on her dragged, feet and muscles ached, nerves seemed to slump instead of quiver.

"I'm afraid you'll have to take a rain check on what we were talking about earlier," said Hebo.

Again she must infer his meaning, obvious though it was. A chuckle rose dry in her throat. "That's mutual too. Let's consider it a loan."

"To be repaid at a high rate of interest."

They laughed aloud, humanly ridiculous, humanly snatching after any hint of gladness. Dzesi purred assent.

They took the shortest route back to open desert. As if standing sentinel, a helicoid towered there, a hundred meters into heaven. They passed through the haze. The sun blazed low above icy hills.

A voice snapped from their spaceband receivers. Lissa knew it, Esker's. An image of the ugly little man sprang up in her mind. He'd be hunched forward, sweat a-glisten on brow and cheeks, eyes burning like yonder sun. "So, you're done for the day!"

Hebo and his companions turned their transmitters on. "About time," he growled.

"Yes, yes. You should have stepped clear and reported every hour or two. We watched, but didn't dare send. Who could tell how the robots would react to a message straight into their domain. Or how it might interact with that force-field? If you'd come to grief, what a treasure we'd have lost!"

"Including us."

"Send your data immediately."

"Look, we can't do that till we're back in the ship and have downloaded. There's a lot."

"That's what I meant, you dolt. No letting it wait till morning. What might happen meanwhile?"

"If you're that concerned about safety, which I can understand," Lissa interjected, "we'll lift straightaway."

"No. You'll stay. You'll send your data, and tomorrow go back for more. You can barely have skirted the fringes of what's there."

She stiffened where she stood. "In other words," she said, "to you we're information-collecting machines. To be worked to destruction."

"No. No. But can't you see, this is an absolutely priceless opportunity? I don't think another will ever occur. We're risking ourselves also, you know. It's worth it. Why, just a study of the hyperwave system—"

"What?"

"There's got to be something of the kind, a transmitter, somewhere on the planet, perhaps at every site. In all our searching, we detected no trace of anything like a relay. Yes, hyperphenomena aren't supposed to occur so deep in a gravity well. But somehow, here, they do. The Forerunners knew, know how to *make* it happen, directly on a planet."

"Well," Hebo blurted, momentarily caught by the passion in spite of himself, "we did find a big something that looked as though it might be some such."

"I thought so!" Esker yelled. "The technology may not be very important to us by itself, but, but what we can learn about the structure of space—natural laws we haven't suspected—don't gamble with your data! Get back to your ship and send them!"

Dzesi snarled.

A flat translator voice broke through, a Susaian tongue behind it. Lissa well-nigh saw Esker shoved aside. She heard the urgency: "Ironbright here. Beware. A strange airborne object has come over our horizon. It's bound for you at high speed. Take shelter if you can. It may be hostile."

LI

Seconds later, the thing flew into their sight. It was dull-blue metallic, maybe three lean meters long, and something in the nose caught the sundown light to a flash like a lens. There was no sign of jets or engines, yet it came too fast, low above the desert, for Lissa to get more than a glimpse.

"Back!" Hebo roared. He caught her arm, whirled her around, and half-dragged her into the force-shimmer. She shook loose and ran on her own beside him. Dzesi loped behind. They slipped through the lattice at the bottom of the tower, slammed to a halt, and stared out.

Dzesi unslung her launcher and latched the rack of little missiles into place. "Easy," gasped Hebo. "We don't know it's a threat." But his rifle was in his hands.

The flyer braked to a halt and hung some thirty meters away, five or six meters up. Its outline rippled in Lissa's eyes. She thought it must be—peering—through the haze, at them.

She felt and smelled the sweat cold on her skin, her heart slugged, but the clarity of endangerment was again upon her and she had no time to wonder why the thing hadn't arrived until now. If it was to study them, stop them if they started doing damage—

Her faceplate darkened itself. Even so, the glare from the lens left blinding after-images. She turned away, and the plate cleared. Dzesi's yowl rang in her receiver. "*Yaroo tsai!*" Then: "It's shooting at us!"

Either Rikhan eyes were less readily dazzled or she had kept from staring straight at it. Yes, a dryland hunter. . . . Hebo must also have been spared, for she heard him: "My God, watch out! That was close!" Once more he yanked at her.

She stumbled back. Vision began to recover. She saw a strut glow red. Melted metal congealed below a deep gouge. Had she not been spacesuited, she would have felt the heat.

Another fire-spot erupted on another girder. And the one beyond it. An energy beam, she knew, sweeping about in bursts of nigh-solar fierceness. "It's a killer," Hebo said. "I think the forcefield's confusing its aim, but it'll probe till it gets us. The robots can make repairs later."

Senseless fury speared through Lissa. Would the Forerunners, the Earth people order this?

"Run," Dzesi snarled. "Scatter. Don't give it a single sitting target."

She's right, Lissa knew, and groped out from under the helicoid. Seeing still better, she dashed for a giant polyhedron. Hide behind it, inside it. But the machine would keep on, though the whole complex be wrecked.

A chant rang wild in her receiver, Dzesi's voice. It pulled her from herself, brought her to a halt beside the structure. She looked back.

Barely, she glimpsed the dart that spurted from the helicoid. Flame and smoke burst against the flyer. Dzesi had stood her ground, with target-seeking missiles.

The shape lurched in midair. Had the explosion put a dent in the hull? It recovered. New incandescences fountained on the lower coils. Dzesi wasn't there. She had climbed, bounded, crouched higher on the frame. She fired afresh. Her song went on.

Hebo came from wherever he had gone. "We'll try for the ship," he gasped. "Quick!"

"But Dzesi—"

"She's diverting it, duelling with it. That's her death-song we hear. Don't let her die for nothing. We can't help. Maybe we can tell her Trek."

Yes, our own weapons are toys, Lissa realized. She ran beside Hebo. Fatigue had dropped away. There was nothing but running.

They left the complex and pelted over rock and sand. The straightest way to *Hulda* kept the fight at the edge of their field of view. Shot after shot rocked the machine. Bolt after bolt pursued Dzesi up the tower skeleton. The song went on.

It broke off. Lissa heard a scream. A firebolt had found Dzesi. The hit was not direct, the wound not immediately mortal. A last missile flew. Maybe she had stared right into the lens to dispatch it. She fell off the lattice, down to the black stone. But this burst was straight to the nose. The machine lurched, veered, crashed, and lay still.

And now *Hulda* loomed ahead. At Hebo's hoarse command, she had extruded a boarding ramp and opened a crewlock. Man and woman staggered into the chamber. They stood embraced while the outer door closed, the alien air was pumped off, ship's air flowed in, and the inner door retracted. Lissa wept.

When Hebo took off his helmet, she saw that his face streamed with more than sweat.

"Anything else around?" he snapped.

"Not in my detection range," *Hulda* answered.

"We'll lift for space right away."

Lissa's breath gasped in and out. She felt stifled. "Let's first shuck these suits," she stammered. "W-won't do us much good if, if we take a hit and the hull can't close."

"Okay." They helped one another. When they were free, they again clung together for a moment before they mounted to the control compartment.

As they fell into their chairs, they looked through the viewscreen, back toward the complex. From here, they saw none of the harm done, or the fallen killer, or any other sign. "Goodbye, Dzesi," Hebo said. "Yes, I'll go myself and tell your Ulas Trek."

"*We* will," Lissa whispered.

No data would be lost either, she thought aside, irrelevantly.

The instruments they bore had downloaded everything into each database. So that much that was Dzesi's would also abide.

Ironbright's image entered the visiscreen. "You escaped," she said. "That is well. We could do nothing to help you, in orbit as we are, but now you shall have our protection."

"We're leaving," Hebo replied, equally flat-voiced.

"Of course. The only prudent action." Even the trans conveyed grimness. "You will rendezvous with us at a thousand kilometers' altitude. Do not attempt to flee. If it seems you are making a break for hyperjump distance, we will destroy you. You may have the acceleration to dodge one naval missile, but you cannot outrun a barrage."

Hebo did not smile; he skinned his teeth. "If you insist. We'll boost and take orbit very slowly. But don't you come any closer to us than—um-m—fifty klicks. If you do, we will scamper. We may or may not get clear, but either way, you'll have lost the information you sent us after."

"Be sensible. You are exhausted, perhaps injured. You need rest, nourishment, care. Your friends are aboard, waiting to welcome you."

"Ironbright, if it weren't an insult to a better species, I'd call you a bitch. Our real friend is dead because you forced us to go down. She, nobody and nothing else, bought our two lives for us. The data are our bargaining counter. Why should we trust you any further than we'd trust a spitting cobra?"

The Susaian rested rock-still for a few seconds that hummed. Then: "Your attitude is wrong but comprehensible, when you are overwrought. We will assume orbit at the distance you request, and until then, if you wish, refrain from further communication. I urge that you refresh yourselves and consider the realities. Our duty is to the Dominance and the Great Confederacy. However, I tell you on my nest-honor that we have no desire to harm you."

Lissa's mind roused. "If you mean that, don't you be in a hurry," she said. "Give us several hours before you approach."

Hours to think. Time to kiss.

Ironbright rippled assent. "Unless something unforeseen occurs, *Authority* will take station fifty kilometers from you at 2100 by her clock. It now registers 1430."

"Fair enough." The best we could hope for, anyhow.

"I shall cease transmission. Leave your receivers open, as we will ours."

"Of course." The screen blanked.

Lissa slumped. "You heard, *Hulda,*" she said dully. "Get us out of here."

LII

They could quench their thirst, bathe, don clean clothes, eat a little. They could not sleep. They hardly dared.

However, it became oddly restful to lie weightless, at peace for this while. The planet glowed huge, starkly beauteous. When their vessel swung around the night side with interior lights dimmed, stars crowded darkness, the galactic belt became a river of silver, nebulae glimmered afar, majesty and mystery that went on forever. Music lilted softly in the background, old melodies that Lissa had always loved, the harmonies of home.

Neither dared they drug themselves to any extent; but mild psychotropes helped the body heal the hurts of stress. At last they could speak almost calmly.

"I can't quite believe the Forerunners, or at least the Earth people—they must be in touch—would suddenly turn so . . . vicious," Lissa said.

"I don't think you have to believe it," Hebo answered.

She looked at him as she might have looked at salvation. "What do you mean?"

"Well, I've had years to turn notions over in my head, and, oh, I don't claim any real knowledge, but maybe I've gotten a sort of feel for the business. Experience seems to bear my hunches out. You're right, a high civilization won't be aggressive or quick on the trigger. It wouldn't have lasted if it were. And it doesn't need to be.

"But it isn't God. It can't foresee and provide against everything."

No, she thought, this is too big and strange a universe. There was an odd comfort in that. Her own kind belonged here too. The same ultimate freedom was theirs.

"Whether the Forerunners originally planned to install a guardian, or Earth suggested it and helped program it, we know it was benign," Hebo went on. "If necessary, it might have disabled our drives as well as our hyperwave sets, but then I bet you it would've sent a message to our planets to come and get us. Ironbright, though, blasted it.

"I wonder if the Forerunners or Earth know. They must have concerns that interest them more than this. Quite likely they, or rather some machine of theirs, calls in periodically, and dispatches somebody or something if there seems to be trouble. The central robot mind here, or whatever centrum they have, may not be bright enough to transmit more than observations by itself. That was supposed to be the guardian's job. Sure, just a guess of mine. Could well be mistaken. Still, the fact is, no almighty outsider has appeared yet."

Hulda was passing dayward. Hebo gazed at dawn over craters, crags, stonefields, icefields, and unseen outposts of an unknown race. "The groundside robots do have adaptability," he said. "They can improvise. Remember my idea that they weren't predesigned, they were developed according to what local conditions had become? They'd have 'known' the guardian was destroyed. They'd have 'known' the intruders sent down a party to prowl around. But how could they know our intentions? Certainly what had happened suggested danger. I think they 'decided' to eliminate it in the only way they could. It took hours to design, make, and program an attack machine. But when it was ready, it had just that single purpose. We're lucky it didn't stop off to shoot at *Hulda* first. Maybe it perceived she was only our carrier and it could deal with her at leisure."

He sighed. "It could not know we had Dzesi with us."

Lissa took his hand. They floated mute for a time.

Dzesi was a warrior, she thought. She'd want us to fight on till we can bring her story home.

As if he heard, Hebo said, "You probably know Susaians better than I do. What do you think we should expect?"

She harked back to Orichalc. "I can't say any more about all of them together than I can about human beings."

"Nor I. Still, your friends among them are bound to have told you a lot. You're a wise lady; you'd discount grudges and prejudices. And your father's a big man on Asborg, bound to have plenty of dealings and many sources of information. You're close to him, you'd have learned from him. Think, darling. What's your assessment of these particular ones we're up against?"

She was silent for another while, which lengthened.

Finally, slowly: "The Dominators are absolute rulers. They live for power. Ironbright's a fanatic. She'd rather lose our data altogether than let us return without having shared it. The superiors at home will approve. After all, from their viewpoint, this has been a, a sheer windfall. *Authority* will have carried out her basic mission, and more. As for the fact that we've contacted Asborg, the Dominators need only declare that they know nothing about us, that we must have suffered some disaster en route. In fact, that will give them an excuse, over and above their claim of discovery, to send a naval force, mount guard, deny access to everybody else."

"While they investigate." Hebo grinned. "For our own protection. Yeah, sure. But do you think they seriously imagine they can cope with Earth, or the actual Forerunners?"

"I think probably they'll be willing to take the chance. So many unknowns. If they are ordered off, they can try to put a good face on it. But they can hope that won't happen, or at least that they can negotiate favorable terms." She paused. "Their regime is in bad trouble. It may well be getting desperate. They'll feel they haven't much to lose, and perhaps everything to gain."

"Uh-huh." Hebo kept his tone level and hard. "Either we download for them, or we die. But what when we have obliged them?"

Her coolness cracked a little. She shivered. "I don't know."

"Ironbright did pledge by nest-honor. The crew must have heard. Isn't that sacred? Isn't breaking it worse than perjury amongst us?"

"Yes. Except . . . fanatics—"

"Or sea lawyers."

Though she didn't catch the reference, it ignited an insight. "Ironbright's exact words were that they have no desire to harm us. That could be . . . interpreted . . . almost any way."

Hebo scowled. "She could say, afterward, we seemed about to take hostile action, and duty required assuming the worst," he grated. "Or we could just be carried back to Susaia as prisoners, with the same disclaimer as if we'd been nuked. Or—what?"

"I don't know, I tell you. She could be honest. Other worlds having the information wouldn't threaten the Dominance."

"Not directly. However, what we learn might upset plenty of ideas, and dictatorships never want that."

"What can we do but avoid giving any provocation, and, and hope?" She wished she had his God to pray to, less for herself than for him and all she loved.

"Yes, I suppose so," dragged from him. I'm sure as hell not going to allow any move that puts you at needless risk." His voice broke. "If I could *know* whether it's needless!"

His fist struck the bulkhead. He recoiled from the impact.

And somehow the sight of him cartwheeling through midair struck her wildly funny. She laughed aloud. Tenderness followed, washing away terror. She dived to him, caught both his hands, and smiled into his gaze. "Whatever else," she murmured, "we do have a couple of hours left."

He looked at her with amazement. "By God, we do. You're purely wonderful."

And later when they floated side by side, amidst music and stars, it came to her that she kept one small power. Very small, but she was not absolutely helpless.

Nor was he, after she told him.

LIII

Orbiting fifty kilometers ahead through the shadow of the planet, *Authority* was to the naked eye hardly a glint in the shining throng. Viewscreen magnification and amplification brought forth the steely form, the guns and launchers, aimed straight at *Hulda*. The human ship lay not quite facing, her hull at a slight angle. "Like an underdog baring his throat to the alpha, not to get bitten," Hebo had jested without much mirth.

Ironbright's image appeared. "Are you ready to send the data?" she demanded.

"When we've settled the terms," Hebo replied curtly.

The head reared on the long neck. "What further is to discuss? You shall transmit at once, before a new emergency arises. Do not abuse our patience."

"We have a few questions first. How can you be sure we'll convey fully and accurately?"

"Afterward we will inspect your vessel and verify."

Hebo made a chopping gesture. "Uh-*uh*. We're not about to admit a boarding party, to do whatever it wants."

"Be realistic. You have personal weapons. You can barricade yourselves if you choose, and wait. One inspector, no more, will actually be hostage to you. After he has reported back, you may depart."

This's no surprise, Lissa thought, and on the surface it's by no means unreasonable. "Nevertheless," she said, and the marvel was how steadily she could speak, "we want to talk with Romon Seafell. We're acquainted, you know; he's been a shipmate of mine and an associate of Captain Hebo's for years. He and we can better make certain that everything is clearly understood and agreed to, than members of two different species can."

Ironbright hesitated. "Romon Seafell is in an agitated condition," she stated after half a minute. "Evidently from concern for you."

You can sense that, Lissa thought, and a fear for himself if he feels it, which he well may, but you can't read his mind. Orichalc might have had some slight intuition, but Orichalc's been with humans a long time, and has a sympathetic heart such as you'll never know, you or your crusader crew. "All the more reason to talk with him," she said. "He must need a friendly human touch." Esker doesn't qualify.

"Are you afraid he'll let out your real intentions?" Hebo challenged. "That wouldn't help either him or us, would it?"

"No," Ironbright admitted. "It would be harmful in that it forced us to fire on you. Do not infer any such thing from his words or his manner."

"We shan't," Lissa replied. "We simply want his reassurance."

"You may have it." The screen blanked.

"A decisive type," Hebo said. "But, yes, like we figured, she doesn't care to stall around one second longer than necessary to get what we can give."

He had made the observation earlier, and was now merely staving off silence. Then, she had wondered if they would be permitted to go home and complain. He had opined that that was no serious consideration. Quite soon after Ironbright returned to Susaia, Dominator warcraft would be here. Asborg could not muster strength that quickly. Neither side wanted war. Whoever arrived first would be in possession—till the Forerunners or Earth acted—and the diplomats could quibble about an "incident" as much as they cared to.

When the matter of a Susaian inspector arose between them, he had in his turn wondered whether that would be a real requirement, or merely a ploy. It would presumably guarantee the correctness of their transmission, and lull their wariness for a critical span.

"We'll have no choice but to go along with it," he had concluded bleakly. "I repeat, no gamble with your life that we don't absolutely have to take." She shuddered and held him close.

In this instant, the visiscreen flicked back to life. Romon stared out at them. He had gone haggard, he trembled, sweat studded his forehead and danced off in tiny star-gleams. "Lissa," he croaked.

Hebo drew back. The other man had no attention for him anyway. "Romon," the woman cried low. "What's the matter?"

"You nearly died."

She smiled above the hammering of her pulse. "That was then," she answered. "It's sweet of you, but I'm fine. I'm worried about you, though."

"I—never foresaw—this. If I'd had any idea you were coming, I'd never have gone—and, and on Susaia I didn't expect so fast an action. I expected they and my House elders would, would discuss things, and make an open agreement. I did!"

Yes, she thought, he can safely say this, because of course Ironbright knows it, and knows we'd know it. What happened here did in fact take all of us by tremendous surprise. She has also been improvising. But, as Torben said, she is ruthlessly decisive.

"I understand, Romon," she responded, still gentler. "Nevertheless it's worked out well, hasn't it? For everybody."

"Lissa—" He couldn't go on.

She whetted her tone. "What ails you? Your ship will let ours go in peace. Won't she?" After a moment: "Won't she? I daresay you've heard the plan. You could scarcely not have, with a trans and the crew being alerted. Or did they lock you away while that went on? Are they behaving suspiciously? Tell me!"

Tears joined the sweat.

"I'm sorry, Romon," she said, softly again. "I didn't mean to hurt you. I realize you've been shocked. In spite of the differences we've had, I've always believed you're a man of honor." Never mind that episode of the flowers. He had doubtless been serving what he saw as the interests of his House. "I'll take your word, Romon, and look forward to meeting you as a friend."

She couldn't offer him love, not credibly. But she could use it.

He swallowed. His shoulders squared. "Yes," he said with a sudden clarity and firmness that she hadn't awaited. "My word of honor, Lissa. Did you imagine I'd stand by and let you be murdered? They admire your courage and resourcefulness here. You know Susaians have their own traditions of the worthy opponent. To the best of my knowledge and belief, once you've done what Ironbright wants, she'll let you go as freely, with praise, as freely as Macbeth sent Duncan home."

She barely heard the breath hiss between Hebo's teeth. "Goodbye, Lissa," Romon said.

"Goodbye for this while," she answered.

"Yes." The screen blanked.

She turned toward Hebo. His face had gone stony. "Well," he said, "that's a relief, isn't it?"

She knew he was speaking for the transmitter. Cold stabbed her.

Ironbright reappeared. "Are you satisfied?" she asked.

Hebo nodded. "Stand by for data download."

Beneath view of the scanner, he touched a receptor spot on the panel. It gave the ship an arbitrary brief signal which had been designated a command. *Prepare to execute Plan Beta.*

Betrayal had been betrayed.

"Ready," said Ironbright.

A radio beam sprang forth. At its baud rate, it bore the work and discoveries of half a planetary day across in less than a minute.

Hebo and Lissa looked into one another's eyes. "I love you," he whispered.

Would they have a little more time while the inspector came aboard? Just a little. Please.

A titan smote them. It rammed them back into their chairs with the force of twenty gravities or more. Blackness thundered across brains. Blood burst from nostrils.

The force stopped. Lissa caught three breaths while the stars whirled around her. Then the next blow hammered her into night.

Afterward she had a feeling that she had somehow sensed the crash; but it was dreamlike, it might have been fleeting delirium.

No flesh could detect and react with the spacecraft's speed. As the missile left its launcher, *Hulda* accelerated. The death flew several meters past her. Before it could turn in pursuit, *Hulda* swung about. In a second burst of power, she hurtled against *Authority.*

Her hull and fields had withstood impact with an asteroid. The enemy vessel was meant entirely for combat. Shards of her exploded in every direction. Some burned down through the planetary sky as meteors.

Outracing the hound, *Hulda* reached hyperjump distance. Acceleration ended. She sprang across spacetime.

LIV

When Lissa swam back to herself, she was unharnessed, afloat in free fall. Hebo's anxious hands went to and fro across her. "Are you all right?" he gasped through the blood that masked him in red and bobbed loose in fire-drops. "Are you okay, darling, darling?"

"I . . . think . . . I am," she mumbled. "You?"

His laugh leaped. "I'm awake."

Stars gleamed in the constellations of home. To one side shone Sunniva.

Later, when they had won back to full awareness, taken analgesics to deaden the pain that filled them and the healing medicines prescribed by the medic machine that examined them, cleansed themselves, and shared from a bottle of whiskey, they could recall what they had done.

"Two-three broken ribs apiece, minor damage elsewhere, nothing that won't mend pretty soon," he said. "Christ, though, that was a near thing. A tad more would've killed us."

She was too weary for triumph. "And we killed so many," she mourned.

"It was them or you. I have no regrets."

"Romon—"

"Yes, he did warn us, knowing it'd cost him his life. But I'm fairly sure he already suspected he and Esker were doomed. What reason would the Dominance have to let them live to tell their story?" Hebo gazed out at the stars. "Well, be that as it may, there at the end he was a brave man. I'll honor his memory."

"How did he warn you?"

"Something few humans know nowadays, and no nonhumans. Macbeth received Duncan as a guest, then murdered him in his sleep."

"We'd better call Asborg."

"Yes, and urge them to call Earth. And to dispatch a squadron to yon system, just in case; but I expect Earth and the Forerunners'll be quick to reclaim their own." Hebo smiled. "I don't expect they'll take what we've got away from us. In fact, they can't, if we squirt the data along with our message. We'll have enough to keep us busy for a good long while to come. Lord knows what we'll find."

"Greatness?"

"Fun, anyway. Discovery is, don't you agree? Now let's start *Hulda* off for Asborg at a nice, easy half a gee, make our call, and rest."

"And rest and rest," she sighed. "Sleep and sleep."

He smiled rather wryly. "I hope we'll be in shape to use some of this last flight better than that. We'll be mighty short on privacy for weeks or months, groundside."

"There'll be time afterward," she promised. "Always."